The Purveyor

Tempie W. Wade

DreamPunk Press

ISBN: 978-1-963928-08-2
978-1-963928-10-5 (open dyslexic font)
978-1-963928-09-9 (ePub)

Chapter One

L as Vegas, Nevada

"Who would have dreamed that what started out as a dusty little water stop on a wagon trail would have turned into all of this? When my father encouraged me to invest in property here in the 1930s, I thought he was out of his mind and the time had finally come to check him into the nearest retirement home. I had serious doubts, but he assured me this was the perfect place to put down roots and establish my name and reputation."

She had a vivid recollection of what the area had looked like when she first arrived, stepping out of her cherry-red 1938 Lincoln Zephyr convertible sedan. Removing her sunglasses, she had watched an errant tumbleweed coming down the middle of the street, blowing directly across the toe of one of her high-heeled pumps. Immediately beginning to have her doubts, she even went so far as to wonder if perhaps her father was having a little fun at her expense, until she remembered— he didn't have a sense of humor. Besides, he would never have steered his precious little girl wrong. Pursuant to his advice, she had marched into the nearest real estate office and purchased enough land on which to build her empire.

Pointing to a construction site up the street, she continued to reminisce. "In 2000, they blew up the one building left from the first casino and resort to be built on the strip back in 1941, to make room for THAT. I remember when the El Rancho first opened. It was a gaudy little thing with an Old West theme, complete with a fifty-foot neon windmill on the top of the main building. It only housed four gaming tables and seventy slot machines back then. The humans couldn't get enough of it and, once they started coming, they never stopped. It boggles the mind to see how quickly it grew into what it has become now. Though, I have to admit, Daddy was right."

"Vegas must have been something special to see back then," he said as he reached for his vibrating phone on the desk, scrolling to check the new message that had just flashed across the screen.

"It most certainly was!"

CEO Harlow Thornhart stood with her back to her assistant, staring out over the spectacular Las Vegas skyline, her crimson eyes casting a sinister reflection in the glass. The window from her sleek, modern office penthouse suite afforded her the best view of the city, especially when the sun went down, and the strip sprang to life. From atop her privately-owned building, she kept a watchful eye over humankind and creatures alike. In a city where two entirely different worlds mingled, one without knowledge of the other; she was the bridge that connected the realms.

"Your new client is almost here," Sawyer called out, slipping the phone into the inner pocket of his jacket and fastening it closed. Crossing the room to the far wall, he entered a six-digit code into a concealed pin pad and unlocked the secured walk-in wine cooler, one that housed a rare collection of unique libations. Pulling open the door, a loud hissing was heard, and a rolling fog emerged, eerily enveloping him from the waist down. "I was just notified by our driver that the limo is less than ten minutes out," he added before stepping inside, wanting to choose something special for the occasion.

"Who is it?" she asked, turning with her arms crossed.

"Matthew Broussard, an extremely wealthy vampire from New Orleans," he replied, returning with two chilled bottles, one in each hand. Pursing his lips, he looked back and forth between them, pondering the choices before him. "Which blood vintage do you think he would prefer —'young French prostitute' or 'middle-aged Roman Catholic Cardinal'?"

"Definitely the Cardinal! Being from Louisiana, I am sure he has sampled every French variety there is, and since we specialize in diversity, we will offer him something he is unaccustomed to enjoying."

"The Cardinal it is!" Sawyer set the other aside and reached for a corkscrew.

"How was your weekend?" she asked.

Her assistant's blond hair was just a shade lighter than it had been when she saw him last, indicating he had spent some time in the sun. There also seemed to be a little extra spring in his black wingtips that evening.

"Wonderful!" he gushed, filling two trumpet-styled wine glasses. "Mason and I flew out to Cali and stayed at this lovely little vineyard to celebrate our twentieth anniversary. The inn was surrounded by two hundred acres of the thickest groves of trees you have ever seen. We hiked deep into the woods and had the entire place all to ourselves. Mason was sweet enough to take down a twelve-point buck and bring me the still-beating heart as a gift. It was so romantic. Words aren't enough to express how much I love that wolf."

Harlow smiled. Sawyer Evans had been her client once upon a time, coming to her in a last-ditch effort to find his 'happily-ever-after'. It was hard enough for a werewolf to find a mate these days but when you added that he was gay, it just made meeting and dating someone twice as difficult. Mason Roark was Harlow's personal art dealer, and as soon as Sawyer had stepped foot into her office, she knew the two would be perfect for each other. Playing matchmaker was not her usual forte, but she had prided herself on bringing those two love birds together. Sawyer chose to give up his life in Seattle and moved to Las Vegas to be closer to Mason at about the same time as Harlow's previous assistant had to be dismissed under less-than-ideal circumstances. The timing could not have been better. Not only was his loyalty and on-the-job performance unsurpassed by any other, but the pair had become the best of friends in the process.

"I am glad to hear it." Stepping to her desk, she asked, "What do we know about Mr. Matthew Broussard of New Orleans?"

"Well, he is extremely wealthy, obviously. It looks like he joined the world of The Diverse around the mid-1800s, but he got his financial start pirating during the Civil War, eventually moving on to discreet smuggling over the years. Recently, he has expanded his holdings by getting into real estate. He currently specializes in locating private high-end properties for select well-to-do humans and members of "The Diverse.""

Harlow chortled at the term and remembered thinking it a little pretentious when she first heard it used by a four-foot-high Yeti in Tibet in reference to himself. He had been the smallest one she had ever encountered, obviously due to some genetic issue, but what he lacked in height, he made up for in confidence. His name was Chodak, and he wanted nothing more in the world than to teach others how to find inner peace through mediation. He had been shunned by his own kind because of his height and was desperate to become a part of a bigger community, yet he found himself mostly alone. One stormy night while looking for a dry place to rest, he happened upon a sickly blind man in a hut in the middle of nowhere. The kindness he held in his heart prevented him from passing by when he heard the pitiful cries for help. Chodak nursed the man back to health, and in return, the man had taught him the secrets of finding an inner peace, no matter what challenges the outer world might be experiencing. The joy he received from this gift made him only want to share it with the world, so he wrapped himself in clothing from head to toe, traveled to the nearest village, planted himself in the middle of the town square, and announced himself as a mystical guru. People flocked from miles around to learn from him and word soon quickly spread of his gift. That was two hundred years ago, and Chodak was still planted in that very same village square teaching new generations how to connect to their inner selves.

Chodak was the first of many brave souls. Before, the creatures of the world hid in the darkness, afraid of humans and of what harm they might inflict upon their kind. But times changed, as they always do. The supernatural beings slowly emerged, calling themselves 'The Diverse' as a way of identifying themselves to other non-humans. Most had chosen to discreetly acclimate to the world around them, becoming a part of it rather than trying to struggle against it. Their numbers were many, but they remained hidden out of fear, afraid of what might happen if humans learned of their existence. If truth be known, the world was a much better place with them in it. While some liked to stir up trouble, most used their unique gifts to make the world a better place for everyone.

"Any inkling as to what he is looking for?"

"Honestly, I have no idea!" Sawyer pulled down the front of his jacket and straightened his bowtie in the reflection of a nearby mirror hanging on the wall. "He refused to give me, or anyone else, any details, saying he would only speak to you personally."

"Wonderful! Another high-maintenance client," she muttered. "Well, at least I know upfront to grossly overcharge him for being the pain-in-the-ass he is inevitably going to be." She heaved a sigh, "Show him in when he arrives."

"Whatever you say, boss!" Sawyer cheerfully bounced off, whistling a lively tune as he went.

Harlow took a seat at her desk and opened the drawer to her right, revealing a built-in mirror on a swivel. After smoothing back a few strands of her long, layered raven-colored hair, she reached into the drawer, located a tube of crimson lipstick, and carefully applied it. Taking the time to check her eyeliner and mascara, she stopped and frowned when she noticed a few small wrinkles forming at the corners of her eyes.

"What the hell is this?" she grumbled and tried to rub them away, to no avail.

"Really?" she scowled, shoving the mirror back down into the drawer and slamming it closed. Leaning back in her chair, she closed her eyes and took several deep breaths, trying to compose herself, as the new meditation app she downloaded on her phone had suggested. Mentally preparing herself for their visitor, she straightened her back, crossed her legs, and positioned herself in a manner exuding extreme confidence, complete control, and absolute power. Dressed in a black business skirt suit, red was the only other hint of color she wore. It came from the soles of her extremely expensive Louboutin six-inch heels, her perfectly manicured fingernails, and the newly applied lipstick on her lips.

Sawyer opened the door a few moments later and escorted her new client inside. "Allow me to present Mr. Matthew Broussard of New Orleans," he announced.

"It is a pleasure to meet you," she greeted while remaining seated, deliberately not extending her hand, instead choosing to simply look him in the eye. She wanted there to be no question as to who was in charge of this negotiation.

"Ms. Thornhart," he acknowledged in a thick Cajun accent, offering a gentlemanly dip of the head and formal bow, "I can assure you, the pleasure is all mine. I want to thank you for welcoming me so cordially, especially on such an impolite and uncivilized amount of notice. I hope my humble request for this appointment has not inconvenienced you in any way."

"Not at all, Mr. Broussard." Harlow gestured for him to sit as Sawyer presented him with one of the glasses. "Roman Catholic Cardinal, for your pleasure."

"Thank you, Ms. Thornhart." He waved the crystal under his nose and smiled, revealing his pearly white fangs. "This is quite a treat indeed!" Sampling it, an expression of delight immediately appeared on his face. "This is an extraordinary vintage and such a rarity these days! It must have cost you a small fortune! Allow me to offer my compliments to your vintner."

"I provide only the best to my clients," she assured.

Entwining her fingers, Harlow rested her hands on her thigh and studied the details of the individual sitting across from her. Mr. Broussard was quite striking, fit, and trim, easily passing for the age of forty, even though she sensed he was closer to two hundred years old. Standing nearly six-foot-three, his dark brown hair was neatly trimmed in a trendy, modern style. Resembling two sapphire gemstones, his stunning blue eyes were the kind human women undoubtedly went mad for. His perfectly flawless skin was tinged slightly pink, indicating he had fed just before his arrival. Dressed in an expensive custom-tailored navy-blue suit, complete with a red silk handkerchief folded and tucked neatly in the breast pocket, she had no doubt he garnered attention from men, women, and The Diverse alike, wherever he ventured. His mindfulness of formal etiquette and seeming sense of propriety only added to his charm.

"Please," holding up his glass, "won't you join me?"

"Of course!"

Taking the cue, Sawyer handed his employer the other glass before taking a protective stance directly behind her. She lifted it in a toast and had a sip. Turning her attention back to her guest, she inclined her head and smiled before setting the glass aside. "Tell me, Mr. Broussard, what can I do for you?"

"Right down to business! I can appreciate that. Well, Ms. Thornhart, I am here in your lovely city of Las Vegas with a close friend for the weekend and before we travel home to celebrate Mardi Gras, I would like an experience to make our stay—memorable. If you are agreeable, I will need a few humans, who we may freely feed on, and ones who will not bring any unnecessary attention, if you take my meaning. Also, we will require a great deal of privacy. My friend and I like to get 'creative' with our meals. I understand you have access to connections who may fit that bill, some who might even enjoy our company and unique mannerisms."

"I do, but why not just take a couple off the street; after all, people go missing all the time? You are wealthy and can afford to rent a place near the desert where it is quiet. What are a few less humans in the world? There are billions, after all, and many who no one will ever miss."

"That was easy enough in the old days," he replied, nostalgia in his voice, "but the absence of individuals tends to be noticed more now, as you well know. I cannot take even the slightest risk of my name becoming associated with any sort of unpleasantness. Reputation is everything in my business, a detail I am sure you, of all people, understand."

"I do. Well, you also need to understand this is quite a tall order and, as you pointed out, on extremely short notice."

"That is why I came to the best in the business."

"I am the ONLY one in the business," she corrected, "and for that reason, it will cost you a great deal. I also have certain, non-negotiable stipulations I insist upon with each transaction."

"Of course! I am willing to pay top price, provided we can come to an agreement on terms."

Harlow regarded him. "For starters, there will be no non-consensual sex involved. I am not a flesh-peddler, Mr. Broussard. I will tell you here and now, I abhor rape and, if I find out anyone engages in that under the guise of Black Thorn Enterprises, or even thinks of mentioning my name in the same sentence, implying my involvement in ANY way, they will pay a costly price."

Mr. Broussard shifted in his seat and nodded. "That condition is acceptable. What else?"

"The humans live. If any one of them is hurt or dies on your watch, I will come for YOU. The mortals I provide will willingly offer their blood and happily participate in whatever games you wish to play, but not one hair will be harmed on any of them. If they come back to me with so much as a paper cut, I will hold you personally responsible. If such a thing does occur, understand you will have sealed your own fate," she leaned forward for emphasis, "and, make no mistake, this devil ALWAYS collects her due."

"Forgive my ignorance on the matter, but how do you manage to ensure absolute discretion if they are allowed to live?" he questioned.

"That is my concern, not yours. I am the best at what I do because I deliver where others cannot. These are my terms, and you are welcome to take them or leave them. It makes no difference to me either way."

"I understand! What about payment?"

Harlow eyed him intently. "Fifty thousand dollars and three—," her eyes drifted to the drawer with the mirror, "make that, FOUR pints of your blood."

"FOUR PINTS!" he exclaimed. "That is an extremely high price, Ms. Thornhart. The money is not an issue, but the blood is another story entirely. Do you have any idea how much time it will take me to recover from that?"

"You are asking for a great deal, Mr. Broussard, and I have a business to fund. Besides, you and I both know you just fed, and a man who looks like you will have no trouble finding a willing victim on the strip as soon as you depart my office. This is Vegas after all, and the freaks do come out at night. Given your appearance and charm, I have no doubt you will be back to full strength within the hour. Besides, think of the glorious stories you will give the humans to tell their friends of their unforgettable encounter with the handsome, mysterious stranger on the strip who took them into his arms and gave them an experience unlike any other. before mysteriously disappearing into the night. I daresay you will become somewhat of a legend."

She waited patiently for his response.

The vampire narrowed his eyes at her as he considered the conditions. "You drive a hard bargain, Ms. Thornhart," a smirk slowly formed on his lips, "but I accept your terms." He stood. "I will wire you the money and sign the contract as soon as you email it to me. Given your reputation for an outstanding experience, I look forward to the delightful services you will undoubtedly provide."

He started towards the door.

"Mr. Broussard," she called out.

The vampire stopped and turned.

"See my accountant on the way out. The blood must be paid in full before you leave, or the deal is off."

"As you wish, Ms. Thornhart." He lowered his head in acknowledgment and departed.

"Four pints?" Sawyer whispered. "What are you going to do with those?"

"A pint of vampire blood is worth its weight in gold. An infusion of one bag will restore youth and give a witch an extra hundred years of life and vitality. I will have no trouble moving those three bags."

"Three? But you asked for four."

Harlow spun her chair around, drumming her fingers on the armrest. "The fourth is for me and these damn crow's feet I seem to have developed, no doubt from the aggravation and stress of this job. I think it's time I treated myself to a little spa day."

"Nonsense! You are as stunning as ever! Don't for one minute think otherwise!" Sawyer cleared away the glasses. "You know what you need? A little vacation somewhere far away from here. When was the last time you took some time off anyway? I know it hasn't been since I came to work for you."

Harlow frowned as she thought back. "I believe it must have been the year 1717 when I ended up spending some time down in Nassau at a little place called 'The Buccaneer's Boot'. Downstairs was a tavern with unbelievably good rum, upstairs was a brothel that catered to humans and The Diverse, and it was THE place to be for a good time. I will say one thing about Edward Teach and Stede Bonnet—those two fellows knew how to party."

"You knew Blackbeard?"

"Who do you think gave him the idea to add the smoke to his facade, giving himself that devilish appearance?" Harlow smirked. "That big oaf had too much rum one night and passed out. As a joke, I carefully braided his beard into little pigtails and tied them off with pink ribbons. Since he was still out of it, I decided to take it one step further by breaking up a candle into little pieces, stuffing them in his facial hair, and adding a long wick. When he started to come around, I snapped my fingers and lit the fuse. The lout nearly shit himself when he woke up and thought he was on fire. Stede and I laughed our asses off, watching him run around the room frantically beating his hands against his face and chest to put out the perceived blaze. When he finally noticed us in the corner roaring with laughter, he realized the joke was on him. He called us every nasty name in the book as he stomped across the floor, but when he reached the mirror and got a glimpse of himself, he decided he liked the look. The next thing I knew, rumors started to swirl about the demon pirate with fire coming from his beard, calling himself Blackbeard, as he raided ships up and down the east coast. After Lieutenant Maynard chopped off his head and sailed it back to Virginia, Lieutenant Governor Spotswood mounted it on a pole as a warning to other pirates. Somehow, a tavern owner in Williamsburg came into possession of it, had the skull lined in silver, and would dare his customers to drink from it."

"That's—interesting!" Sawyer did his best to conceal how truly mortified he was at the notion.

"I thought it was a rather creative idea myself. Somehow, I think he would have approved. I 'acquired' it from a museum in Salem a couple of decades ago. I keep it above my bar at home and, every now and then, have a drink from it in his honor.

"Is that what that thing is? I always wondered but never asked because I wasn't sure I wanted to know the answer! I was right!" Sawyer shook his head, deciding it was a suitable time to change the subject. "Would you like me to summon Cherise?"

"No, it's Thursday. She is performing at the club tonight. Have the car brought around, and I will stop in for a drink on my way home."

The Black Rose was the last remaining vestige of the golden age of Las Vegas, discretely hidden away among the overwhelmingly abundant flickering neon everyone seemed to be so fond of these days. Cut from a very different cloth, it harkened back to a time when men wore sharp, custom-tailored suits and ladies got dolled up in expensive, glamorous evening gowns to spend a night out on the town, sipping cocktails and listening to the sweet sounds of live performers like 'Ol Blue Eyes' himself. Crossing the threshold into this place was like stepping back in time to the 1950s—and that's exactly how Harlow intended to keep it. Ripped jeans and graphic tees sported by the younger generation, as well as those god-awful polyester kulaks and socks with sandals favored by the older crowd were expressly forbidden. On the right night and under certain circumstances, it might even get you killed. A formal dress code was posted at the entrance and strictly enforced. Beer didn't grace the menu at this exclusive establishment, only lavish cocktails and expensive, top-shelf whiskeys were offered here.

There was one other thing that made The Black Rose unique—it had become a haven for The Diverse and the handful of humans who knew of their existence to socialize and enjoy a relaxing night of entertainment without the need to conceal their true natures. Inevitably, even though it was out of the way and never advertised, some clueless mortal would somehow manage to wander in, completely unaware of who the true patrons of the club were. The regulars knew exactly who, and what, they were dealing with.

Harlow entered through her private entrance, emerging from her office and into the crowd unnoticed. Cherise was on stage, poured into a tight, low-cut silver gown, perfectly accentuating her curvaceous figure, topped off by a white mink fur stole. The crowd sat quietly entranced as she crooned a slow, sultry version of 'Fever' into the vintage mic, one gloved hand wrapped around the stand, the other reaching out towards the enraptured audience. From afar, she could have easily passed for Marilyn Monroe, especially given she had chosen to style her richly-colored blond hair in the same iconic fashion that night.

Taking a seat at the bar, Harlow recalled her one-time meeting with the young actress in the summer of '62. The pair had met at a glitzy soiree thrown by one of the humans Harlow had made a lucrative deal with. Normally, she didn't attend such things, but a few up-and-coming politicians were in attendance, and they were always good to have in your back pocket. Harlow had stepped outside for a smoke, only to realize her case was empty. Miss Monroe had kindly offered one of her own. She had been one of the few humans Harlow had taken an instant liking to, and the ladies had bonded over a few shared bottles of Dom Perignon. Miss Monroe, ironically, had an appointment with her two days after she was found dead of apparent suicide. Given some of the things confessed to her after a few drinks the evening they met, Harlow had her doubts as to that account. She often wondered how differently things might have turned out for the performer had she managed to work her into her schedule just a little bit sooner.

Shrugging her thoughts off, she waved the bartender for a drink. After all, the actress had been just a human, and humans weren't meant to live forever. Removing a Treasurer Luxury Black from her case, she waited for Samuel to place a martini in front of her before placing it between her lips. Producing a vintage lighter from beneath the bar, he lit her cigarette and asked, "Can I get you anything else, Ms. Thornhart?"

"No," she inhaled and blew out the smoke, "just let Cherise know I need a word with her between sets."

"Yes, ma'am," he replied, waiting for her to sample her drink, as was his custom. Taking a sip, she smiled. "Perfect as always, Samuel. You never disappoint. Thank you."

"My pleasure," he smiled bashfully, pleased by her compliment. His appearance and demeanor closely resembled a younger version of Morgan Freeman, the now slightly graying older gentleman had come here from Atlanta on vacation many years ago and fallen in with the wrong crowd, leaving him hooked on cocaine, penniless and beaten half to death in a back alley. It just so happened to be HER back alley, and she never much cared for attention from the local authorities. Taking him under her wing, she had gotten him cleaned up with the help of a mystical healer she kept on payroll with the company. Overcome with gratitude, and far too ashamed to return to his family in Georgia, he had pledged his undying loyalty to her, asking only for a chance to turn his life around. It just so happened, he was quite skilled as a master mixologist, so she gave him a job as a bartender in the club. Samuel had remained a loyal employee for the past thirty years, eventually working his way up to becoming the manager. The gang members who beat and robbed him, on the other hand, had all met tragic ends one week later when their flophouse mysteriously caught fire and burned to the ground—with them inside. The local authorities merely looked the other way when they discovered the doors had been bolted from the outside. After all, having a few less drug dealers in their city made their job easier.

"Those things will kill you, you know. You really should give them up," she heard a man say from just to her left. "I am Jim, by the way."

From the mirror behind the bar, she could see the reflection of one of those oblivious humans who had wandered in, his arm extended, waiting for her to shake his hand. The short, slightly balding man with a bad comb-over, was at least fifty and sporting a round pot-belly that was dangerously close to popping the bottom button holding his shirt together. The deep white skin indention on his left hand indicated he had wrenched off his wedding band only moments before finding his way inside the bar. Not only was his breath stale but, overall and in general, he reeked of desperation and disappointment.

Harlow turned and blew a perfectly round ring of smoke directly into his face. Coughing and sputtering, he waved his hand to clear the air in front of him.

"Let me save you some time and trouble, Jim," she said, now looking straight ahead, pausing to take another puff, "I already have a drink, so I don't need you to buy me one, especially since I own the fucking bar. I am not interested in hearing anything about your life as a traveling pharmaceutical rep, your three children, or your wife in Ohio who just doesn't understand you anymore. In fact, I don't want to have ANY sort of conversation with you and for the record," she turned and looked him directly in the eye, "I wouldn't fuck YOU if an asteroid hit the Earth tomorrow, destroying every last human being—AND DILDO—left on the planet. You are not going to have a pleasant evening here, Jim, so you might as well take your chances at one of the casinos lounges up the street. This isn't your type of crowd, and this is NOT going to be your lucky night."

"I—um—I—" the man stuttered as he reached for his wallet to pay for his drink.

"Forget it! It's on the house. Just get the fuck out of my club and out of my sight!"

Observing the exchange, Samuel winced feeling a certain amount of pity for the poor man. It was one thing to be turned down, but entirely another to have your manhood eviscerated on such a level. After all, the clueless bastard had no idea who he was dealing with. He carefully set aside the glass he was drying, reached beneath the bar, and slid a business card across the counter. "Go see Kandy. She will take care of you."

The man's eyes widened, and his face burned bright red from embarrassment.

"Kandy is," the bartender leaned forward on his forearms and whispered, "extremely talented, well-endowed, and appreciative of a hard-working man like yourself—plus her rates are more than reasonable. She might even give you a discount if you tell her Sam sent you. I promise you won't be disappointed."

The man snatched the card, offered an appreciative dip of the head, and hurried towards the door.

"Does Kandy give you a percentage of every client you send her way?" Harlow questioned.

"Not a percentage, per se," he replied, sporting a mischievous grin as he tossed the towel over his shoulder, "but we do have an arrangement that is mutually beneficial to both of us."

"In other words, she pays you in trade." Harlow rolled her eyes. "What is it about Vegas?"

"You seem to like it," Cherise chimed in as she took the bar stool next to her.

"It does have its advantages." Harlow slid over her cigarette case to share. "Are you and a few friends interested in a job?"

"What did you have in mind?"

Cherise was one of those humans who walked in two worlds. Her mother had been a witch who read Tarot cards on the strip, and her father was a black-jack dealer for one of the larger casinos. There wasn't much this young lady hadn't seen or experienced in her short lifetime. It also happened to make her the perfect person for Matthew Broussard. Cherise had once dated a vampire for a brief period, but it was long enough to discover the pleasures that went along with letting one of their kind feast on her blood. In humans, it created a high more pleasurable than any known street drug ever could provide and with no dangerous after-effects on the body.

"A vampire and his friend are in town for the weekend, and they are looking to have a little fun. The gig pays five thousand a piece, and for you, an extra ten grand to include your finder's fee for bringing your friends along. It is short notice, and they will require a great deal of attention, as well as discretion, all weekend."

"What exactly are they looking for?" Cherise lit a cigarette.

"A few games and a little bloodletting—the usual. You know the type. Of course, as always, you are under my exclusive protection while you are engaged with one of my clients."

"Sex?" she asked hopefully.

"Not in my contract, but you already know that. What you and your friends choose to do of your own accord, and for extra income, is none of my concern, as long as it is consensual on both ends. I don't need to know the sordid details. Interested?"

"What does he look like?"

"Let's just say you won't be disappointed. I don't know of any woman who would be."

"Well, you know I can't resist a vamp," Cherise replied with a tinge of excitement in her tone, "and my girlfriends and I could do with a little fun. Count us in."

"Splendid! I will have Sawyer send you the details, along with the key codes. You can entertain them out at the Mountain Pass house. It should be secluded enough for their needs."

"Looking forward to it!"

Harlow stubbed out her cigarette as Cherise returned to the stage and motioned for Samuel to call for her car before finishing her drink.

"Home?" asked Mitchell, after settling into the driver's seat of the Karlman King SUV and starting the engine.

"Not yet. Drop me off on the strip. I have something I need to take care of first."

"Find a high-stakes poker game that piqued your interest?"

"Not tonight. There is another more pressing matter that needs attending."

Glancing in the rearview mirror, he looked over at her for a moment. "Need me to come along?" he questioned.

"No, I can handle it," she replied with a sly smirk.

Mitchell was a former Navy Seal she had hired as her driver and personal bodyguard, even though protection was the last thing she needed. As Broussard had pointed out, appearances were everything, and as the CEO of a company worth hundreds of billions of dollars, she could never be seen without implied security.

Harlow emerged from the car and searched the crowd for Jim, the man who had wandered into the bar earlier. Kandy tended to work out of the lounge of The Aurora. As she started that way, she barely noticed the family dressed in shorts and matching Vegas t-shirts arranging themselves for a photo op in front of one of the fountains.

"Can you help us?" asked the father, leaping directly into her path, excitedly holding out his phone. Focused on the entrance to the casino, she didn't acknowledge him at first and was completely unaware he was addressing her until he dramatically waved both hands directly in front of her face to get her attention.

"Hello, there!" he sang in a mid-western accent. "Pardon the intrusion. I am Ed, this is my wife, Sheila," the woman waved, "and these are our kids, Ed Jr. and Sherry. This is our first trip to Vegas, and we were wondering if you could take a picture for our scrapbook."

When Harlow realized he was addressing her directly, she scowled. "NO!"

Spying Jim, she attempted to brush him off and go around, but he was persistent.

"Aw, come on!" he pleaded, stepping in her way. "It's really easy. All you have to do is press this little button," he pointed, "right here."

"GET OUT OF MY WAY!" she snarled.

"It will only take a second," the man insisted. Pressing it into her palm, he ran back over to join the others.

Harlow cocked her head to one side as her nostrils flared, enraged by this human's audacity. Surely, this puny creature had no idea how close he was to meeting his maker. Her eyes fixated on his as she held out her hand and squeezed, crushing the phone into a hundred pieces before dramatically dropping the fragments to the ground.

"Oops!" she derided, full of disdain, "I must have pressed that damn button a little too hard." Stepping on the shards, grinding them into the pavement, she emitted a low guttural growl and walked past him to continue on her way.

Ed's eyes widened in disbelief, her show of strength along with the loss of his phone rendering him speechless. Glancing nervously over his shoulder, he herded his family away from the scene, back towards the safety of their hotel room.

Jim had made his way inside.

Harlow reached the entrance at the exact same moment the ghoul who was following him did. As his hand reached for the door handle, Harlow grasped his wrist.

"What the hell do you think you are doing?" she demanded.

"I was just going in to have a little late-night snack," he replied.

Harlow pushed him away from the entryway, towards the side alley before shoving him against the building with a force he had never encountered before, cracking numerous bricks in the process. "You are not eating a human who just left my bar!"

"Why not? I saw how you treated him. Surely you don't care what happens to him!" he asserted.

"You're right! I don't! Stuff an apple in his mouth, rub his ass down with buttered seasoning, and slow roast the bastard on a spit, for all I care, but do it next week and far away from here. Did you forget about all the cameras in this town? I will not have the authorities coming down on my club because it was the last place that bastard was seen alive. I don't need, nor want, that kind of attention!"

"I'm sorry, Ms. Thornhart, you're right," he muttered, recognizing his mistake. "I wasn't thinking. I will be more careful next time, I promise."

Pressing her finger into his chest, he squirmed when it began to burn with an intense heat, like the tip of a hot poker. Leaning in close, she whispered in his ear, "I am only giving you a pass because you are new here. The next time you make a mistake like this in MY town, it will be the last one you ever make. You may think yourself immortal, but rest assured, there is not a creature walking this Earth I don't know how to kill, and if you think I don't have the gumption to do it, think again."

The young ghoul nodded, averting his eyes. "Yes, ma'am. Whatever you say."

"Get out of here!" she ordered and watched him scamper off into the crowd.

Shaking her head, she turned to leave. That's when she noticed Jim coming outside with Kandy on his arm. He had a huge smile plastered across his face; she was stuffing a wad of cash into her bra.

Walking back to the car, Harlow scoffed, "Why didn't I just let him eat you?"

"Where to?" asked an amused Mitchell as she slid into the back seat.

"Home! I have had entirely enough of humans for one day—" she wrinkled her nose when she realized she was addressing one and added, "no offense."

"None taken," he said with a sly grin, glancing into the rearview mirror. "I suppose humankind has sort of gone to hell in a handbasket as of late."

"Take my word for it, Mitchell, it is not a recent thing. Humanity has been doomed from the very beginning. If I am being completely honest, I am amazed the species has survived this long."

Chapter Two

Harlow dropped her keys on the table by the door and slipped off her shoes, tossing them aside one by one. Greeted by a roar from the large black panther who had wandered into the hall, she stopped to scratch the creature behind the ears.

"Good evening, Bathsheba. I trust you have had an uneventful day." The feline responded by purring before slinking off in the direction of the pool.

"I agree! I think that is an excellent idea!"

Strewing her clothes across several rooms, she sauntered through the mansion, completely bare by the time she reached the neon blue pool overlooking the city. Bathsheba had made herself comfortable, leisurely sprawled along the edge, draping one paw over the side and stirring, causing ripples to form. Harlow dove in headfirst, finding the water a bit cool, but refreshing. She took a lap before going to the center and swimming downward, coming to rest on the bottom in a meditative pose.

The water calmed her, helped to clear her mind on the most stressful of days. In all her years in this world, she had found it to be the only place she could go where the rest of the world was shut out. Closing her eyes, she remained perfectly still in the same position for nearly an hour. Her eyes popped open, however, when she sensed a presence.

Knowing she would get no peace until he had been dealt with, she surfaced to find the handsome devil casually leaning against the retaining wall with his hands in his pockets. Barefoot and dressed in a pair of black trousers, topped with a white button-down shirt opened halfway, he looked like someone who had just stepped out of one of those ridiculous cologne commercials.

"Cern!" she said as she walked up the steps and reached for a towel, drying off her face. "You know I don't like to be disturbed at home. What do you want? I am not in the mood for any of your Fae fuckery today."

"A little Fae fuckery is exactly what I had in mind," he purred in a sultry voice, strolling towards her, sporting a sexy smile along with those gorgeous golden eyes. "It occurred to me that I owe you a favor."

"You owe me eighteen favors, but who's counting?"

Lowering his head, he lightly brushed his thumb across his lips beguilingly. "I was hoping to work one or two of them off."

"Oh really!" Harlow tossed the towel aside and crossed her arms. "What did you have in mind?"

"By doing what I do best, of course."

"You want to—"

"Yes! This former Fae god would like to offer his services for the evening, devoting his undivided attention to pleasuring the one and only Ms. Thornhart."

The memory of when she first met Cernunnos, also known as 'the horned one', the old Celtic god of lust, rushed back. He had found his way to her doorstep when he fell out of favor with his family. Desirous of a new life, one without the responsibilities that came with his position, and far away from his mother, he had begged her to help him essentially fake his 'death', so he could begin anew. Seeing the advantage of having a god with a body like his at her disposal, she had agreed. He had been most grateful for her assistance and had spent the following three days expressing that appreciation.

"You think you will be repaying me when you are undoubtedly getting the better end of the deal? THAT would have to be considered favor number nineteen."

"Fine! Consider it favor number nineteen!" He shrugged. "I have grown bored bedding humans, and I need a little excitement in my life. Lucky for me, I know from personal experience, there is no one more exhilarating in the boudoir than Ms. Harlow Thornhart. What do you say? Toss this old dog a bone."

Harlow reached out and pressed her finger to his lips. The tip of his tongue darted out, seductively encircling the digit before taking it all the way in, suckling, his eyes fixed on hers. He grazed his teeth against it as she pulled it out and dragged it down his chin, past his neck, and to the opening of his shirt. Her sharpened nails sent buttons popping free, one by one as she continued, finally coming to rest at the top of his trousers. Her eyes drifted to his growing bulge as she considered his proposal. It had been a while since she had blown off any steam, and Cern certainly knew what he was doing in that department.

"I say," she said as she leaned in, "if you want to spend the night with me, you should be on your knees begging—and while you are down there..." Her sentence was interrupted when he grabbed by the waist and pulled her into a sensuous kiss. Dragging her fingers around to the back of his head, she smiled before suddenly grabbing a fistful of hair and roughly shoving him downward, into a better position to serve her needs. A carnal groan escaped him as his knees hit the ground. His excitement grew when his lips gently went to the top of one foot, then the other, taking a moment to silently worship the perfection that stood before him. His chaste kiss turned more urgent, his tongue beginning a slow, decadent swirl in a line upward to his prize. Harlow closed her eyes and laughed with delight as a wicked idea came to mind.

"How would you like to pay off some of that debt?"

"All I have is yours!" Cern's eyes drifted up dreamily. "There's nothing more valuable in this world than the sweet taste of Harlow Thornhart on your lips."

Two

"Put these in the vault," she said, handing Sawyer two vials when she returned to the office on Monday afternoon.

One held a few strands of hair and the other, a thick, glittery green substance that seemed to move of its own accord. He eyed that one warily. "What should I label them as?"

"One is the hair of a Fae god," a sly smirk crossed her lips, "and the other—well, let's just say you are probably better off not knowing. Just list it as 'Cern' and put that one in my private collection." She spun her chair around to face the window and lit a cigarette.

Sawyer held the vial away from his body and screwed up his face. "You are right, I really don't want to know." Sliding aside an original Johannes Vermeer painting concealing the safe, he secured it inside. "Let's just put that in here for the time being. I will take it down to the sublevel vault later—after I locate a hazmat suit and a barrel full of industrial-strength hand sanitizer to dunk myself in."

"Since when is a gay man afraid of 'that'?" she teased.

"Most gay men, including myself, aren't accustomed to it glowing in the dark," he retorted, eyeing it warily before closing the safe. "Are you sure it is not radioactive?"

Harlow grinned. "Messages?"

"Just the usual stuff, but I handled them. You do, however, have one interesting message from a shapeshifter looking for employment. The financial company she was working for was downsized and laid her off. Ironically, she had already been contemplating a career change where she could use her natural talents, which led her here."

"A shapeshifter?" Harlow's interest was piqued. "There aren't many of those left around, are there? It might be good to have one on the payroll.

Screen her and if you think she might be a good fit, set an appointment so I can meet with her."

"I will take care of it." Sawyer started towards the door. "Oh!" he exclaimed, pausing and snapping his fingers. "That paranormal fellow with the occult museum down the street called."

"What did he want?"

"He is looking for something new and exciting, a headlining artifact to bring in the tourists. He didn't seem to have anything specific in mind, just anxious to get his hands on whatever interesting item we can dig up—anything but clowns. Apparently, the man despises them."

"Who in their right mind doesn't?" she muttered and exhaled a puff of smoke. "Rummage around the vault and see what we have lying around down there. I think there may be a haunted doll or two, or perhaps even a few things from the home of that serial killer that recently died. Just make sure it's not anything he's going to hurt himself with. After all, he is one of our few clients willing to overpay without complaint. I need to keep ones like him around."

"Whatever you say! I will head down there and see what I can scrounge up. You know that man is going to owe you his soul before it's all said and done."

"He can't pay with what he doesn't own." Harlow glanced over her shoulder. "Do you know how many have already staked a claim on that thing? In true Vegas style, they will have to hold a tournament cage match just to determine who wins that prize when his time comes. I am happy to take his money while he's still alive and breathing."

"Well, let me see what I can find," he called out as he reached for the door.

"Sawyer! Any word from Cherise?"

"No, actually, I haven't heard anything," his brow creased, "and that's not like her!"

"No, it isn't!"

The fact that Cherise hadn't checked in didn't settle well with Harlow. Using the untraceable private line at her desk, she punched in the young woman's cell number, but it went straight to voicemail.

Dialing a different one, he answered immediately, as he always did. "Yes, ma'am! What can I do for you?"

"Mitchell, drive up to the Mountain Pass house and let me know what you find. Cherise and her friends were supposed to be there this past weekend entertaining some clients and she hasn't reported back in. I'm—concerned."

"I will leave immediately and call you as soon as I get there."

An hour later, while standing on the balcony enjoying another cigarette, her phone buzzed.

"Well?"

"I could describe what I found, but I think you will want to see it instead. It's not good."

Before he finished his sentence, she was already retrieving the keys to her sports car from the drawer. Harlow crossed the room, stepped into her private elevator, and hit the 'G' on the panel. "I'm on my way!"

Emerging from her exclusive underground garage, she went to the fastest car in her collection. Though she rarely drove, when she did, it was only the best. Sliding into the leather seat of the black Koenigsegg Gemera, her pulse quickened, and she smiled. After all, a car that did 248 mph was bound to get anyone behind the wheel a little excited. Tires squealed and heads turned as she exited the private garage. Racing down the strip at an unnatural speed, she was at the Mountain Pass house in a matter of minutes.

Mitchell was waiting outside when she arrived. A grim expression filled his face as he opened the car door and held it for her. The man was a former Seal, stoic in nature, and tended not to let his emotions show, yet she could sense something about what he had seen that day had greatly disturbed him.

"Show me!"

Stepping across the threshold into the large open design living room, Harlow felt the crunch of shattered wine glasses beneath her stilettos. The smell of blood, mingled with alcohol and a little something else assaulted her senses immediately. Broken furniture was strewn across the floor and the walls were covered from floor to ceiling in red symbols she recognized a little too well. Brushing her fingers across one of them, she drew her hand closer to her nose and inhaled. There was no mistaking it; they had been drawn with human blood. None of what she was seeing was sitting well with her.

"What are those?" Mitchell asked as he stepped around the shards of glass covering the floor. "I have never seen anything like it before."

"Sigils. They are symbols drawn and used by those who practice witchcraft for spells. These particular ones are used for concealing what someone does not want to be seen by magical methods. For instance, if someone was trying to scry for a person in a house with these surrounding them, the pendulum simply would not detect them." Confused as to why a vampire would be using them, she looked around the rest of the room, "Did you search the house?"

"I did." Holding out his hand, a solemn expression on his face, he directed her towards the staircase, allowing her to go first. "Just to the left," he instructed when they reached the top of the landing.

Harlow already knew what was coming, having detected the stench of death and decay as soon as they started towards the second floor. Numerous spots of blood soaked the carpet, forming a trail into the master bedroom. Peering inside, she could see the three shriveled bodies of the women lying across the bed, dumped unceremoniously after having been drained of their bodily fluids.

Frowning, Harlow walked around the room, carefully taking in every detail of the scene. Searching the faces of the victims, she breathed an internal sigh of relief when she saw Cherise was not among them. Her reprieve was brief, however, when she spotted a Polaroid picture being held in place on the wall by a butcher knife from the kitchen. The image was of the young woman sprawled in a chair, her eyes barely open, clutching an empty wine glass. That's when it dawned on Harlow what the other smell combined with the alcohol had been—Rohypnol, the date rape drug. Below it, a message was scrawled out.

'If you want her, come and get her! Laissez les bons temps rouler!'

Harlow's blood boiled as her anger overwhelmed. The sheer audacity of that vampire had her seeing red. How dare he come into her city and challenge her in such a manner? Snatching the photo from the wall, she turned and stormed out of the room, calling out orders as she went.

"Get the response team out here to move these bodies and have them find a more suitable place—and explanation—for their deaths, one that is not connected to Black Thorn Enterprises in any form or fashion. Then have the cleanup crew wipe this place down with a flame thrower. I want nothing left behind. After you get them started, meet me back at the office. We have a situation that needs handling."

"Yes, boss!"

"I want eyes on Broussard NOW!" she bellowed into the speaker, jamming the gas pedal down as far as it would go. Mitchell had called Sawyer before she arrived and filled him in, so the assistant was already working on the problem.

"The IT department is checking satellite imagery now," responded a frazzled Sawyer. She could hear him typing away furiously. "It looks like his personal jet took off from a private airstrip near there about eight hours ago."

"What about Cherise? Any sign of her?"

"I can't tell. The plane was stored inside a hanger, and the car pulled directly up to a darkened canopy connected to it. I am afraid we are at a disadvantage trying to track a creature who needs to move under the cover of darkness."

"Did the surveillance cameras outside the house pick up anything?"

"I am afraid not. Every single piece of footage from their time there was mysteriously blacked out. I have some of the IT people looking at it, but they are fairly certain there is nothing to retrieve."

"What's his destination according to the FAA?"

"The registered flight plan says New Orleans."

"Ready the jet. Make the arrangements and have a car waiting on the tarmac. Call Mitchell and tell him to grab his things. We leave within the hour."

"On it, boss!"

Harlow hung up the phone and growled, gripping the steering wheel tighter. Only one thought filled her mind as the words spewed forth from her lips. "Enjoy your last few hours in this world, Matthew Broussard, because you are a dead vamp walking!"

Chapter Three

New Orleans, Louisiana

It was around 3 a.m. when they touched down. A black Suburban was waiting on the tarmac when they arrived. Mitchell drove them directly to the hotel Sawyer had booked for them.

La Maison des Divers was a restored home from the seventeenth century tucked discreetly away in a secluded part of the French Quarter. Built in the Queen Anne style, the sprawling, white three-story residence boasted a gabled roof, three domed turrets, dormer windows, and a stunning, circular wrap-around porch. A ten-foot-high black wrought-iron fence formed a perimeter around the property, enclosing the large oaks and magnolia trees dripping with Spanish moss that filled the landscape, affording the estate a great deal of privacy. A small plaque on the secured front gate was the only identifier of this exclusive manor. It was a home away from home for The Diverse, where they were free to relax among those of their own kind without fear of reprisal.

"Ah, Ms. Thornhart," cooed the leprechaun manning the front desk, "Welcome back to New Orleans. We are honored to have you stay with us again. It has been far too long since you have graced us with your presence." He ambled down from the raised platform that had been built with a custom set of handrails and steps, allowing him to greet his guests face to face. Taking his carved wooden cane in hand, he came around the front counter. Reaching into the front pocket of his dark green suitcoat, he produced two gold keys and motioned for them to follow. "Your private suite is ready, as is the room next door for your driver. A complete office has been set up per your assistant's request, and, as always, we are at your disposal for whatever your heart desires."

"Thank you, Carter."

"Are you here to enjoy Mardi Gras?" he inquired politely, escorting her up the beautiful grand staircase that had been intricately carved with depictions of the gods and goddesses from Greek mythology.

"No! I am here on business to kill someone who crossed my path," she replied matter-of-factly.

"Oh!" Carter smiled uncomfortably and looked straight ahead. Then, as an afterthought, "It's not me, is it?"

"Why? Have you done something that warrants such a punishment?" she snapped. "Oh no, no, no!" He assured. "Well, not unless you count lifting a few gold coins off the tourists—or the occasional pair of shoes that I may or may not have pilfered from some unsuspecting visitors—but certainly nothing as serious as what you are suggesting." The shiftiness in his tone did not go unnoticed.

"From human tourists or members of The Diverse?"

"Why, the humans of course!" he replied, somewhat insulted. "What do you take me for? I would never do that to one of our kind."

"Then, have at it as much as you like! I could care less!"

Mitchell cleared his throat from behind to remind her he was still there.

"Except for this one who is off-limits," she clarified. "He is with me and under my protection."

"Shoes?" Mitchell questioned.

"Leprechauns have a shoe fetish," she explained in a hushed tone over her shoulder. "They have an uncontrollable urge to steal the ones that catch their eye. They have also been known to take the odd foot or two, if it's a particularly good pair of shoes and the owner puts up too much of a fight."

Mitchell grimaced. "How exactly do they take the feet off?"

"Trust me! You really don't want to know. They can be nasty little creatures when their greed gets the better of them."

Mitchell eyed the leprechaun warily and frowned.

Carter smiled warmly back at him, revealing a monstrous set of sharp, jagged teeth.

"Have I mentioned, those heels are to die for?" Carter remarked as his eyes drifted to her pumps.

"These are one-of-a-kind, made from the skin of the LAST leprechaun who coveted my shoes. Have I mentioned I have been in search of a matching handbag to go with them?" She fired back. "If I recall correctly, you seem to resemble him a great deal."

Carter immediately shifted his gaze straight ahead, an abysmal expression filling his face. "Your room is just down the hall. Let's get you comfortably settled in, shall we?"

Harlow paced the room, mentally exploring the options of which method she would use to put an end to the vampire.

"I need the address Broussard gave to us when he booked the appointment," she bellowed into the speaker phone on the desk, her assistant on the other end.

"I just sent it over to your phone, as well as Mitchell's, but you should know, it's the address for his office, not the one for his home."

"What? Why is that all we have?"

Sawyer sighed. "It was an oversight on the part of the IT department. Given the amount he paid up front and the extremely short notice, no one took the time to verify the minor details. It simply slipped through the cracks."

"Find out who let it slip, and I will deal with that person when I return."

"I already did. It was Rowan Webster, and he is extremely apologetic for his mistake. He is, at this very moment, digging into Broussard's background while hacking into Cherise's emails, texts, and voice mails trying to get any and all information the vampire might have sent her directly." Pausing, he felt the need to add, "Rowan feels horrible about what happened and would do anything to make up for it."

"You know what? I don't care where he WAS. Just tell me where he IS at this very moment!"

"We don't know for certain," Sawyer winced as he uttered the words, holding the phone away from his ear in anticipation of what would inevitably come next, "It is proving more difficult than we could have anticipated. He seems to be two steps ahead of us."

"How the hell is this one fucking vampire from New Orleans managing to outmaneuver every single person in my company?" "I think that is a question that deserves further investigation, and you may not like the answers we find," Sawyer confessed.

"What do you mean by that?" she barked.

"I mean," he blew out the breath he had been holding, "it appears he may have had some help on the inside. He knew exactly how we would handle the transaction and the steps we would follow, as if he may have had knowledge of our internal procedures and protocols."

"You think we may have a spy in our midst?" she bristled, mostly because the thought had already crossed her mind.

"It would explain quite a bit."

Harlow let out a low, guttural growl. "Start the interrogations and find me the one who is responsible for this. I will take intense pleasure in dealing with him or her personally upon my return." "What are you going to do while we are checking on that?"

"Oh, I have a few ideas, but right now I need to know where Broussard is! I am going to pay a visit to the only address we have on file for him and see what I can find."

"Watch your back, boss!" Sawyer cautioned. "You may not realize it, but New Orleans can be a dangerous place, especially for those who are different."

Chapter Four

Sitting around the rickety table at the rundown fishing camp, Chase Devereaux eyed his two younger brothers, Randy and Logan, from behind the cards he held. He had learned a long time ago how to read their body language with a great deal of accuracy.

The old wooden floor creaked when Randy reached around and scratched the back of his neck, a guaranteed sign he was bluffing. That hunch was confirmed when he wiped his mouth with his palm after clearing his throat for no apparent reason, his face remaining stoic. It was one of the things that made him a great interrogator in his job as a police detective—IF you didn't know what to watch for. He wasn't the one to beat.

Logan anxiously drummed his fingers on his right thigh while rocking his chair back, balancing it on two legs, his surefire tell for having a rather decent set of cards. Judging by the lively tune he was humming and the grin he was attempting to suppress, Chase was willing to bet money he was sitting on four of a kind. That kid was never able to keep a straight face, even if his life depended on it. The weak link among the siblings, Logan was always the first to spill the beans whenever they got in trouble, becoming the one their mama went to when she needed someone to rat out one of the others. Two chocolate chip cookies and that boy folded like a cheap suit.

"I call!" Logan said, tossing five poker chips into the middle of the table, having a tough time hiding the excitement on his face. "What have you got?"

Randy slapped his cards down in disgust. "A pair of twos."

"Ha!" Logan fanned out his cards and waved them in front of his face. "Four of a kind. Beat that!"

"What about you, big brother?" asked Randy, looking on with disgust as Logan reached for the winnings.

Chase narrowed his eyes, and a slow smirk spread across his face. Spreading out the cards one by one on the table, he announced, "Royal flush!"

Logan froze. "Damn it!" he grumbled, reluctantly relinquishing his hold on the winnings.

"Better luck next time," Chase chuckled, raking the pile of chips over in front of him. "It looks like the next round at the bar is on me."

"I was hoping to BE at the bar by now," Randy complained. "How much longer is this going to take?"

A bone-chilling howl split the air, a somber response to his question. He tensed and slowly turned towards the window. The three brothers became quiet and exchanged guarded looks.

"It's headed this way," Logan muttered, casting a wary glance towards the door. "It must have finally picked up on the blood trail." Randy got up, went over to the makeshift fireplace, and tossed on two more large pieces of wood before adding a little lighter fluid. "Well, it's about damn time. We laid it at sunset. I have to be back at the police station in a few hours." Using the poker, he stoked the flame until it blazed brightly.

"And I have the early morning shift with the EMTs," added Chase, peeking through a knothole in the side of the shack.

"How did you manage that?"

Chase and Randy both turned to glare at Logan who was trying unsuccessfully to conceal the grin on his face. "Hey, it's not my fault you lost the coin toss."

Randy crossed his arms. "I suppose it's his OWN fault for flipping a man with a two-headed coin, you little shit!"

"Two-headed coin?" exclaimed Chase. "You cheated your older brother, the one who has looked out for you your entire life? The same one who kept Johnny Reardon from kicking your ass when you kissed his girlfriend behind the restaurant on Valentine's Day? How's that for gratitude?"

"For the record," Randy chimed in, "I would have LET him kick your ass. It was Valentine's Day, after all."

"I don't know what you're talking about!" Logan winced, quickly getting up. "I need a beer!" and went outside to get one from the cooler on the porch.

"You didn't really fall for that, did you?" Randy asked as soon as he was out of earshot.

"Of course not!" whispered Chase with a wink. "I know you and our little brother better than anyone else. I just needed a break from working in the ER. You know I hate being cooped up in there, especially on weeks like this, so whenever I need to get out for a while, I always offer to flip him for his shift. That lucky bastard hasn't lost yet."

Randy chuckled and shook his head. "You always did know how to get what you wanted out of us."

"It's a gift bestowed on the eldest brother at birth," Chase laughed.

The howl came again, this time much louder.

Logan returned with three bottles, handing one to each of his brothers. After popping the tops and chugging them down, Logan confirmed their suspicions. "He's about a hundred yards out. Time to go to work boys!"

Moving quickly to gather their long blades from where they hung on the wall, the trio filed out the front door. The brothers knew they were the only thing standing between the rogue rougarou that had been terrorizing the area for the past month and its next victim. Not much attention had been given to it when it was just killing small animals, but when it moved up to taking the lives of two fishermen a few days ago, the brothers knew it was time to step in.

They returned thirty minutes later, splattered in mud, blood, and other bodily fluids with their prize in hand. Chase reluctantly tossed the severed head of his childhood classmate onto the fire and frowned as the lifeless brown eyes of his old friend stared back at him accusingly. Striking the final blow to the ferocious beast had caused him to turn back into his human form. No one had been taken more off guard than Chase when it happened, and he was having a hard time reconciling his conscience with what he had done.

"Who would have thought it was Billy Harmon?" asked Logan, using the same towel to wipe his face and his blade clean.

"We used to fish together as kids," Chase spoke in a low tone, his eyes fixated on the flames consuming the head. "When we were thirteen, he was the one who gave me my first hit off a joint while we looked at the Playboy's he took from underneath his daddy's mattress. His wife and kids are going to be devastated. I don't know how they are going to get through this especially since he was the only one working."

"We will figure out a way to see the family is taken care of." Randy gripped his brother's shoulder comfortingly. "It had to be done, Chase, or others would have died. If we hadn't taken him down, the blood of the innocent would have been on our hands."

"Yeah, I know but it doesn't make it any easier."

"How long do you think he'd been one?" Logan asked unexpectedly.

Chase shrugged. "It couldn't have been very long because he had no control over himself whatsoever. He was acting more like a wild animal who had no idea what he was doing. My best guess? He was turned only a couple of weeks ago."

Randy sighed heavily. "Which means, there is another one out here somewhere who did the turning."

"They are all over Louisiana, as you well know," Chase turned. "It's only the ones who cause problems that we need to concern ourselves with."

"It's getting late. You two should head home," Logan suggested. "You might even manage a couple of hours of sleep if you hurry."

"What about you?"

Logan threw himself across the ragged, dusty sofa, tucking his folded hands behind his head. "I am going to stay for a bit, just to make sure nothing else is lurking about. After all," he grinned, "I don't have to be at work in the morning."

At sunrise, Chase sat on the edge of his bed and rubbed the sleep from his eyes. He hadn't got much rest. Whenever he drifted off, childhood memories of Billy would fill his dreams and, when he woke, he was forced to re-live the previous night's events all over again.

Going over to the window, he pulled back the curtain and looked out. This was his favorite time of day when only locals filled the streets while the tourists were still in their hotel rooms sleeping off the prior night's revelry. Still feeling melancholy, he decided the best therapy for his current frame of mind would be work, and his mood instantly lifted when he remembered it was his day in the city.

Chase had been Chief of the Emergency Room for six years now. He loved the job most of the time. It was during Mardi Gras when he liked it a little less. After all, taking bets on who would be puked on the most by drunks in one night tended to get old quickly. His personal record had been seven incidents in one eight-hour shift. Ride days with the EMTs meant he got to get out among the locals who really needed help, and that was where his heart truly was. After a quick shower, he dressed and grabbed his wallet and keys.

His spirits continued to improve with the smell of chicory coffee filling the hall as he locked the door of his loft apartment. Descending the stairs and rounding the corner, he smiled when he saw a familiar face waiting with two bags of beignets, along with cups to go.

"Thanks, Mama! I don't know what I would do without you!" he said with a huge grin and kissed her on the cheek.

"Starve to death—that's what you'd do!" she chided, rubbing his arm.

"How can I starve to death when I live above the best restaurant in New Orleans with the finest cook in all of Louisiana in the kitchen?" Taking the bags and the coffee, he headed towards the door. "Love you, Mama!"

"Love you too! Now, go save some lives. Have a good day, and cher, be careful!" she called out, beaming with pride as she watched him go.

Jacquelin Devereaux was proud of all her boys, but especially that one, who had worked his way through medical school on scholarships while still helping to look after the family. Chase had been so young and carefree when his father passed, but something in him had changed that day. He never once complained about having to step up and assume the position as 'man of the house', helping with his siblings while she worked late hours at the restaurant to pay the bills. The community had rallied around them, but she had no idea how she would have managed. He had been her rock when she needed him the most, and now he took as good a care of the locals as he had of them.

As soon as he was out of sight, her expression faded and was replaced with something a little more disconcerting. Sliding her hand into her apron pocket, she nervously ran her thumb over her mother's rosary, which she had taken from her jewelry box in the wee hours of the morning. A worrisome feeling had settled into the back of her mind, overcoming her sometime during the night. It was one stronger and unlike anything she had ever felt before. Over the years, she had learned to pay attention to those little inklings, having saved her a great deal of grief on more than one occasion, but something about this time was different. Trouble was on the horizon, and she wasn't sure if they were prepared for what was to come.

A voice on the television in the background caught her attention. Grabbing the remote from the counter, she turned up the volume to better hear the perky blonde giving the weather forecast.

"You might need that umbrella if you are headed out to work or the Mardi Gras festivities tomorrow folks. A little low has formed off the coast, basically blowing up out of nowhere, and it looks like it might be headed straight for the city."

"What are you doing here, doc?" asked Simone Martin, looking up from the paperwork on her desk as Chase strolled in. She was one of the regular EMS workers on duty for that shift.

"Didn't you get the memo?" He kicked the door closed behind him. "I am your partner for the day."

"Uh-huh!" Simone rested her forearms on the desk and smiled. "That brother of yours suckered you into filling in for him again, didn't he?"

"I lost a coin toss, fair and square," he replied with a grin, kissing her on the cheek before handing her one of the bags, "but it's alright, I don't mind. After all, I get to spend the day away from the hospital AND with a pretty lady. I got no complaints!"

"Flatterer!" Catching a whiff of the food as she unrolled the bag, a wide smile spread across her face. "I can't say that I mind either. That brother of yours never brings me breakfast and, God knows, I LOVE your mama's cooking!"

"The best in Louisiana!" he agreed, setting a cup of coffee in front of her.

"How is it you are still single, Chase? You are thoughtful, handsome, a doctor, and you deliver the best food in town. You are every girl's dream."

"According to my last girlfriend, I work long hours, spend too much time with my family, and at this stage in my life, should have a place of my own that's not above my mama's restaurant where she cooks for me every day."

"First of all, there is nothing wrong with any of those things and second, that woman was a high-maintenance bitch. You are better off without her and should be on your knees thanking your lucky stars you dodged that bullet!"

He laughed and pulled up a chair next to her, popping a beignet in his mouth as he pointed to the computer screen. "What are we looking at today?"

"I thought we might stop by the nursing home this afternoon and check in on my granddaddy. His blood pressure has been up, and he won't take his pills unless I come by and fuss at him every couple of days.

"I think maybe George does it on purpose so his granddaughter will keep coming by to see him," Chase suggested. "Didn't he do the same thing when his sugar was up a little bit last year?"

"Yes, he sure did, now that I think about it! You know what? You might be on to something there!" The thought hadn't even occurred to her. "Oh, that sneaky little cuss! I am going to have to teach him a lesson."

"Or you could just play along and let him have his fun. As I recall, his blood pressure wasn't terrible, and his sugar levels are in the prediabetic range, which isn't especially worrisome since he DID just turn ninety-seven. You could cut him some slack, maybe spring him for a night of Mardi Gras? After all, he can only have so much fun where he is now."

"You're absolutely right! I think I will do just that when I am off tomorrow," she agreed. "Thanks for pointing that out."

"Happy to help." He turned his attention back to the screen. "What else have we got?"

"As far as calls, it's been a fairly quiet morning for a change, not that I'm complaining. I just hope it stays that way. Honest to goodness, if I get puked on by one more person with alcohol poisoning, I am calling in sick for the rest of Mardi Gras."

"I hear you, and don't get me started on the stupid things they do before that!" Chase grimaced. "A few days ago, I actually had to cut a set of beads off a drunk guy's dick after he tied them in a knot right before taking a Viagra."

"Sweet Jesus in Heaven! What the hell is wrong with these people?"

"Mardi Gras madness!" Chase chuckled. "It happens every year without fail. I think you and I both could do with a slow day."

Two minutes later, the radio went off.

Chapter Five

It was 7 am and Mitchell was catching a few hours of sleep, one of the many faults that went along with being human. Harlow decided it was best if she checked out Broussard's office alone, a place not far from where they were staying. Slipping on her long coat, she stepped outside and quickly covered the three-block distance in no time.

The streets were unusually empty, only a few humans here and there, most of them attired for work, all extremely friendly, politely saying 'hello' and 'good morning' as they passed by.

Harlow rolled her eyes each time.

Finally, locating the large brick building, she made sure no one was watching and slipped down the side alley. It appeared to be deserted, all the signage having been removed. Working her way around to the back, she tried to peek inside, but the windows were covered with blinds that were closed. Finding a locked metal door, she crushed the handle in her hand and ripped it off the hinges before tossing it aside with ease.

The cream-colored walls were bare, only the outlines of where things had once hung were left. The wood floors had been swept, but still showed signs of wear and tear from many years of being used. The space had been emptied of everything except for a single office chair, intentionally left in the middle of the room and turned away. A low guttural growl escaped her when she saw the seat was currently occupied. With the wave of her finger, she spun it around. In it sat the white shriveled corpse of Matthew Broussard, his severed head resting on his lap. By the fresh smell wafting on the air, he had only been dead a couple of hours. Oddly enough, his body had been completely drained of blood, not even one drop left on the floor. He did, however, have a single sheet of paper with something printed on it stapled to his forehead, his eyes open and fixated upwards as if pointing to it. Ripping it free, she read it aloud.

"From the desk of Harlow Thornhart, Black Thorn Enterprises."

Her head snapped up when her keen sense of hearing picked up on the faint sound of sirens. Her attention shifted to a small panel at the door, and she realized a silent alarm had been triggered when she came inside.

"It looks like someone was expecting me."

Exiting the building, she bawled up the paper and threw it into the trash dumpster outside. With the flick of her hand, the metal container went up in flames. As she started away, the grinding of moving metal could be heard. Stopping and turning, she noticed a small surveillance camera tucked in the eave of the building to be the cause of the noise. It was focused directly on her.

Playing to her audience, Harlow outstretched her arms, palms up, inviting whoever was watching to reveal themselves. When no one appeared, she shrugged, waved goodbye, and snapped her fingers. The device exploded as she walked away.

"What the hell is going on here?"

Harlow ducked into the first restaurant she came to, passing a police car as she stepped across the threshold. It was a few doors down with the name 'Deveraux's Kitchen' painted on the front window. Taking a table in the corner, one that gave her a clear view of the street, she settled in and watched the emergency responders rush to Broussard's office. Though she didn't technically need to eat, she thought it best to not bring attention to herself by sitting inside without ordering. Besides, she had discovered over the years that sugar and caffeine were two of the few things she actually enjoyed in this forsaken world.

"Good morning! My name is Livi. What can I get you started with?" asked the waitress who came over to greet her. Busy writing on her pad, she didn't bother to look at who she was addressing.

"What do you suggest?" Harlow asked, taking off her sunglasses and screwing up her face at the checkered tablecloths. A plastic menu was tucked between the metal napkin dispenser and the ketchup bottle in front of her.

The woman glanced up from her pad and gasped, taking a step back when she saw Harlow's eyes were a mix of crimson and black. "I take it you are from out of town?"

Cocking her head to one side, she smarted, "What was your first clue?"

"The fact that you asked what you should order for one." Using her pencil to bring attention to the menu, her eyes remained fixated on Harlow. "We are famous in the French Quarter for one thing in the mornings—our café au lait and beignets."

"Fine! Bring whatever you humans eat."

"Humans?" Livi blinked hard and shook her head. "Alright, I will get that right out. Say, can I ask you about those great colored contacts you're wearing? They are pretty awesome and would be perfect for my Halloween costume. Did you need a prescription for them?"

"I am not wearing any contacts."

"You're not?"

Harlow shook her head. "No! This is my natural color."

"Oh!" Livi drew her lips into a frown. Using her pencil to point over her shoulder, she added, "I am just going to go grab that order," before hurrying off.

When Livi returned with her cup, Harlow leaned back in the chair with her arms folded. "Do you know someone by the name of Matthew Broussard? I believe he handles real estate or something of the sort around here."

"I know the name, but that's about it. I also haven't lived here long, so I'm not the one to ask. Jacquelin is the owner, and she knows everyone around. I can send her over if you like."

"Please do!" Harlow pulled a hundred-dollar bill from her phone case and slid it across the table. "It's important."

Livi readily accepted and tucked it in her apron. "Sure thing."

Harlow took a sip from her cup, a surprising expression crossing her face. "Not bad! Not bad at all!"

An older woman was chatting with someone at the counter. Harlow watched Livi pull her aside and they both looked in her direction as she whispered something. The woman's eyes widened, and her jaw tightened.

"Catholics!" Harlow muttered under her breath, sensing the uneasiness rolling off the woman. She could see the outline of the rosary she was clutching in her pocket. "Why does it always have to be Catholics?"

"I am Jacquelin Devereaux," the owner said coolly as she came over and placed a plate of beignets in front of her, keeping her distance. "Livi said you had a question for me."

Harlow forced the warmest smile she could muster. "Yes. I am looking for information about someone by the name of Matthew Broussard. Do you by chance know anything about him?"

Jacquelin hesitated, her hand unconsciously drifting to the incredibly old, jeweled gold cross hanging around her neck. "Why would you need to find him?" The older woman must have subconsciously sensed Harlow was somehow different.

"I have some business with him I am anxious to conclude." Hoping to hurry things along, Harlow remarked, "That is a lovely necklace you are wearing." Reaching out, she asked, "May I? I am a bit of an expert on antiques and a sucker for beautiful jewelry."

Jacquelin offered a curt nod and watched carefully for a reaction as Harlow leaned forward, slipping her palm beneath the cross. "It has been passed down on my husband's side of the family for generations and has been blessed by three different Popes."

Harlow smiled when she felt the old woman's body relax a bit. She knew exactly how to handle humans like this one. Jacquelin had just enough faith and conviction to believe someone unclean of nature would never be able to touch such a sacred item and come away unscathed.

"It was made in the late 1800s by Gerald Bouchon if I am not mistaken," Harlow continued. "He was a fine maker of religious jewelry in Rome at the time, but unfortunately not very well-known. And unlike some of his fellow artists of the period, he did not become famous after his death, which is a shame because he was quite talented. It has been said that he created some of his best pieces for certain members of the Vatican to use in the expulsion of demons during exorcisms."

"How do you know so much about it?" Jacquelin pulled out one of the chairs and slowly sat down.

Releasing it, Harlow leaned back. "I few pieces of his have come into my possession over the years and I recognize his distinct style. I am a purveyor of the unusual, if you will—a buyer and seller of some of the world's most extraordinary items. Your piece is quite exquisite."

"Well, you certainly seem to know your trade."

"It is imperative in my line of work. Please, if you know anything about Broussard, I would be most grateful for the information." The woman's brow creased. "There is a lot of talk about that man and none of it is good."

"I understand, and I consider myself duly warned."

Jacquelin glanced around to make sure they were alone. "He had an office a few doors down, but it was sold a couple of months ago out of the blue and the word is he left no forwarding address. I don't know where he lives, never have, but there are rumors that his mama's side of the family had a place out in the middle of nowhere near Belle Chasse before the Civil War. I am not sure there is even anything left out there other than water and gators. No one ever goes near it because it is rumored to be haunted by a pirate. I'm sorry, that's all I know."

"Thank you! You have been a huge help." Harlow did her best to seem sincere as the elder woman got up and started away. Taking a beignet, she held it up for a closer inspection before taking a nibble. When the sweetness hit her taste buds, she moaned and popped the rest in her mouth, relishing the flavor.

Jacquelin paused and turned, a sudden thought occurring to her. "You know, the new owner might know where to find him."

"Oh really?" Harlow swallowed and lifted her cup to wash it down. "Who might that be?"

"It's some company out of Las Vegas, though I don't know for the life of me what they would be doing all the way down here." Tapping the side of her temple, she tried to recall the name. "I believe I heard someone call it Black Heart—no! Black Thorn Enterprises?"

Resting the cup back on the saucer, Harlow gritted her teeth. "Thank you," she repeated, keeping a cool demeanor on the outside. Inside, she teemed with rage.

Jacquelin smiled and returned to work.

Harlow's phone began to buzz. Looking down, she saw it was Sawyer.

"Have you found him?" he asked when she answered.

"Oh, I found him," she whispered in a low tone, "but he was already dead."

"What? Who the hell killed him?"

"I don't know, but someone is playing games with me, and no one plays games with Harlow Thornhart!"

Chapter Six

Detective Randy Deveraux was the first officer on duty to arrive. Removing an extinguisher from the trunk of his car, he doused the dumpster fire in the back before it could do any damage to the building. Noticing the backdoor had been tossed haphazardly aside, he withdrew his Glock from his side holster. Aiming his weapon, which he kept loaded with silver bullets just in case, at the ground, he quickly peeked around the corner.

"POLICE! MAKE YOURSELF KNOWN!" he shouted.

Pausing to listen, he relaxed a bit when he was met with dead silence. A rapid sweep of the area revealed he was the only living soul in the building. Holstering his gun as he crossed the room, he frowned when he saw Matthew Broussard, or what was left of him, sitting in the chair. Circling the body and squatting down for a better look, Randy found it oddly peculiar there was no blood, especially given he had been decapitated and the head was resting on his lap. It appeared he had been deliberately drained. "What the hell?" Standing, he went over the rest of the place but found nothing. Radioing for an ambulance, he specifically requested a certain unit knowing he would need the assistance of his brother who had taken a shift that morning.

Chase and Simone pulled up just as he returned to his vehicle.

"What have we got?" asked Simone, grabbing her gear from the rig. "And what's with the extinguisher?"

"DOA inside and a small trash fire out back," Randy replied. "I just need the doc here to officially pronounce him dead so I can get the forensic team involved."

"Oh! Well, we will just make sure," and she started inside.

Randy stepped in front of her, cutting his eyes to Chase.

"It's a mess in there, plus, we don't want to contaminate the crime scene."

Simone looked back and forth between the brothers, unsure of what to do.

"Why don't you run down to Mama's and grab us some more coffee?" Chase suggested. "I will take care of things here, and then we can head back to the station. It won't take long, I promise."

"Grab me one too," Randy added. "Tell Mama to put it on my tab."

"Yeah, right! Like your mama charges any of you boys," she said with a grin as she stuffed her bag back into the truck.

"What have we got?" asked Chase once she was out of earshot.

Motioning him inside, he explained, "Matthew Broussard, minus his head and all of his blood."

"Broussard?" Chase stopped short when he saw the corpse. "Damn! This is new!"

"I don't suppose there is a chance this was just some kind of weird sex thing that got out of control?" Randy crossed his arms. "After all, it is Mardi Gras, and we have seen stranger things than this."

"I guess there's always a chance," his brother replied dryly. "Not likely, but there's always a chance, I guess."

"Depraved serial killer, rival vampire, or do we have someone else hunting these things who just showed up in town, not realizing we were already here?" Randy went over for a closer inspection.

"Got me? Usually, these creatures are better about covering their tracks. The decapitation aspect is new."

"Yeah," Randy agreed, "not to mention the blood drain. Do vampires drink other vampires' blood?"

"You're asking me? How the hell would I know?"

"You're the oldest brother. Aren't you supposed to know everything?" Randy teased.

"Well, I know he is dead," Chase muttered. "I will fill out the paperwork so you will have it for your report. What do you want me to list as the cause of death?"

"Suicide?"

"Suicide?" Chase scrubbed his jawline and stared at Broussard. "So, this guy killed himself by chopping off his own head," looking around, "with no blade of any kind and it just happened to land in his lap?"

"Wouldn't be the first time we have stretched the truth."

"At least you had the good sense to keep Simone out of here." Chase blew out a hard breath. "Alright, text me whatever you want me to put down in the report. What about the folks in forensics?"

Randy shrugged. "I haven't called them yet. Maybe some embers from that dumpster fire out back will spill out and cause this place to mysteriously go up in flames before they arrive. Lucky for me, my brother the doctor was here to witness the scene before that happened."

"Alright, whatever you think is best." Chase slapped Randy on the back. "Keep me posted."

Harlow stormed back to the hotel to find Mitchell awake and working on his laptop.

"What's wrong?" he demanded when he noticed her less-than-calm demeanor.

"I have just found out that Broussard's former office space, and the place I just discovered his headless corpse in, was sold to Black Thorn Enterprises!" she snarled, slamming her hand on the nearby bureau, shattering the marble top. "Find out what the fuck is going on!"

Mitchell picked up his phone and started making calls as he typed on his computer. By mid-afternoon, he had an answer.

"It looks like the building was sold to Black Thorn Enterprises three weeks ago," he said, pointing to the screen. "Money was transferred from your private corporate account straight into Broussard's and immediately rerouted to an offshore one."

Resting one hand on the desk and leaning over, she asked, "Who made the deal and signed the paperwork?"

"This says you did."

"I most certainly did not!"

"Everything was done with, and came from, your direct account."

"No one has access to that other than me!"

Mitchell frowned. "That's what's so disturbing. Sawyer may be right—there may indeed be a spy in the company."

Harlow paced the floor. "Who would be stupid enough to try and pull something like this on me?"

Her driver leaned back in his chair. "I don't know, ma'am, but until we find out, it may be best to work on the assumption no one can be trusted knowing what your next move will be. What would you like me to do?"

Regarding him, she paused to think about the answer. This situation would require more than her security guard could handle. She needed someone a little more powerful in her corner. He would likely get hurt. Finally, she replied, "Go home, Mitchell."

"You mean back to Vegas?" He was genuinely taken aback. "Begging your pardon, but why would you want that? I would never betray you if that is what you are implying!" Harlow rested her hand on his shoulder. "I know, and I don't believe for one minute you ever would. You and Sawyer are the only two I do trust. I need you to go help him find out who our mole is."

"I can do that from here." "You will be safer there."

"I can't just leave you alone!" he protested. "Who will look after you?" Harlow smiled. "You and I both know I am the last person in this world who needs protection. I have been taking care of myself for what seems like an eternity. Truthfully, I am more worried about Sawyer. If someone is plotting against me from inside my company, they may use him to try and get to me. Go look after him—as a personal favor to me."

"Alright, ma'am, whatever you say," he conceded, "but what are you going to do in the meantime?"

"Hmmm!" Harlow picked up a travel brochure from the desk, advertising some of the local shops in town. "I think maybe I will pay a visit to an old friend and call in a few favors."

Chapter Seven

Chase clipped the final suture on his first case of the night and laid the scissors aside. "Be more careful with your fishing pole next time," he said to ten-year-old Andy Monroe as he removed his gloves. "Did you at least catch anything before you hooked yourself?"

"A couple of little catfish, nothing worth frying up," the boy replied, holding up his hand to admire his soon-to-be new scar. "When can I go back?"

Rocking back on his stool, Chase glanced at the boy's mother. "Well, you can't get those stitches wet for a couple of days and you need to come back in a week for me to take them out."

"A whole week?" the boy whined. "What am I going to do for a whole week?"

"Your homework maybe?" his mother chimed in. "If you had been doing that instead of sneaking off to that fishing hole, we wouldn't be here now."

Andy rolled his eyes.

"Listen to your mama," Chase lectured and stood, "and look at it this way, this will just give those fish an extra week of getting bigger before you hook them." He stopped to ruffle Andy's hair, then pointed at his hand. "Keep that clean and out of the swamp water until you see me again. I would hate to see you lose it. I don't imagine one-handed fishing would be all that easy."

"Thank you, Chase," said his mother gratefully. "Tell your mama and the rest of the family we said 'hey'."

"Yes, ma'am, and call me anytime if you need anything. You know how to reach me, here and at home."

Chase rested his forearms on the desk as he filled out the chart. His back was to the entrance. He heard them long before he laid eyes on them.

"Fuck!" he grumbled. "I am too tired for this shit tonight."

Three drunk women had stumbled into the waiting room of the ER and found their way past security to the nurse's station—a blond, a brunette, and one with her hair dyed bright green. Each of them wore at least a dozen strings of beads around their neck.

"BARTENDER!" the blond sang and banged on the desktop with her hand. "I— need—I—want a hurricane," she slurred.

Barely glancing over, Chase continued writing his notes. "We are fresh out. I suggest you try The Frisky Gator down the street. I am sure they are well-stocked for the night."

"They said they were all out and asked us to leave!" the one with the green hair replied, poking out her lips in a pout.

"I am sure they had their reasons," he muttered.

"Say," the brunette slinked around the desk and, unexpectedly, slung her arms around his neck from behind, "you're cute! Want to party with us?" She giggled and laid her cheek flat against his back. "I can guarantee this will be your lucky night."

"As tempting as that is, I am going to have to pass!" He gently peeled her hands away and stepped aside. "Some of us have work to do. George!" He called out for the security guard. "These ladies seem to have lost their way. Can you point them in the right direction?"

"Ah, come on!" the blond complained, jumping up and down like a child having a tantrum. "We just want to have a little fun."

"You are in the wrong place for that, unless you consider cleaning out bedpans a good time. There are several bars up the street, ladies!" he assured them. "I am sure there's plenty of fun to be had at one of them, where they will be more than happy to serve you."

"Alright! Alright! That's enough of that!" George made his way over to the women and shooed them towards the exit. "Sorry, doc, I was on my break. I will get them out of your hair." The three women grumbled as he moved them along. When they reached the exit, the ladies turned, let out a boisterous 'whoop', and lifted their tops, flashing everyone in the waiting room. The blond then leaned forward and vomited all over her own shoes.

Chase groaned and shook his head. "Get someone to clean that up, will you George?"

"Sure thing, doc!"

"Mardi Gras!" Carly, the head nurse on duty complained as she came over to join him. "Why is it everyone loses their freaking minds during Mardi Gras?" She had been there for thirty years, and nothing surprised her anymore.

"Don't forget, it's also a full moon," Chase pointed out. "It's a double whammy!"

"Lord, help us all!" Carly chuckled. "Is Andy ready to go?"

"He is! I just need to sign his discharge paperwork, grab him some antibiotics from the back, and remind him to keep it clean."

"You think he will?"

"No, and that's why I am sending him home with a week's worth of meds."

"You don't want to send it out to the pharmacy?" Chase closed the file he was working on, frowning. "They can't afford it. His dad got laid off last month and they lost their health insurance." He thought for a moment before taking a quick peek around. "As a matter of fact," he dropped the folder in the trash, "if anyone asks, you have no idea where his file went and without that, they can't be billed."

"You are going to get in trouble with administration for that one of these days," Carly whispered with a grin, "but I reckon God will look the other way. I know I will."

Chase leaned with his back against the desk and winked. "Get in trouble for what? I don't know what you are talking about."

Carly laughed as she went to get Andy's medicine.

"You can get fired for that you know?" Randy scolded, holding up two bags of food, shaking them.

"Who else are they going to get in here who is dumb enough to run this place and work the night shift in New Orleans during Mardi Gras, with a full moon to boot?" he asked as he took the bag and waved his brother into an empty examination room. "What's for supper?"

"Burgers and fries. Mama was sold out of everything else."

"I'll take it!" Chase grabbed two rolling stools, shoving one towards Randy, and sat down on the other. He pulled down the roll of paper and tore it off so they could use the examination table to spread out their food on.

"What's the word on the body from this morning?" Chase asked.

Randy stuffed a fry in his mouth. "Officially, it is being called a suicide because somehow the damn place burned down before the boys could get out there. Go figure! It was a good thing you and I saw the rope hanging from the rafters before it did, or we would have had to conduct a full investigation. Besides, the powers that be upstairs wouldn't have wanted the news of a murder to get out and panic the public during Mardi Gras. As far as anyone is concerned, he was an emotionally unstable man who wanted to give himself a quiet sendoff with as little effort and inconvenience as possible."

"Yeah, because chopping off your own head is such an easy way to do it!" Chase remarked sarcastically.

"The reality is, you and I both know exactly what this really was, and we are going to have to handle it ourselves."

"We just need to figure out who did it." Chase unwrapped his burger. "Any ideas?"

"The building belonged to Matthew Broussard up until a few weeks ago when he sold it to a company in Las Vegas." Reaching around to his back pocket, Randy pulled out a folded piece of paper and dropped it on the table. "The signature on the paperwork belongs to one Ms. Harlow Thornhart."

"We have always had our suspicions about him, but what do we know about her?"

"Not a lot. Only that her name appears on that one piece of paper."

"What do you mean?"

"I mean, she doesn't have a passport, a driver's license, a credit report—hell, not even a social security number."

"How does a person exist without any of those?"

"That, big brother, is a good question."

"Maybe it's a fake name?"

"I thought that, too, but I looked up this company that bought the place. It's called Black Thorn Enterprises and Harlow Thornhart is listed as the sole owner of it. From what little I can gather, this company is worth hundreds of billions, yet no one has any idea what they actually do."

"That's a little weird," Chase remarked. "But then again, this whole thing is. Who else would want to drain the blood but another vampire?"

"It doesn't make sense, but we need to figure out what's going on before anyone else turns up dead. I guess we need to start by shaking some tree branches and seeing if this Harlow Thornhart falls out. Given what little information there is about her, chances are she is a creature of some sort too."

"Speaking of which," Chase pulled his phone from his back pocket and checked the screen, frowning, "have you heard from Logan?"

"Now that you mention it, I have not. You?"

Chase shook his head. "Not a peep!" He scrolled through his contacts and hit send, but it went straight to voice mail. "He always lets me know when he is back in town."

"Maybe his phone died, or he went home and crashed."

"Yeah, you're probably right."

Carly knocked on the door. Sticking her head inside, "I am sorry to bother you on your break, Chase, but there is a heart attack patient on the way in. The ambulance is five minutes out."

"Thanks, Carly," he sighed, "I will be right there." Grabbing one final fry, he stood.

Randy jammed the last of his burger into his mouth. "I have to go, too." Rolling up his trash, he raked it into the nearest can.

"Keep me updated," Chase said as he did the same.

"Will do!"

Chapter Eight

The bell over the door rang as Harlow stepped inside. It was near midnight and a few tourists were mulling about, admiring the many oddities the shop had to offer. Picking up a shrunken head, Harlow scowled. This was the cheap souvenir stuff made in China. The good merchandise used by real practitioners was always kept in the back, out of sight.

"Can I help you find something?" a teenage girl running the cash register asked as she stared down at her phone.

"I am looking for Marie."

"Ms. Lavine is in the middle of a Tarot reading." She stopped to blow a bubble with her gum. "There are two others ahead of you in line, so you will have to wait your turn."

"I don't wait in lines! Tell her Harlow Thornhart is here to see her."

"Look, lady! I can't interr—" Slowly, the girl looked up to find Harlow glaring back at her scornfully.

"DO IT!" she commanded.

The girl let out an audible squeak and dashed out of the room, screaming, "Ms. Lavine, someone up front needs to see you. I am taking my break! On second thought, I quit!"

Harlow turned to the remaining customers in the store and growled, "GET OUT!"

The place cleared out in five seconds flat.

"Oh look, it seems a spot just opened up," she remarked sarcastically as her attention went to an unusual box displayed behind the glass of an antique cabinet. Bending over, she noted it contained several aged bottles, the labels nearly worn off, a large wooden cross, and three sharpened wooden stakes.

"Don't tell me you left Vegas to come down here to do a little vampire hunting?"

Harlow smiled and straightened up. "That's exactly what I intend to do. You sell many of these?" "Oh, those things?" she scoffed and flipped her hand. "I can't keep them in stock. They won't kill a mosquito, but the tourists seem to be fond of them. If you are looking for the real thing, I have probably got something in the back that will work a little better, not that Harlow Thornhart needs it." "I would have preferred to use my bare hands on this particular one anyway. Too bad someone beat me to it." Harlow crossed the room and embraced her old friend. She went by the name Marie Lavine these days, but Harlow would always know her as Marie Laveau, Voodoo Priestess of New Orleans.

"You are looking well!" "Thanks to you, cher, I will be celebrating two hundred and twenty years in September!"

Her old friend's skin was now a gorgeous warm sepia color after so many years of treatments with vampire blood. Her long, dark hair hung in loose curls, cascading down her back and over her shoulders, pushed back with a wide headband while she was giving Tarot readings. It helped to better display her unusual emerald-green eyes, offering a more mystical appearance overall.

Marie kissed her cheek before going over to lock the door and flipping the closed sign. "Now, let's go catch up."

Marie took her by the hand and led her to the back. Sliding aside an old armoire, the pair stepped through the concealed entrance into the tunnel that connected the shop to her home one block over. Making their way through, they emerged in her parlor from beneath a burning fireplace, one that moved to the side with the reciting of a few magical words no mortal could manage. Marie went to her collection of spirits on the nearby buffet and poured two glasses of something that produced smoke when uncorked as Harlow settled in on the sofa.

"You still live in this old place?"

"I am rather fond of it and it's easy enough to continue bequeathing it to myself with each generation." Marie handed her a glass. "Each time I pay you a visit and have my youth restored, I just change my name and pretend to be a long-lost granddaughter showing up to collect my inheritance."

"You would think these stupid humans would eventually figure it out!" Harlow sipped the concoction.

"It's New Orleans, baby. Nobody questions the weirdness. It's a little like Vegas, now that I think about it," Marie paused and smiled, "and the humans aren't so bad once you get to know them."

Harlow sneered. "If you say so."

"What brings you all the way down to my neck of the woods, cher? I know it has to be something important to pry you out of that high rise of yours overlooking the city." Setting her glass aside, Harlow heaved a sigh. "Matthew Broussard."

"Broussard? Why on Earth are you bothering with that old vampire?"

"He came to me in Vegas and paid a great deal of money for a few humans to feed on. He then killed three of them, kidnapped one, and, oh yes, just turned up dead in his former office, which apparently now belongs to me. According to the paperwork, I purchased it a few weeks ago even though this is the first I have heard of it. You know how I operate, and I always make it a point to keep my name out of everything."

"That is quite interesting—and surprising. Broussard is dead? Huh! He had a thriving little business here and went to great pains to keep up appearances. Everyone here knew him as an upstanding citizen. He has been quietly concealed in New Orleans as long as I have. It just makes me wonder why he would come to you and risk it all now, especially given your reputation. Surely, he knew what he was getting into." Marie tapped her lips as she pondered something. "I wonder if it has to do with that witch he took up with?"

"What witch?"

"I don't know her name—no one seems to—but she turned up a few months back. I have never laid eyes on her. In fact, I don't recall anyone mentioning they have, but the rumors have been swirling up a storm."

"That would explain why I couldn't find him. She was using sigil magic to conceal them. I found them drawn on the walls of the house they were at. I just can't figure out why. It's almost as if—" a sudden realization had hit her mid-sentence, "as if, he WANTED me to come here. And if I hadn't come by choice, attaching my name to a building with a dead woman inside would have most certainly forced me to make the trip, especially given my determination to not have my name associated with any sort of trouble—only I am not sure Broussard would have known that."

"You think you were being lured to New Orleans? Why would he do that?"

"Home field advantage?"

Marie laughed. "What idiot is trying to trap Harlow Thornhart? That would be suicide. Who would be so utterly foolish?"

"Someone who doesn't know who they are dealing with."

"Well, given he was recklessly taking human lives as you say, there's a good chance one of the locals beat you to him."

Harlow frowned. "Who would dare take that pleasure from me?"

"There is reason to believe there are a few hunters of The Diverse around town, though nobody knows who they are. All we know is that when someone steps too far out of line, they usually end up disappearing, never to be heard from again."

"I don't believe that is the case with him. You see, his body was completely drained, which implies another vampire or possibly even a witch who was after his blood."

"How many pints do you think he had in him?"

Harlow shrugged. "Nine, ten maybe?" "That's quite a cache!" Marie's eyebrows shot up. "If you have a way to store it, that's a whole lot of extra years for a witch. It would certainly be worth killing for."

"Why involve me?"

"That's a good question." Marie reached for the bottle and topped off their glasses. "And one we will figure out later. Right now, I want to catch up."

The two women talked and laughed, reminiscing until dawn.

At around 6 am, Harlow's phone rang. Looking down at the caller ID, she anxiously hit answer, placing it on speakerphone. "Cherise?"

"Harlow!" sobbed the woman on the other end. "Help me! Please!"

"Cherise! Where are you?" she demanded, straightening up, focused.

"I don—I don't know. It's a big, strange house and it looks like it is surrounded by a swamp. Please, Harlow! You have to help me! I'm so afraid!"

"Are you hurt?"

"No, I don't think so, but I feel strange, like something's not right."

"Cherise, who is holding you hostage?"

Before she could reply, the phone sounded like it was dropped, and her voice became muffled.

"Cherise! CHERISE! Answer me!"

A loud scream was heard before the line went dead.

"Damn it!" Turning to Marie, she explained, "That was my missing employee. She's alive but in danger. I need Sawyer to get a trace on that call asap."

Harlow started to pull up his number, but Marie placed her hand over the phone.

"Don't bother!" she said as she stood. "If it was Broussard's place, then I know exactly where she is. Come on, I'll drive!"

Chapter Nine

By the end of his shift, Chase still had not heard from Logan and was starting to get a little concerned. He went home and collapsed on the couch, not bothering to undress, the double shift having got the better of him. The next thing he knew, sunlight was streaming through the windows as his phone buzzed, waking him up. It was a call from Randy letting him know he was waiting outside. Grabbing his keys, he locked the door and slipped down the back entrance, not in the mood to explain things to his mother.

"We just got a 911 call from the old Mandeville place," Randy explained as he got in, "and the caller says Harlow Thornhart is trying to kill her."

"What the hell is this thing?" Harlow demanded, gripping the handle near her head.

"It's called a Jeep, and we need it to get where we are going."

"How do you stand it?" Harlow bounced in the seat as they drove over the bumpy, makeshift road, far from civilization and the comfort of something as simple as pavement.

"Are you kidding me? Do you remember what it was like riding a horse and buggy? This is a whole lot more fun!" Aiming for a large puddle, Marie laughed as mud sprayed the side of the windows.

"Is this really necessary?"

"If you want answers regarding Broussard, it is. His place is out here in the middle of nowhere. Years ago, this was all underwater and his original stomping ground. No fiercer pirate ruled these waters, and he took everything he wanted, amassing quite a fortune for himself. When one of the big storms came through, the terrain was changed, and he found his ship, which had been docked close to the house, was now on somewhat dry land with no way to move it to the open sea without tearing it apart. Instead, he bought a newer, faster vessel and left the old one right where it was, using it to add on to the main part of the house. He even left it intact, so that the bow of the boat became the new front of the house, complete with the massive deck to walk out on. Each night, he would light up the original lanterns igniting that swamp with an unearthly glow, unlike anything that had ever been seen before. Pretty soon, it got the reputation of being haunted, probably started and spread by Broussard himself to keep folks out of his business."

"There is no record of Broussard having property out here. I had my people check that first thing."

"That's probably because it would have never been listed as his. The place belonged to his mama and, as far as I know, it has remained in her family's name. I suppose it was better for him to keep it that way since he was trying to stay hidden. Only the local families that have been around for several generations know about the connection. Analise Mandeville, his mother, was something else."

"Mandeville?" Harlow thought for a moment, trying to recall something she once heard. "Where do I know that name from?"

"It's an old family. Analise arrived here from France with her extremely wealthy and overly pious father when she was fifteen, along with her Irish Catholic nursemaid. He died under rather mysterious circumstances two years later, leaving her the sole heir to his massive fortune. Rumor was, Analise had a mean streak a mile wide, and she and her father had an argument earlier that day. Apparently, he wanted to send her back to France to live in a nunnery. She wasn't too keen on the idea."

"Not that I can blame her. It seems the timing of his death was quite fortuitous. How did he die anyway?"

Marie grinned. "They 'say' he got drunk on wine and stumbled onto a hungry alligator."

"What's so suspicious about that?"

"For one, they say he never had more than one glass of wine a day, and two, how many gators do you know that can manage to find their way inside your house, climb the stairs, and lock themselves in your bedroom?"

"Ah!" Harlow smirked. "The girl had style."

"Before Landon Broussard came along, she also had three husbands, all meeting untimely ends in unusual ways within six months of their wedding night."

"A black widow? I think I am starting to like her even more," Harlow remarked. "How long did our dear Landon last?"

"Six whole years—until Analise found out he had taken a lover on the side. That night, she paid a visit to the woman's home, cut out her heart, and had it served to Landon baked into a pie the next day. After putting five-year-old Matthew to bed and sending the servants away, she planned a nice romantic dinner, taunting him with the knowledge of what was in his pie, after he had thoroughly enjoyed two slices. He was so furious, he reached across the table and strangled her to death with his bare hands, completely unaware she had added a little something extra to his dessert—oleander. They found them both lying dead on the dining room floor the next morning."

"What a shame. I would have liked the opportunity to have met her. What happened to little Matthew?"

"He was raised by the Irish woman, who also happened to dabble in the dark arts in her spare time. I expect he picked up a few tricks and a fondness for witches along the way."

"How did he get turned into a vampire?"

"Honestly," Marie swung a hard right, "I am not sure. I don't believe I have ever heard that story, although I must admit, I am a bit curious myself."

Chapter Ten

Leaning over Rowan's shoulder, Sawyer scrubbed his jaw, worry creasing his brow. Mitchell had a grim expression on his face, standing with his arms folded looking on. "You are sure this is where the leak was coming from." "I am!" Rowan sat on the floor behind the main server he had pulled away from the wall with a pile of cords in his lap, concentrating on an odd-looking half-stone buried inside the drive. "This has got to be a connector stone, though I have never actually seen one before, only heard the stories. They are extremely hard to come by because they are said to only have been forged by Vidar himself."

"Who is Vidar?" Sawyer questioned.

"He was Thor's half-brother, both being sons of Odin himself, and the god of silent vengeance. He believed in quietly taking revenge, but was adamant about doing so justly; so, to ensure he always had the correct information before acting, he created these. Climbing the highest mountain in Asgard, he would find a perfect stone, split it evenly down the middle and enchant it. Essentially, this is the ancient version of a surveillance bug, the difference being this one works on, and with, magic."

"How rare are we talking?" Mitchell asked.

"I have only heard of two. Vlad the Impaler had a set, as did Ivan the Terrible. It was thought they were all lost to the ages given they look like—well, rocks. The only difference is they all have a tiny half cobalt crystal in the middle, glowing brightly when the halves are joined."

"How does it work?"

"It appears this stone is absorbing all the information from our system and transmitting it to the other end."

"And how does the person get it from here?"

"That is where it gets a little more interesting. See where that cord comes out of our computer and runs right through the stone? If it works like I think it does, it is sending all that data to another processer somewhere, and here's the beauty of it," the analyst explained, "with a simple spell, that person can attach the other half of the stone to their own system and gather whatever passes through this end. It's basically an open line to everything we have, and virtually undetectable."

"How long do you think it's been here?" Rowan brushed off his hands. "Judging by the dust, it could have been an extensive amount of time, years even. I only found it because I had been here all night, accidentally spilled my coffee, and pulled it out to clean up the mess. " "Can you remove it?" The young tech pulled back the hood on his sweatshirt, revealing his pointy ears, and cut his eyes at Mitchell as he unfurled his tail. "Can the gremlin who graduated from MIT with honors take out the big bad magic stone?" he asked sarcastically. "I think I can handle it."

"Good! Ms. Thornhart is going to want to see that, and it might just get you off the top of her shitlist. Call me as soon as you are done so we can take the jet back to New Orleans."

"YOU can take the jet," Sawyer clarified.

"No, WE will. The boss is concerned about your safety. I have strict orders to keep an eye on you, and I will not have her upset with me."

Sawyer shook his head. "I need to be here. You go ahead, I will be fine."

"I know you will because you are coming with me, even if I have to drag you kicking and screaming."

Sawyer became visibly upset. "New Orleans is not the place I need to be."

"You can take it up with her when we get there." Mitchell gripped his shoulder. "Look, Sawyer, the boss could be in some real danger here and

I, for one, don't want it on my conscience if something terrible happens. I know you don't, either."

Sawyer closed his eyes and made a face. "You're right. Let me grab a few things and I will meet you at the hanger."

An hour later, they were in the air on the way to Louisiana.

Chapter Eleven

The Mandeville abode was truly a remarkable sight—half-vessel, half-house combined and manipulated into a stunning, unique piece of architecture. The front part truly appeared as an old buccaneer ship sitting in the water, complete with the rope rigging, lifted white masts, and even a crow's nest. The river had reclaimed a small part of what it had once gifted to the dry land, even if it was only a few inches. It was just enough to create ripples as it crashed against the hull. The part of the house closest to where they parked was fashioned in true plantation style, built high up so it would not flood when the water rose. A lovely veranda extended the entire length of the house, overlooking the river on the far side. Time had taken its toll, peeling the paint and rotting a few boards, but the ageless beauty of the structure was not lost. If anything, it only added to its charm.

Getting out of the car, Harlow closed her eyes and listened closely. The sounds from the swamp were the only signs of life she was able to detect. Inhaling sharply and letting it out, she muttered under her breath. "There's no one here."

"How do you know?"

"I know!"

The women climbed the massive set of outside steps and emerged on what would have been the deck of the ship, now a platform overlooking the water.

Marie glanced over her shoulder towards the main part of the house. "It looks extremely quiet in there. I think it is safe to go poke around a bit. Let me see what I can find."

Harlow walked to the far end, resting her hands on the boat rail to get a better look at the area. She sensed him before the wind shifted slightly and she caught his scent. "I do declare," she mumbled in an exaggerated southern accent, "I believe the authorities have arrived."

Her back was to him when she heard him shout, "POLICE! HANDS IN THE AIR!" Slowly turning, she was amused to see a stranger aiming his gun directly at her heart.

—and she burst into laughter.

"I said HANDS UP!" he repeated, this time with more determination.

"I know, I heard you the first time!" she managed, resting her palms on her thighs, now laughing even harder.

"I don't see what's so funny." Randy steadied his gun, gripping the handle tighter.

"The fact you are trying to stop me with THAT is hilarious." Harlow walked straight to him, wrapped her fingers around the barrel, and crushed the weapon into dust. "Thanks for the giggles! I haven't laughed that hard in at least a century."

Randy's eyes widened as she stalked past him, down the outside stairs, and out of sight.

"There's no one inside," Marie called as she stepped outside, stopping short when she saw the detective appearing dumfounded.

"Aw shit!"

"Marie?"

"Oh hey, baby! What are you doing here?"

Harlow was almost back to the Jeep when Chase appeared out of nowhere and moved to block her path.

"Get out of my way!"

"I'm sorry, ma'am, but I am afraid I can't let you leave. My brother and I have a few questions for you." Dropping to his knees, he flicked a lighter, igniting a circle of flames around them nearly six feet high. "And I'm willing to bet you can't cross that witch's circle."

"Did you just call me 'ma'am'?" she barked. "Do I look like a fucking 'ma'am' to you?"

Chase shrugged and bobbed his head back and forth.

"I have GOT to take the time to have that vamp blood treatment," she mumbled. Turning her attention to him and the flames around her, her eyes narrowed. "So, tell me," she said with an exuberant amount of confidence, "what do I collect when I win this bet?"

"I don't make deals with witches."

Harlow nodded as she locked eyes with him and strode across the flames as if they didn't exist. Stopping in front of him, she waved her hand, extinguishing the fire instantly. Pausing to regard him for a moment, she took the time to appreciate the fact there was indeed a fine specimen standing before her. She rarely bothered to notice human men, but something about this one was different. His face was quite pleasing, a strong jawline with a hint of stubble topped off by striking brown eyes. Noting his well-maintained physique, overall, she found him somewhat enticing—for a human anyway.

Leaning forward, her lips to his left ear, she grazed his lobe with her sharp teeth and whispered, "Your little holy oil fire won't work on me. You see, I am not a witch." His scent was intoxicating, a mix between mint and tea tree oil, which must have come from his shampoo. It wasn't Clive Christian by any stretch of the imagination, but it wasn't a turn-off either. She seductively dragged her nails across his neck, to the top of his blue t-shirt stretched tightly across his chest, stopping when she heard Marie from over her shoulder.

"Don't hurt him!"

Harlow growled, tapping her fingertips against his firm torso as she pondered her next move. She also found herself somewhat bewildered when she noticed he hadn't flinched, standing his ground, exuding no element of fear. His heart rate hadn't increased, not even by one beat—but something else had. Her eyes drifted downward, and a slow smirk spread across her face. A large bulge had formed below the belt of his faded jeans. "Well, would you look at that!" she mumbled before turning around, expecting an explanation from her old friend.

"Allow me to introduce Dr. Chase Devereaux and Police Detective Randy Devereaux, two of the finest, upstanding citizens of our fair city." Marie discreetly skirted the witch's circle and looked back and forth between them. "So, let me guess, you are the family of hunters keeping The Diverse in check in New Orleans."

"Marie, how do you know about The Diverse?" Chase questioned, shifting to adjust himself, hoping no one else noticed.

Cocking her head to one side, Harlow answered dryly, "You seem to be a smart boy. How do you think?"

"I have come across a few in my time," her eyes went to Harlow, pleading for her to go along with her story. "I have managed to make friends on both sides." Shifting the conversation, she addressed Randy, "I knew someone local was hunting down rogue members of The Diverse, but I had no idea it was you. How long have you been doing this?"

"All our lives. It sort of runs in the family."

"How many times have we worked side by side down at the homeless shelter and handed out boxes at the food bank? I had no idea you boys were doing this in your spare time. Does your mama know?"

Chase relaxed, put his arm around her shoulder, and kissed her cheek. "Who do you think taught us?"

Harlow rolled her eyes and made a gagging sound. "This is all very touching, but I am here on business."

"So are we. The station got a call from a woman saying someone was trying to kill her." Randy became serious. "I need to search the house."

"Don't bother, there is no one here, living or dead."

"She's right," Marie agreed.

"Did you or your friend here have anything to do with Matthew Broussard's death?" he demanded.

"No, and that is the truth, Randy! I swear it! We are just trying to get some answers."

"What kind of answers?"

"For some reason, someone is trying to make it look like I committed crimes that I had nothing to do with," Harlow replied, "and I want to know why. In addition to that, one of my employees was kidnapped and I want her back. I received a call from her saying she was out here, but no one has been here for a while."

"We thought it was Broussard," Marie continued, "but it looks like someone else is behind it."

"Who are you?" Randy addressed the odd woman directly.

"Harlow Thornhart."

Randy stepped closer. "YOU are the Harlow Thornhart we have been looking for?"

Chase folded his arms, looking her up and down, his curiosity piqued. "WHAT are you?"

Harlow extended her hand and lightly brushed the back of it along the side of his face, a devilish grin on her lips. "Your worst nightmare—a creature you have no way of controlling or killing."

A chilly, light mist of rain began to fall as if nature itself were sending a message to the two to separate. Their eyes met and remained fixated on each other until Marie stepped between them, breaking the spell. "The house is empty. How about we go inside and talk?"

Harlow and Marie climbed the stairs together, going inside to wait for the Devereaux brothers while Randy radioed the station to let them know it was a false alarm. The first room they came to was most unusual. The set of doors on the far wall of the library opened onto the deck outside. Given the layout of the room and the wooden beams, they deduced this had been the captain's quarters on the banked ship.

"You are friends with these humans?" asked Harlow, searching through the bottles of libations along the side wall.

"Yeah, I am. I have known the family forever. Randy is the head detective at the local police station. He comes out on his own time to watch over the shops on our street when Mardi Gras rolls around, and the tourists get rowdy. Chase is the chief physician over at the Emergency Room at the hospital and donates his time to the free clinic to offer medical help to those who can't afford it. Their youngest brother, Logan, when he is not working his EMS job, volunteers at the homeless shelter. Their mama has never failed to open the family's restaurant to feed folks each time a storm comes through and knocks out the power. Hell, they even have one brother who is the parish priest at one of the local Catholic churches. Like it or not, they are good people."

"Good people who kill The Diverse when they perceive they have done something wrong." Harlow screwed up her face and tossed a bottle of rock-gut whiskey into the banked fireplace. "What makes them judge and jury?"

Playing devil's advocate, Marie asked, "What makes YOU qualified to be the judge and jury when you are the one who is delving out the punishment?"

"I am Harlow Thornhart—I need no other reason," turning, "and don't tell me you have gone all soft over these humans!"

Marie located two glasses and brought them over. "You forget, cher, before I met you, I was human."

A sudden understanding washed over Harlow. Placing one hand on her hip, she groaned judgmentally. "Which one of them are you slumming it with?"

"I wouldn't call it 'slumming'," looking down and rubbing an imaginary spot on the table, Marie attempted to appear innocent, "Randy and I, on occasion, may share a night, now and again."

"Your booty call? He's your fuck buddy?"

"That sounds so crude. I prefer my 'Netflix and chill' partner."

Harlow cringed. "Tuh-may-toe, tuh-mah-toe," she enunciated. "He is still a human?"

"Like you have never hooked up with a human?"

"No, as a matter of fact, I have not!"

Marie laughed but found herself taken aback when she realized her old friend was not kidding. "Never? In all this time, you have never once taken a human, male or female, into your bed?"

"Never! Not even when I was drunk beyond comprehension!"

"I have to admit, that surprises me! I find it a little hard to believe the great Harlow Thornhart hasn't left a trail of broken hearts in her wake over the centuries."

"I have, it just hasn't included humans."

"Why is that?"

"I have my reasons," she replied, clearly uncomfortable with the subject.

"Aren't you curious what it would be like?"

"No! If I have an itch that needs scratching, I have a former Celtic god of sex at my disposal. What could a human possibly do that he could not—and a thousand times better?"

Reaching for a bottle of scotch, Marie pulled out the cork and poured. "Well, don't knock it 'til you try it! You might be pleasantly surprised."

"I highly doubt it!"

"Well, it seems I have a new mission in life." Marie grinned. "Harlow Thornhart, I will not rest until I have hooked you up with a mortal man."

"Don't waste your time—or mine. How good could one possibly be?"

"Everything's fine out here at the old Mandeville place," Randy said into the phone. "Probably just some kids playing a prank. I'm going to give the place a good once over to make sure, so I won't be back until later."

"Don't stay out there too long," said the officer on the other end. "There's a storm coming, and you know how easily the roads flood out there."

"Storm? What storm?"

"A low blew up off the coast out of nowhere this morning. The weather service is blasting out alerts like crazy. It caught them completely off guard, too."

"That's a little strange, but I will keep it in mind. Thanks!" After hanging up, he cast a wary eye to the heavens. Gray clouds had started to move in, and it appeared the sky, which had been just a little drizzly, could open at any time.

"What's strange?"

"Apparently, there's a storm coming. We had better conclude our business here if we are going to stop off and check on Logan." Randy angled his head towards the house. "What do you think?"

Chase leaned against the car and crossed his arms. "I trust Marie. We've known her forever and I don't think she would lie to us."

Randy nodded. "Yeah, Marie wouldn't lie to me of all people."

"What do you mean by that?"

"Um—nothing," Randy stuttered. "I just meant—"

Chase's eyes suddenly flew open wide. "Are you and Marie involved?"

"NO—maybe—on occasion?"

"And you never said anything?"

Randy shrugged. "I am not sure what there is to tell. We hang out every now and then. What about the other one?" he asked, hoping to shift the focus off his personal life.

Chase sighed. "I think the verdict is still out on that one. There is definitely something different about her."

The pair started towards the house. "Did my eyes deceive me earlier or did you get a boner when she whispered in your ear?"

Just the mention of her, and he started to feel the betrayal from his body once more. He tried to think about anything but the mysterious, enchanting, not to mention incredibly attractive, creature he had just had the pleasure of meeting.

"She must have bewitched me somehow to distract me," he stated stoically. Subconsciously reaching for his lobe and clearing his throat, he added, "Besides, have you looked at her?"

"Yeah, I have," Randy slapped his brother on the back, "and it's a wonder I didn't get one, too. I don't think I have ever, or will ever, have a woman that looks like that give me the time of day. What do you suppose she actually is?"

"I don't know," Chase shook his head, "but we should probably figure it out. After all, she walked through that witch's circle like it was nothing, and I don't know of any creatures who can cross an ignited ring of holy oil like that."

"Alright ladies," Chase announced as they came into the library, "we are listening."

Harlow took a seat, glass of scotch in hand, and crossed her legs seductively. "Why should I tell you anything?"

"You can answer our questions here or at the station," Randy threatened.

Harlow laughed. "What are you going to do, Barney Fife? Force me into your car with the one bullet you carry in your pocket. Maybe Opie over there can lend you a hand."

"How do you know about Barney Fife and Opie?" asked a baffled Marie.

"You know I don't sleep, and late-night television leaves a great deal to be desired."

Clearing his throat, Randy tried to get back on track. "What exactly was your relationship with Broussard?"

Taking a large sip from her glass, she simply glared back at him in response.

"Harlow, maybe you should tell them everything," Marie encouraged. "They already know about the existence of The Diverse and they may be able to help, especially since a human life is in danger. I know you want to get Cherise back safely. At this point, you don't have anything to lose."

Inhaling deeply, Harlow paused to gather her thoughts. "Broussard came to me in Vegas wanting a few humans to party with, which I provided."

"Prostitutes?"

"Absolutely not! They were hired for a little bloodletting, which I might add, these ladies were more than a little excited to happily participate in. I don't force anyone who works for me to do anything they aren't completely on board with. Instead, he trashed my house, concealed himself with witch magic, and killed three of them before kidnaping Cherise. When I came after him, I found him dead in his former office, which apparently belongs to me now, even though I have no knowledge of the purchase."

"What are you—like a Jinn—or something? Do you grant wishes?"

"No!" she snapped, her tone one of disgust. "Do I look like a fucking genie to you? Do you see a bottle lying around here anywhere from which I just popped right out of like Barbara Eden?"

"You do know there are more than four channels now, right?" Marie mumbled. "Maybe you should try giving cable or Netflix a whirl."

"Look lady, I don't know what the hell you are! I am just trying to understand what's happening here!"

Harlow closed her eyes, taming her ire. "I am in the business of buying, selling, and trading unusual items for The Diverse and humans alike, depending on the highest bidder, and on who has what I want the most at the time."

"What was Broussard's price?"

"Blood and money, and if I had known he was going to be this much trouble, I would have charged him triple."

"How did you two end up out here?" asked Marie.

"We got a call," Randy answered, "from a woman claiming Harlow Thornhart was trying to kill her."

"Me? Who was it?" Harlow demanded.

"It was a woman. That's all I know."

"That doesn't make sense. How would anyone know we would come out here?" Marie pondered aloud. "I am one of the few people who knew about this place, and this person would have had to have known you would come to me for that information." Seeing the confusion on Chase's face, she added, "Harlow and I go way back. We have been friends for many years."

"If they had access to the files at Black Thorn Enterprises, they would have known about our connection." Pieces were falling into place in Harlow's mind as she spoke. "Sawyer and Mitchell seem pretty convinced we have a spy in our midst there, and that would certainly explain a great deal."

Chase frowned. "What are we missing?"

Harlow and Marie exchanged wary looks.

"Broussard is rumored to have been involved with a witch the past few months," Marie explained.

"And he would have not been able to pull this off without her," Harlow added. "So, who the hell is she, and where is she now?"

"You forgot one other question," Randy pulled out a chair and took a seat. "How did this person know you would come out here THIS morning at THIS time?"

Harlow growled, coming to an alarming realization. "We were all being led here!"

The electricity abruptly flickered, and a crack of thunder shook the floors.

"That didn't sound good," Marie remarked as she got up and went to the window. Pulling back the curtain, she found it impossible to see anything outside because of the deluge of rain that had burst forth from the sky. "I don't recall hearing anything about bad weather this week."

Randy went over to join her. "When I called the station, they mentioned the weather service issuing warnings for a coastal storm coming ashore. It looks like it popped up out of nowhere."

"There is a reason no one saw this storm coming." Harlow looked down into the bottom of her glass. "It was brewed up just for us."

"You think our witch conjured it?"

"I am certain of it. Why else would it hit at the exact same time we were all here unless it was meant to delay us? Whoever did it needs us out of the way for the evening."

"Why does another witch have it in for you so badly?" Chase asked, fishing for information.

"I told you, I am NOT a witch!"

"Then exactly what are you?"

"That is none of your concern, and I know exactly what you are doing. Stop trolling for information. If you think you have figured out a way to outsmart me, think again. I have been around for longer than you know, and I am already miles ahead of you."

"Chase does raise a good point," Marie worked her way back over. "Who would trifle with you and why?"

"A personal vendetta?" Randy proposed. "Have you had any unsatisfied customers lately?"

"I have NEVER had an unsatisfied client, only ones I refused to take on."

"Which ones would those be?"

Harlow pulled a cigarette from her case and stared out the window as she tapped it. "Ones who had nothing to offer in return."

"Well, you will have some time to think about it," Chase pointed outside. "It looks like we are going to be here for a while. Water has already covered the road, and it doesn't look like it's going to stop anytime soon."

The flickering power died completely.

Randy reached for his phone and checked it. "No service. It looks like we are cut off for the time being."

"Damn it!" Chase hurried over to the window to see for himself. "What about Logan?"

"I'm sure he's fine. He can take care of himself."

Marie's ears perked up. "What about Logan?"

Chase hesitated to answer and looked at Randy who simply shrugged.

"We took down a rougarou the other night and he decided to hang out at the fish camp to make sure everything was taken care of. We haven't heard from him since."

Marie came to a grim understanding. "The two fishermen on the news who died—the ones they said spilled out of their boat and were attacked by gators? I take it that's not what really happened."

"That was the official word," Randy responded, "but it was actually a newly turned werewolf who couldn't control himself. We couldn't risk him killing anyone else."

"Anybody I know?"

"Billy Harmon."

"Damn it all!" Marie grimaced. "He has a newborn and twin six-year-olds at home. If he had lost control there, it could have been devastating, to say the least. How are you going to explain it to his wife?"

Randy sighed heavily and sat down. "His car will be located in the water in a few days where it will appear he ran off the road and died instantly. That way the double indemnity clause will kick in on his life insurance policy. The family is going to need all the help it can get. It's the least we can do."

"I suppose working for the police department makes it extremely convenient when it comes to killing The Diverse and covering your own asses in the process," Harlow scoffed. "How many times have you used your job to hide your dirty little deeds?"

"How many times have I treated patients and consoled families in the Emergency Room because some of your Diverse have no conscience?" Chase fired back. "It's easy to sit there and defend them when you don't have to see their handy work up close and personal. Come back and tell me what horrible people we are after you have had to look a mother in the face and break the news to her that her three children are dead, like I had to a couple of months ago. I had to lie to her and tell her it was carbon monoxide poisoning when in truth, a demon sucked their life force out of their bodies while they slept. You know what else I had to do?" Chase paused and cleared his throat. "I had to identify her remains by the suicide note she left because there was nothing left of her face after she blew her brains out. In it, she blamed herself for their deaths because their furnace was old and needed to be replaced, but she had chosen to spend what extra money she had on Christmas presents for them instead."

"I know from personal experience there are good and bad on both sides," Marie said quietly.

"And I am guessing The Diverse doesn't have a police force of their own, given the number we have to handle ourselves down here." Chase started out of the room. "I am going to look for some candles. It will be dark soon."

"I think I will go help him." Randy stopped when he reached the doorway. "You know, since we're stuck here for probably the night, it might be a good opportunity to try and find out more about your witch. If what you have told us is true, there's a good chance she stayed here and left some clues behind."

"He's right," Marie pointed out when he was out of earshot.

Somewhere in the background, the sound of a generator roared to life and the lights came back on.

"You are perfectly fine sharing space with these two brothers who would kill you in a heartbeat if they knew who you really were, especially given some of the things you have done over the years."

"Well, let's not enlighten them, shall we?" She got up and went over to browse some books on the shelf. "And don't be so hard on them. Their daddy was killed by a rougarou. All those years, I honestly thought they believed he died from falling and hitting his head, but after today, I am sure they know the truth."

"What happened to the werewolf?"

"You know what? I don't rightly know. I don't even know who it was because it happened at a time when I was away becoming my 'granddaughter'. The boys were probably too young to remember the details, but I expect Jacquelin knows exactly what happened."

"Ah yes, the ever-faithful, rosary-clutching Catholic mother I met at the restaurant. I never get enough of her type."

"Wait until you meet the brother who is the parish priest," Marie goaded. "I am sure you will adore him!"

"I can't wait!" Harlow refilled her glass and drained it.

Randy found Chase in the kitchen, angrily rifling through drawers just as the generator kicked in.

"I thought you had her riled up enough for her to let it slip."

"Yeah, me too." Exhaling sharply, he leaned against the counter, the memory of the family's deaths still a little bit rawer than he realized. "What do you make of all of this?"

"I trust that lady about as far as I can throw her, but if a witch is running around killing people strong enough to kill a vampire and conjure a storm, I think we are going to need all the help we can get. I don't know much, but I am fairly sure I don't want to be on our dear Ms. Thornhart's bad side."

"It would be nice to know how to protect ourselves against her if the need arises though." Chase raked his hair back and focused on the problem at hand. "Maybe I am approaching this all wrong, after all, you get more flies with honey."

"See any chocolate bars?" Randy started checking the cabinets. "Maybe she is just 'hangry'. You could try cooking her a romantic dinner to soften her up a bit," he teased, producing several cans of beef stew. "How are your reheating skills these days?"

Grimacing, he replied, "After spending a few minutes with her, I think I would have better luck serving the blood I just found in the fridge."

Chase and Randy came into the library with armfuls of firewood.

"Lucky for us, there was a screened-in porch loaded with this. It should help knock the chill off. The temperature is dropping pretty fast."

Setting it on the hearth, he left Randy to get the fire going while he pulled a candle from his back pocket. "I did find this, but I guess we don't need it now."

Harlow poured the remainder of the scotch into her glass, emptying the bottle.

Marie took it from her and handed it to Chase with a grin. "For ambiance."

Chase laughed, stuffed a candle in it, and placed it on the mantle. "How's that?"

"Perfect!" Marie patted him on the back.

"Damn it!" Randy exclaimed. "The wood is damp, and it doesn't want to light."

Harlow rolled her eyes. "Must I do everything?"

The brothers watched incredulously as she rolled her palms to and fro in a circular pattern, a spark appearing, before morphing into a ball of fire she held in her hand.

Addressing Randy, Marie waved him to one side and said, "You might want to step back."

He moved aside, rolling back on his haunches half a second before Harlow threw the ball into the fireplace, instantly drying the wood and creating a roaring blaze.

"That's handy," Randy muttered, glancing over his shoulder at Chase, his brow creased with concern.

"You're welcome!"

"Show off," Marie muttered before turning to Chase. "Did you find anything else?"

"I just made it as far as the kitchen. There's canned food in the cabinets and fresh blood in the fridge."

"Human or vampire?" Marie asked, extremely interested in the answer.

Randy's head popped up. "Does it really matter?"

Marie shrugged, attempting to appear disinterested.

"Of course, it matters," Harlow explained. "Vampire blood is far more coveted than human. It can do far more in the magical realm than yours ever could, and people and creatures alike are willing to pay a premium price for it."

"For what reason?"

Harlow stood up and walked over to the table holding the array of alcohol. "For one, vampire blood is one of the few things that can keep a witch young. One pint is worth a hundred years of youth and vitality, not to mention certain other properties that may be transferred in the process, like an enhanced sense of taste and smell." Her eyes drifted to Marie, addressing her personally without letting on to the others. "What's in the kitchen is human. I smelled it when he opened the refrigerator."

"You smelled it?" Randy questioned. "From all the way in here? How many pints have YOU had?"

"I don't need another creature's blood. My senses are a bit sharper than most, just like my teeth." Grabbing a bottle of Tequila, Harlow started towards the hall. "I think I will have a look around and see if anything jumps out at me."

"You want the candle in case the power goes out again?"

Harlow scoffed. "Why would I need that when I can see perfectly fine in the dark?"

"She can see in the dark, too?" Randy whispered to Marie. "Are we safe with her?"

"As long as you don't piss her off or get in her way—or breathe too loudly." Plastering on a smile, she patted his cheek. "Don't worry, baby, you will be fine."

"What exactly is she anyway?" asked Chase.

"I don't know, and that's the truth." Marie sighed heavily. "I am not sure anyone truly knows. Harlow has always been less than forthcoming about that information, but what I do know is that she has walked the Earth longer than any creature, and she is more powerful than anyone will ever know."

"How did you two come to know each other?"

Shifting uncomfortably in her seat, her eyes went to the floor, and she shrugged. "Oh, just from being around. You know how it is. I get all sorts of unique clientele wandering in the shop. She and I hit it off the first time we met."

"That didn't answer my question," Chase remarked quietly.

"You know, I think Harlow has the right idea. I have always been curious about this place. I think I will have a look around myself."

Marie located Harlow in the hall upstairs, leaning against a doorway staring inside one of the bedrooms.

"Which one do you think it was?"

"Which one what?" Marie asked, resting her hands on the jamb, following her gaze into a room seemingly frozen in time. Given the untouched dust on the floor and the décor from the late nineteenth century, it was clear that it was the first time that door had been opened in decades.

"The one with the hidden alligator."

"Good question!" Marie chuckled. "Here's another good one. Can the legendary Harlow Thornhart not snap her fingers and send this storm back to where it came from?"

"Oh, I can, but our witch doesn't know that and doesn't need to just yet. It takes a great deal of strength and energy to conjure one of those, and she will need time to recover. Now, she believes she is safe for a bit with us trapped here. We will let her go on thinking that for now. Besides, something tells me there is some useful information hidden around here."

"Like what?"

"I will know it when I see it." Harlow grimaced at the discolored wallpaper on the wall. "You know, it wouldn't have killed Broussard to update the place a bit."

"Some people like to keep things the way they were, so they don't forget how it used to be." The two women worked their way over to a faded portrait hanging on the wall next to it. A beautiful young woman with flaxen hair stared back at them with a small boy perched on her lap holding a wooden horse. "That must be Analise and young Matthew."

The portrait next to it was of an older man, clutching a Bible. "And this must be 'daddy'."

"Mandeville," Harlow repeated. "What is it about that name? I know I have heard it before."

"The Mandeville family goes back a long way," Chase said from behind them. "All sorts of crazy rumors about them have been passed down for generations. I guess some things never change, like people getting bored and making up gossip to spread around."

"Like what?" asked Harlow.

"My favorite was that they came here from overseas to hide some priceless family treasure," he looked around, "which, now that I'm here, doesn't seem all that farfetched. Neither do the stories about this place being haunted. No one with any good common sense would be nosing around here. I guess that explains why the four of us are spending the night," Chase said dryly.

"Don't tell me you are frightened of a few ghosts?" A sly smirk crossed Harlow's lips.

"The dead don't scare me. It's the living that gives me nightmares."

"Speaking of worrying about the living, I think I will go check on Randy. It's probably best we don't leave anyone alone here." Marie started towards the stairs, a smile spreading across her face. "You two play nice while I'm gone."

"Find anything interesting?" Chase asked as soon as Marie left.

"Only dust bunnies and poor decorating choices, so far," she replied, inclining her head inside. "No one has stepped foot in here for quite a while."

Chase nodded towards the bedroom at the end of the hall. "Maybe his coffin is down there."

"His coffin?" Harlow slowly turned to face him. "What on Earth makes you think he has one of those?"

"Isn't that what vampires sleep in?" Chase asked, struggling to keep a straight face.

"No, they do not! All the ones I know sleep in king-sized beds with extremely high-count Egyptian cotton sheets. Their skin is more sensitive than most."

Chase chuckled, unable to contain himself any longer.

Harlow crossed her arms and glared at him when she realized he was teasing. "Humans!" she huffed.

"What's so wrong with being human?" he asked as they started down the hall.

"Tell me what's so right about it. You're born, you live miserable lives and then you die, all in the blink of an eye. You work your precious time away just to barely scrape by and put food on the table for the other, miniature versions of yourselves you choose to bring into this world, ones I might add who vomit and shit all over you in the process. Then you get old, sick, and die. It's a vicious, never-ending cycle. I also might add, your kind has done far more damage to this planet than The Diverse could ever conceive of doing."

"You don't seem to have a very high opinion of humankind, in general, so why come down here to try and save the one human Broussard took?"

"That's business. Cherise was under my protection, and I take my reputation seriously. Broussard made it personal. I will not tolerate—in any form or fashion—the perception that someone has gotten away with crossing Harlow Thornhart. As far as the human, in respect to my professional relationships, there are a few I have come to tolerate over the years. Cherise is an asset I am not willing to lose. She has made me a great deal of money."

"What about Marie?"

Harlow ignored his question, gripping the doorknob and flinging the door open. "Well, this is interesting."

Stepping inside, they were amazed to see this oversized room was completely different from the others. Harlow flipped the light switch to find it had been updated and modernized. The light gray walls surrounded a king-size bed resting in the middle, neatly made with matching bedding. A large screen TV hung on the wall above the gas fireplace at the foot of the bed. Off to the side, in front of an enormous, picture window overlooking the river, was a sitting area with two large chairs and a coffee table. To the right was a sleek, black desk outfitted with a state-of-the-art computer set up. Upon closer inspection, it was revealed the suite also had an equally up-to-date bathroom, covered in glossy black tile complete with a smart shower. A closet was just beyond that, filled with neatly pressed designer suits, expensive shoes, ties, and a drawer of Rolex watches.

Harlow removed a couple of the most lavish ones and tossed them to Chase, who deftly caught them. "Here, I don't think Broussard will be needing these."

"I can't take a dead man's belongings."

"Why not? They aren't doing him any good. You could feed all the orphans in New Orleans for the price of one of those. In fact," Harlow scooped up three more and shoved them into his chest, "feed all the homeless in Louisiana. Some good might as well come from that bastard's death."

Harlow rested her hands on her hips and looked around. "This room has been scrubbed clean. There isn't a whiff of anything. It's almost as if our witch knows exactly what to do to avoid detection from me specifically."

Tossing the watches on the bed as he passed by, Chase made his way over to the computer. "Maybe not everything," he mumbled and took a seat to begin typing.

"What are you doing?"

"The computers at the hospital are always going haywire and we lose data all the time. I have become somewhat of an expert on retrieving that stuff. Someone tried to wipe this one clean, but what most people don't realize is that nothing is ever completely gone if you know the right place to look." Fifteen minutes later, he leaned back in the chair and spun around. "This diagnostic needs to run for a few hours and then we should be able to come up with something."

"A doctor and a computer whiz—I'm impressed. While we are waiting, let's see what else we can find."

A quick search of the upstairs revealed several more bedrooms, but nothing of consequence. As they started down the stairs, Harlow stopped and glanced over her shoulder when something caught her attention.

"What is it?"

Harlow shook her head. "Nothing. I just thought I heard something."

Joining the others, they found Marie and Randy happily cooking in the kitchen.

A look of repulsion crossed Harlow's face when she saw Marie wearing an apron, looking more like Julia Child than a Voodoo priestess.

"What the fuck are you doing?"

"We humans have to eat," Marie replied with a wink.

"There were some rice and canned beans in the makeshift pantry," Randy explained, pointing with his thumb over his shoulder, "and this woman can make a gourmet meal out of anything."

Harlow rolled her eyes.

"Find anything interesting upstairs?" Randy directed the question to his brother.

"Maybe!" Chase looked over Randy's shoulder to see what was cooking. "Broussard's bedroom suite has a computer setup. It was wiped, but I am running it now to see if we can retrieve anything."

Harlow's head suddenly turned sharply to one side when she detected an unusual smell in the air. Searching the room, she spied a door at the far end of the kitchen. Hurrying towards it, everyone stopped to watch. Finding it locked, she crushed the doorknob and pushed the door inward, revealing a rudimentary set of concrete steps descending into a root cellar. Ignoring everyone's shouts of caution, she hurried down them, stopping short when she reached the last one which rested on a dirt floor. By the time they caught up with her, she was holding a set of chains that she had ripped from the wall.

"This is where they kept Cherise," she spat, enraged. "Her scent is all over the place."

Chase located a pull switch and tugged, turning on a single light bulb to illuminate the area. A new sleeping bag was lying in the corner near the wall where the chains had been. Kneeling, he located a few drops of dried blood on the fabric, along with a broken necklace.

"Is this hers?" he asked, picking up a gold chain with the charm of a dragonfly attached.

Harlow took it from him and held it up. "Yes, it is. She never takes it off."

Getting up, he brushed his hands off and looked around. "Well, the good news is there isn't much blood here, which means no major carnage, so there is still hope. Chances are, they're keeping her alive to use as bait for you. That would explain why this area wasn't scrubbed as well. Whoever is behind this wanted you to know they still have her."

"We will figure it out, cher," Marie said encouragingly, taking Harlow by the shoulders, "and we will find her. After all, Harlow Thornhart never loses." Guiding her towards the steps, she added, "In the meantime, supper is almost ready. Let's sit down while we eat and figure out the next move."

"What the fuck is this?" demanded Harlow, staring at a bean impaled on the fork she was holding in the air.

"Red beans and rice."

"You people eat this stuff down here?"

"Yes, we certainly do!" Marie replied and spooned another helping on her plate. "Try it, you might like it, just like some other things if you cared to give them a chance before judging them so harshly."

"I think it's delicious," Randy raved.

"You would," Harlow snarked. "You are trying to get laid by the cook tonight."

Randy looked down into his plate, averting his eyes.

Chase grinned and stuffed a forkful in his mouth. "So, how long has this been going on?"

Quickly shoveling in a mouthful of beans to avoid answering, Randy shrugged and looked at Marie.

"Since last summer when the storm came through and we were trying to evacuate everyone on my street," Marie answered. "Everyone else got out just in time, but we were trapped on the second floor of my shop when the water rushed in. It turned out to be a lovely night."

"And you haven't said a word," Chase cut his eyes at his brother.

"It's nobody else's business," Randy retorted, wiping his mouth with a napkin. "Besides, we have liked keeping it to ourselves."

"Or maybe Marie is ashamed to be seen with you," Harlow remarked casually, pushing around the food on her plate with the fork.

"Why on Earth would I be?" demanded Marie, narrowing her eyes.

"It's just that you two are so different and in so many ways."

"I don't think so. In fact, we have a lot in common," Randy interjected. "We have both grown up in New Orleans. We love the city and the people in it. Taking care of it is what brought us together." He slipped his hand over on hers. "Marie is the best thing that ever happened to me."

"I am?" Marie visibly shook and her face filled with disbelief.

"You are!" he reiterated tenderly.

Smiling sweetly, she added, "And Randy is a wonderful man that any woman would be lucky to have—I am lucky to have."

"Oh, please forgive me," Harlow rested her hand on her breast, feigning contrition. "I had no idea you two were so in love. I suppose you have perfectly good reasons for not telling your family after nearly a year of being together. Perhaps you are waiting until after the wedding, or the birth of your first child?"

Marie turned to glare at her old friend. "Ignore her! When she goes too long without getting laid, she gets a little cranky and tries to make everyone else as miserable as she is."

"My needs were more than sufficiently satisfied at least a dozen times over the weekend but thank you for your concern." Harlow winked and blew her a kiss.

"Alrighty, this conversation went off the rails pretty quickly," Chase mumbled and cleaned his plate.

"What about you, Chase?" Harlow rested her elbow on the table and faced him. "When was the last time you got lucky?"

"Um—not as recently as any of you," he replied awkwardly.

"Well, that became painfully obvious when we were outside. You might want to consider buying a looser pair of jeans to accommodate yourself if this goes on much longer. Come on, confess! How long?"

"Don't give her the satisfaction of an answer," urged Marie. "You will regret it. Harlow Thornhart is a master manipulator, and she will have you so tied up in knots you won't know whether you are coming or going."

"I do love tying a good knot when the occasion calls for it," Harlow reached for her glass and smiled over the rim, taking far more pleasure than she should in making Chase uncomfortable, "preferably to the wall in my red room."

"Since we aregetting everything out in the open now," Randy waved his fork in the air, "how long HAS it been, big brother?"

Realizing there was no way out of this conversation, Chase huffed and slid his plate away. "Not since Amber."

"Amber Sparks? THAT Amber? You two broke up three years ago." Randy propped his elbows on the table. "Are you trying to tell me you haven't been with another woman since then? Bro! Why didn't you say something? I could have hooked you up with—someone."

Marie slapped his shoulder.

"I am perfectly fine!" Chase reached for his glass and drained it.

"I don't know," Harlow teased, "I hear human males can have all sorts of health issues if they go too long without 'cleaning out the pipes'. You should probably do something about that before it causes permanent damage."

"Perhaps Harlow could help you out with that," Marie suggested, amusement alight in her eyes.

"We have already had this discussion. You know I NEVER fuck humans."

"There's no time like the present to start." The two women had locked eyes, having an additional conversation without words. "Maybe today is a good day to turn over a new leaf, try something new, live a little."

"Do I have any say in the matter?" Chase asked as he abruptly stood, clumsily knocking over his chair in the process.

"NO!" they replied in unison, still staring at each other.

"Who is this Amber?" Harlow questioned.

"For the love of God, can't we just let this go?"
"No! Who is she?"

"She was just a girl I went out with for a while."

"Was she a stripper?"

"A stripper?' Chase appeared confused. "No! Why would you think that?"

"Well, with a name like Amber Sparks, what else could she possibly be? Randy covered his mouth with his palm, snorting as he snickered.

"Was it serious?" Harlow continued her interrogation.

"I really don't want to talk about it."

Harlow addressed Randy. "WAS it serious?"

Randy eyed Chase guardedly. "Yeah, it was," he said quietly.

"What happened?"

Chase sighed, knowing she wouldn't stop if he didn't answer. "Things just didn't work out. She hated that I spent so many hours at the hospital, and I couldn't get past the fact she screwed someone else. The end!"

Harlow settled in excitedly, but Marie reached over and grasped her hand, reigning her back in. "Let this one go," she whispered. Harlow expressed her disappointment by wrinkling her nose.

"Okay! I guess I should just clean up my plate," Chase said as he carried the dishes to the sink, essentially ending the conversation.

"Why?" Harlow called over her shoulder. "I don't think Broussard will mind the mess."

"She's right, just leave it," Marie agreed, rubbing her arms. "I don't think he is going to complain. You know what? It's getting chilly in here. What do you say we move to the library where that warm fire is burning?"

After the four polished off a vintage bottle of wine they had found tucked away in a safe place, Marie and Randy found an excuse to disappear into one of the bedrooms on the first floor. Chase and Harlow sat quietly, an awkward silence filling the air between them. The sound of heavy rain coming down on the tin roof became deafening but was soon replaced by laughter, the kind that came from the joy of two lovers doing what they do best.

"Maybe we should go check on the computer progress," he suggested.

Grabbing a bottle of rum, Harlow agreed, "Yes, let's!"

"It needs about another hour," Chase announced after checking the screen.

Harlow stretched out across the bed, propped on one elbow, regarding him. "Thank you," she said begrudgingly.

"For what?"

"Helping with the computer. I know you have an aversion to The Diverse and this must be difficult for you."

Hooking his arm over the chair, he turned. "It's not that I have an aversion to them as much as it is a desire to protect the people they harm. I know there must be many who live peacefully, bothering no one, and I take no issue with that. If they are a benefit to the community, I will be the first to welcome them. I am a live and let live kind of guy, but when they cross that line, we have a problem."

Harlow could tell their earlier conversation was still fresh on his mind.

Against her better judgment, she decided to repay the favor by offering him a little peace of mind.

"It wasn't your fault, you know?" she said unexpectedly.

"What wasn't?"

"That woman's suicide." His back straightened and he noticeably tensed as she continued. "She is responsible for her own actions, as is every creature on this planet, human or Diverse. Blaming yourself serves no purpose."

"I can't help but think if I had just told her..." he trailed off.

"Told her what? The truth?" Harlow scoffed. "Let's say you did tell her what really happened. What do you think she would have done?"

Chase shifted in the chair. "I don't know. Taken a different path?"

"Let me tell you what she would have done. It would have been one of two things. Either she would have started drinking, eventually moving on to drugs when the alcohol stopped dulling the pain and ended up dead well before her time from either an accidental or intentional overdose. Or, she would have become angry, and hell-bent on revenge, seeking out the creature who stole her children away. Armed with no knowledge of what she was dealing with or how to destroy it, she would have been cut down within moments of picking a fight. No matter which path she chose, the outcome would have undoubtedly been the same. You just saved her from some extended misery."

"I don't know. If I had checked on her sooner or sent someone to stay with her, maybe she would have gotten through the initial shock and chosen to use her pain to somehow help others who suffered such a loss," he countered.

"You have far too much faith in your fellow humans," she chided and stopped to take a swig from the bottle she had brought up. "And you are also missing the point. SHE, and she alone, made her choice. Stop blaming yourself for the shortcomings of others. Your life will be far less disappointing that way."

He got up and went over, taking a seat on the edge of the bed. She handed him the bottle and he took a large drink from it, making a face as it splashed against the back of his throat, burning as it went down.

Scooching over, she made room for him and patted the bed.

Chase reclined, resting the bottle on his leg, staring at the ceiling as he considered her words.

"Why did you become a doctor?"

"You really want to know?"

"I seem to recall asking!"

"I watched my father die after being attacked by a rougarou," he answered with no emotion in his voice. "I was seven at the time and helpless to do anything to save him. I never wanted to feel that way again, and if I can prevent someone else from experiencing such a thing, then I will."

"Tell me what happened."

Chase inhaled sharply and blew the air out slowly, the memories from that night flooding back. He could still see it all clearly in his mind's eye. "I was upstairs in bed. My brothers were sound asleep, but the full moon was shining through the window, and I was wide awake. I got up to go get a drink of water from the bathroom. That's when I heard my daddy arguing with someone. Slipping down the stairs, there was the sound of a heavy 'thump' that came from the direction of the kitchen. That's when I saw him. It was quite a shock for a kid who still believed his dad kept the monsters under the bed at bay. God, I was terrified."

Harlow rested her hand on his arm. "For the record, you never have to fear the monsters under your bed. They are only there because a temporary portal appears but closes before they can get through. Since people began sleeping in beds, I have only heard of three, maybe four, getting through and taking a child back with them."

Chase blinked hard and his face went pale. "Dear God! I think that is the most horrific thing I have ever heard."

"Please, continue," she urged.

Shaking his head, Chase returned to his memory. "I flattened myself against the wall, held my breath, and prayed he wouldn't see me—but he did. The werewolf stopped, looked directly at me, and let out a howl before running out the front door, away from the house. When I was sure he was gone, I hurried in to check on my dad. There was a little bit of blood dripping down the front of my father's face, pooling at the back of his head as well as on the table. He was frantically trying to tell me something but was unable to form words. I held his hand and cried as his body stilled and he passed. My mother came in from the family restaurant an hour later and I was still there, resting my head on his chest, sobbing and begging him to wake up."

"He saw you? The creature, I mean! You are certain?"

Chase nodded.

"That's peculiar," Harlow cocked her head to one side, "and your father was left alive?"

"Yes. Why?"

"That doesn't really make sense. First of all, allow me to clarify a common mistake humans make all the time. Rougarous and werewolves, though very much related and alike, are two slightly different creatures. Werewolves are made by other werewolves, typically having no control over their emotions or their actions when there is a full moon, most of the time not even remembering what happens while they are changed, especially when the blood lust takes over. It is usually decades before they can manage to exhibit any measure of control whatsoever without intervention by someone who knows how to help them. Your friend Billy Harmon sounds like he was a werewolf. The ones who are born into it, not made by another, are what you are referring to as a rougarou."

"Wait! Some people are born like that?"

"There are, though it is extremely rare. I have only heard of a handful of actual cases over the years, but they do exist, nonetheless. It happens when a curse is placed on the mother when she is carrying the child and, often, she has no idea she has even been hexed. It doesn't manifest itself until the child starts to mature. That is why rougarous are typically a regional legend, only born into areas where black magic is practiced. These individuals also grow up hearing the stories. When the mutation begins to manifest, these creatures learn quickly to conceal themselves as a matter of self-preservation. Rougarous also tend to have more control over their actions. They can change at any time, full moon or not, and they know exactly what happens when they are in that form. If your childhood memory is accurate, and he left you alone, it was likely you really did have a rougarou in your home. That is a remarkable situation in itself."

"Does it really make a difference?" he asked quietly. "Either way, my father is still very much dead."

"No, I don't suppose it does, but if you ever go looking for the responsible party, you should know it could literally be anyone—your banker, your kindergarten teacher, or even your next-door neighbor. It is useful information to have in the back of your mind."

"I will remember that."

"Who taught you about The Diverse and how to hunt them?"

"That was our mama. Daddy's side of the family had been secretly watching over people here for years. He was the one who taught her. I don't think there is anything she doesn't know about them now. Not only did she raise us by herself, while running the restaurant to pay the bills, but she also taught us how to defend ourselves against the things that go bump in the night."

"I met your mother when I arrived in New Orleans. She was," Harlow paused, choosing her words carefully, "an interesting woman."

"I bet your mother is an 'interesting' woman, as well." Turning his head to face her, he asked, "You do have a mother, don't you?"

"Do I look like I was hatched from an egg? Of course, I do—everyone has a mother!"

"What's yours like?"

Harlow snatched the bottle back. "I wouldn't know. I have no memory of her whatsoever. The bitch dumped me off on my father as soon as I was born, so he raised me himself and taught me everything I ever needed to know."

"What happened to her?"

Harlow drank from the bottle. "Don't know, don't care! I am not even sure she still exists in this world. I have never felt the desire to find out."

"Is your father still around?"

"Yes, though I don't get to see him as much as I would like. He is busy building his own empire."

"You should go visit him while you can. You never know when it will be the last time." His tone was filled with an unmistakable amount of sadness.

Harlow cut her eyes over at him and she felt something soften within herself. "What was the last good memory you had of him?"

A warm smile spread across his face. "Earlier that day. He had taken time off from work just to spend it with me. I had just joined a baseball team, and he wanted to work on my batting skills. We went to the park where we spent most of the day before grabbing hot dogs from one of the vendors there and heading home. He had a headache and wasn't feeling well, but I was the happiest kid on the planet."

"I'm sorry for your loss," she said sincerely.

"And I'm sorry you never knew the love of two parents. No child should ever have to live like that."

A peculiar expression crossed her face. No one had ever spoken to her in such a manner, and she wasn't sure how to feel about it.

Their eyes drifted to each other as something akin to a magnetic force began to draw them together.

"What do you have against sleeping with humans?" he asked breathily.

"I have my own reasons," she hissed through her teeth, her hand coming up to lightly touch a wisp of hair that had formed a soft curl against his forehead, "but, since we have nothing else to keep us occupied, I may be willing to make an exception for one night."

His heartbeat quickened as she grazed his cheek with her fingernails, wanting nothing more than to be close to him. Their lips were just about to touch—when the computer chimed.

The mood was spoiled. Each rolled away from the other and off the edge of the bed.

Chase landed on his feet and went to work.

"I found it!" he announced moments later.

Harlow went over to join him, leaning over his shoulder. "What does it say?"

He blew out a hard breath when her hair brushed against the nape of his neck, breathing back in the scent of her intoxicating perfume, detecting traces of vanilla and orange blossoms.

She smiled, inwardly pleased when she sensed the rush of adrenaline from their bodies being in such close proximity.

"It looks like there is a ton of stuff from Black Thorn Enterprises. Isn't that your place?"

"Yes, it is! How the hell did Broussard get access to my files?" her attention now focused.

Chase typed away, flipping from one screen to another, completely absorbed in the task at hand. "This is going to sound crazy, but it looks like he somehow intercepted all incoming and outgoing information, funneling it through here."

"I have the tightest security in the world. That simply isn't possible."

"I am afraid it is. Look," he pointed, "isn't this your personal calendar?"

"Yes, it is!" Harlow's phone suddenly buzzed. "I thought we didn't have service here?" she said as she looked at the screen.

"There must be a cell booster powered by the generator around here somewhere."

Seeing it was Sawyer on FaceTime, Harlow answered.

"Oh Harlow, thank goodness! I have been trying to call you for hours. Why haven't you been answering?"

"Long story! Do you have something for me?"

"We found the leak."

"Explain!"

Sawyer held up the stone. "This was hardwired into our computer system. Rowan says whoever has the other one has been tapping into all the information in our system."

"That's how they were getting in," Chase remarked.

"Those stones belong to me!" she exclaimed. "They were placed in the vault nearly fifty years ago after I acquired them from the Kremlin."

Sawyer shook his head. "Harlow, I know that vault like the back of my hand and I have never seen those before. They must have been moved before I came onboard."

The connection started to break up and the video feed shook. "Are you on the jet?"

"Yes! Mitchell and I are on our way to you. Rowan said you would be able to use this to trace the person on the other end, but there's a bad storm over the city. I am not sure we are going to be able to land."

"I will handle that. Come straight to La Maison des Divers as soon as you touch down. I will meet you there."

"Will do, boss. See you soon."

"You do remember we are stuck here, right?" Chase pointed out after she hung up.

"Not for long!" Going to stand in front of the window, she waved her fingers back and forth while saying a few words he did not understand. The rain ceased instantly, and the clouds parted, revealing a bright full moon. With a clap of her hand, the water that covered the road, receded back into the river, leaving the way clear.

"How the hell did you do that?" he muttered in disbelief.

"I am Harlow Thornhart, and I can do things you can only dream of," she winked and turned on her heel. "Get the others. We are leaving, but there is one thing I need to do first."

Harlow strode into the first bedroom she had come across that night, twitching her nose when the smell of mustiness became more distinct. The dust stirred and moved as she crossed the threshold. "I know you are here," she demanded with resolve, "and I am short on time. Show yourself!"

From the farthest corner, a dim light began to emit, spinning and twirling into an oblong formation before finally taking the loose shape of a man, bent over at the waist as if weary and worn from age. The Bible-clutching being emerged into the middle of the room.

"Let's forgo the pleasantries, shall we? I have a witch to kill, and you have something you need to get off your chest. I take it you are Analise's father?"

The man offered a slow, curt nod. "I am Gordon Mandeville."

"What are you still doing hanging around? You should have crossed over a long time ago. What's keeping you here?"

"I am not sure I can trust you," he responded firmly.

"It seems you couldn't trust your daughter, either, so what do you have to lose with me? Look, no one else is coming back here, and with the death of Matthew Broussard, who I am assuming was the last survivor of the Mandeville family, I am afraid I am all that you get."

He studied her for a long moment, as if mulling things over. "If I entrust this to you, I am going to need something in return."

"I am sure we can work out an arrangement."

The elder gentleman glanced over his shoulder. "I was the last true guardian of a sacred artifact my family has protected for centuries. I brought it to Louisiana, thinking the remoteness of the area would provide the perfect place to conceal it, and I was correct in my assumption. Analise would have been the next in line to guard it, but she murdered me before I had a chance to pass on the secret. I suppose that was a good thing, for if she had come into possession of it, there is no telling what sort of havoc she would have wreaked in the wake. I had assumed knowledge of its existence died with me, until three nights ago when the relic was removed from its encasement." Gordon glided towards the door. Harlow followed him down the stairs and into the main hall of the original part of the house where the others were waiting. They all stopped and stared as the ghost came to rest in front of a panel beneath the staircase.

"Who's your friend?" asked Marie.

"Gordon Mandeville, Analise's father."

"Are you seeing this, too?" Randy nudged Chase, who nodded in return. "Just when you think you have seen it all."

The specter pointed to three of the spindles on the stair rail. Taking a closer look, Chase could see there were several notches carved on them.

"Rotate them each a quarter turn," Gordon instructed.

Chase obeyed and with the final pivot, the panel popped free, revealing a secret room. Cautiously stepping inside, they were astonished to see an empty gold sarcophagus, covered in protection sigils, the lid lying in pieces on the floor.

"The witch took it," Gordon explained.

"What exactly did she take?" asked Chase.

"The only thing in this world that can kill any creature that walks upon it!"

"The Sword of Lucifer," Harlow finished the sentence before he could. "That's where I knew the name from. The Mandeville family has been in possession of it for centuries. That particular information was buried deep in my archives and kept in my personal vault."

"We were able to prevent it from falling into the wrong hands all this time but," he closed his eyes as if in physical pain, "with my passing, there was no Mandeville left to watch over it. No one after me even knew it was here."

"Who is she?" Marie questioned.

"I don't know. Matthew brought her here believing she could be trusted, but she betrayed him in the worst way possible just to get it, and with it, she will do great harm to humankind. That sword retains a power no creature can control for very long. It corrupts whoever wields it, making them crave power and destruction. This specially crafted ark contained it, prevented it from affecting anyone, but now that it's out in the world, I am not certain it can be reigned back in."

Harlow stared down at the container, letting her fingers glide over one of the symbols. These weren't witch sigils.

She faced Gordon. "Rest! Let me take it from here. I will personally secure the sword and ensure it never falls into the wrong hands again."

"How? And why would you?"

"I have some unique tools at my disposal," she faced him, "and because that witch has picked the wrong bitch to fuck with!"

"I hope you have the honor and fortitude to do as you say you will," Gordon's eyes drifted around the room. "And now, I must ask for that favor in return."

"Name it."

"When I found this place, it was wild, untamed, and the most beautiful location I had ever seen. I wanted nothing more than to live out my final days being a part of it rather than becoming an intrusion upon it, but that dream was taken from me. I have no legacy left in this world. My descendants have brought nothing but dishonor and shame to the home I spent so much time building as my personal sanctuary. I only ask that you give back to the swamp the land it was generous enough to loan to me to enjoy for such a fleeting time. See to it that this house is no more."

"You have my word, sir."

"Thank you, and I wish you well on your quest." With those words, Gordon Mandeville slowly faded from sight.

"Harlow, what the hell is going on?" Marie demanded. "Who are we dealing with?"

"I will explain when we get back to the hotel." Turning her attention to the brothers, she added, "The road is clear. You two may go. I know you are anxious to find your brother."

"Logan is a big boy, and he can take care of himself," Randy assured.

Chase agreed. "And if this is as bad as the old man says it is, you are going to need all the help you can get—even if we are human."

"Did you just tell me 'no'?" Harlow snapped.

"Yes, I believe I did!" Chase crossed his arms, planting his feet in a firm stance. "Like it or not, you need us, and you won't be rid of us so easily!"

"I don't need anyone!" she countered, stepping to meet him face to face.

The corners of his lips twitched up. "Too bad! You're stuck with us."

"He's right," Randy interjected. "It's not just The Diverse who are in danger if this is true. I think it's better if we all stick together on this. We may be able to bring some things to the table others cannot."

Harlow cut her eyes to Marie, who shrugged. "Give them a chance. They just want to help."

"Fine!" she conceded and started towards the door. "You have exactly two minutes to clear out of this house."

"What happens in two minutes?" asked Randy.

Harlow started to form the fireball between her palms. "I am keeping my word."

The Mandeville estate burned brilliantly in the background as the two cars sped away.

"You know Marie is being less than forthcoming with us, don't you," Chase said to his brother as they drove away from the flames.

Randy sighed heavily. "Yeah, I know, but she's Marie. No matter who or what she is, I lo—," he caught himself, "—trust her. I trust her."

"I am pretty sure you were about to say you love her," Chase taunted, ruffling his hair. "Aw! My little brother has fallen in love! Mama will be thrilled!"

"Shut the fuck up!" Randy shoved him away. "Marie and I are good together," he confessed, "and we have some things to talk about given all we learned today, but I think she'll be worth it."

Chase reached across and gripped his shoulder. "I think you're right. No matter what Marie turns out to be, I do believe she has a good heart and that's all that matters."

"You always were better at reading people and creatures than anyone else. What about this Harlow? What kind of a read are you getting on her?"

"I don't know, Randy. She is something alright, I just can't figure out what. It's hard to keep a clear head around her."

"Did you get another boner while you two were upstairs?"

Chase turned to look out the window, refusing to answer.

"Dude!"

Silence filled the car for the next two miles.

"What do you suppose she would be like in the sack?" Randy asked, breaking the silence.

"I wouldn't know. She doesn't fuck humans, remember?"

"Yeah, but if she did, what do you think it would be like?"

"I think she would be like a praying mantis," Chase replied. "Give you the best night of mind-blowing sex you have ever experienced in your life and then, literally, bite off your head for a midnight snack."

Randy grinned. "Yeah, but what a way to go!"

"What happened with you and Chase upstairs?" Marie elbowed Harlow, the car she was driving not even veering an inch from the movement.

"What went on with you and Randy downstairs?" Harlow pitched back.

"Oh cher, I rocked his world!"

"I know, I heard! I also tasted a little vomit in my mouth when I heard you squeal like an ungreased pig who took it up the ass. Why in the world would you go and fall for a human?"

Marie laughed. "Who the hell else am I going to fall for? A vampire? We see how well love worked out for Broussard. I did try dating a ghoul once, but I kept finding little pieces of him all over my house—and not the good pieces, either! And don't even get me started on how much werewolves shed. If you think getting cat hair off a sweater is hard, you should try getting wolf fur off your black velvet couch! They don't make one of those lint roller things large enough. Besides Harlow, I am over two hundred years old. Maybe it's about time I took a chance on love, after all, I'm not getting any younger."

Harlow brushed a strand of hair away from her face. "Not without my help, you're not."

"You know, you have never told me exactly what you have against humans. I mean, I know all the usual blah, blah, blah reasons, but I am truly dumbfounded as to why you have never taken one to bed. Explain that to me! There are so many in the world, you could have a different dick every night. It's not like they don't flock to you. I know quite a few of them are sleazy and disgusting, but there are some good ones out there too."

"Marie, I am not having this conversation with you!"

"Alright! Have it your way, but I will say this—even when I am with Randy, I can't help but notice the fine ass on Chase whenever he walks by."

"Hmph!"

"Since we are changing the subject," Marie's said in a more serious tone, "what's the deal with this Sword of Lucifer? I've never heard of it before."

"Very few have. It's safe to assume it's one of the world's best-kept secrets. You know the story about the battle and how the archangel Michael cast Lucifer down from Heaven? What everyone tends to forget is that there was indeed a brutal clash before that happened, and as in every fight, each combatant is armed. This was no different. History is always written by the victor, which is why you have only heard of Michael's weapon, a long two-toned golden broad sword, polished to a shine brighter than the sun, and one the wielder can set aflame by merely uttering a few words. Gifted to Michael by God himself, it can only be used against that which it perceives as evil, meaning it can never be raised against a human, for as long as a person is a living soul, there is always redemption should the owner choose to accept it. According to legend, it rests in Heaven and is only taken from there in times of great need.

"The Sword of Lucifer, on the other hand, is quite different. Forged by the devil himself, this blade was made by mixing bronze with his blood, giving in an eerie glow and creating a bond between it and its creator. It doesn't have the limitations of Michael's sword in that it does not distinguish between good and evil, meaning it can be used against anyone or anything. Because it was part of Lucifer during the fall, literally and figuratively, it is forbidden from returning to Heaven. To prevent another uprising, it is also never allowed to enter Hell, meaning it only has one other place it can reside."

"Here!" Marie was starting to understand the ramifications.

Harlow nodded. "Knowing how dangerous it could be in the wrong hands, the angels chose to entrust its care to a few faithful servants. It didn't take them long to figure out, with Lucifer's blood flowing throughout the blade, humans would become easily susceptible to the temptation and begin to develop an insatiable lust for power."

"That's why it was enclosed in the sarcophagus! I knew there was something odd about those sigils on it."

"They are written in Enochian, the language of the angels, to keep the power contained within the crypt and conceal it from Lucifer and his followers. Once they solved that issue, they decided to entrust it to a family with strong religious roots and blessed their descendants financially so they could concentrate on keeping it safe."

"Until Analise came along. I guess they never saw her coming."

"Exactly!" Harlow turned her head to stare out the window. "I have heard the stories all my life, but never dreamed I would ever get the opportunity to see it for myself. It looks like I am going to get an up-close and personal view."

For the first time since they met, Marie found herself worried about Harlow.

Chapter Twelve

Sawyer was staring down at the street from the window and Mitchell was typing away on the computer in the room when they returned at 2 am.

"Sawyer Evans, Mitchell, meet Marie Lavine, and brothers, Chase and Randy Devereaux."

Sawyer's head snapped up, clearly taken aback. "Did you say 'Devereaux'?"

Noting the apprehension, Harlow regarded her assistant with curiosity.

Chase shook Mitchell's hand and then turned to Sawyer. "It's nice to meet you."

He was always so cool and collected. Harlow had never seen him so out of sorts before and she was puzzled.

Sawyer's widened eyes drifted to his outstretched hand as if it were an abomination. Quickly recovering, he offered his own in return. "And you as well."

Chase's gaze lingered and he tightened his grip. "Have we met before? You seem familiar?"

Shaking his head, "I don't believe so."

With the pleasantries out of the way, Mitchell got down to business. "I have the stone here. I take it you know more about how this works than we do?"

Harlow tossed it up in the air and caught it. "I do, but I don't need this to tell me who is responsible for what we are dealing with. I already know." Casting it aside, she took a seat.

The room went quiet as she explained.

"Thirty years ago, before Sawyer came along, I employed an extremely talented young witch by the name of Daphne Savant. She was with me for nearly a year when I caught her helping herself to some of my personal stash of magical herbs. Begging forgiveness, she swore it was a simple mistake, and promised to replace them, but I dismissed her just the same on principle. Anyone else, I would have killed on the spot, but in truth, the things she took weren't all that special to begin with and I thought I saw some potential in her. A few days later, I realized my herbs weren't the only things she had helped herself to. A few of my rarer items had mysteriously disappeared, as well. When I paid a visit to her apartment, she had cleared out, concealing herself with some wickedly strong sigil magic that even my best witches weren't able to work around. That spell work came from a book gifted to me by an ancient coven in return for their protection during the witch trials. I haven't thought about her since, but when Sawyer mentioned he had never seen the stones before and that the leak was coming from inside Black Thorn Enterprises, the pieces fell into place. That bitch used the information from my personal files to track down the sword."

"What sword?" asked Mitchell.

"The Sword of Lucifer. The one thing in this world that can kill anything in it."

"Everything?" Harlow offered a curt nod.

"Why is she doing this?"

"That's a good question and one I intend to get an answer for." Harlow looked around the room. "We have the advantage of time until dawn. It will take her that long to recover from the storm she conjured. First and foremost, I want Cherise safe and then I will deal with Daphne personally. No one else touches her. She is mine!"

"How are we going to find her?"

"We don't have to—she will find me. In the meantime, I suggest everyone go home and let me deal with this on my own."

"No way!" Chase argued. "You are going to need us. Chances are, she has this woman close by wherever she is. She also doesn't know that Randy and I are lending a hand, so she will never see us coming."

Harlow cocked her head to one side. "You would be willing to do that to help me?"

"You ARE trying to save a human."

Something akin to a smile started to cross her lips before she cleared her throat and forced it away. This 'human' was starting to grow on her, whether she wanted to admit it or not.

"Alright," she conceded, "but since you are human, you cannot function without sleep. I want all the mortals in the room to go and get some rest. We can discuss strategy in the morning."

Chase, Randy, and Mitchell all headed for the door while Marie hovered near a cart of liqueurs that had just been restocked, looking over the selection.

"You coming, Marie?" asked Randy.

"Um—of course—," she stuttered when she realized her mistake, "all us humans have to stick together!" Turning for only Harlow to see, she grimaced. Facing Randy, she faked a yawn while stretching her arms above her head. "I'm exhausted, baby! I will be out as soon as my head hits the pillow."

Harlow rolled her eyes and went over to close the door behind them.

"I should go, too," Sawyer said quietly.

"Not so fast!" Harlow extended her arm, blocking him and the door. "You and I need to have a chat!"

"You flinched!"

"I what?"

"You flinched when I said 'Devereaux'," Harlow repeated as she took a seat, directing him to the one across from her, "and I have never seen you at such a loss for words. Why?"

Sawyer rested his elbows on his knees, raking his hair back with both hands nervously. She waited patiently for an answer.

"I recognized the name, that's all. I was born here, and I know the Devereauxs hunt our kind."

"In New Orleans? You never mentioned that."

Sawyer got up to pour two glasses of Jack Daniels from the cart and handed her one. "I don't have such pleasant memories of this place. I have gone out of my way to forget everything about it. I suppose I am just a little unsettled here. How did you end up with the brothers anyway?"

"Randy is a police detective, and his station got a call that I was trying to kill Cherise out at the Broussard place. Chase just happened to be with him. They were looking for their brother, Logan, who apparently went missing after a hunt."

"Missing?" He slowly sat down.

"They said they hadn't seen him in a couple of days."

"What were they tracking?"

"They took down a newly turned werewolf who killed a couple of fishermen. Their brother was hanging out to make sure whoever sired it wasn't still around."

"They shouldn't have left him alone. Do they think he's alright?" The concern was evident in his voice.

Harlow rested her glass on the arm of her chair. "Why do you care about a human who kills your kind without batting an eyelash?"

"I don't!" Sawyer shrugged, quickly shifting his mood, attempting to seem unbiased. "I was just—curious."

"Are you certain there isn't another reason?"

"There is," he confessed and sucked in a breath. "I haven't had much sleep the past few days. I am not thinking clearly. Maybe I should get some rest too." Setting his glass aside, he rose. "I have procured the room across the hall since Mitchell has the one next door. I think I will go lie down. Good night."

"You know what I find odd, Sawyer?"

He stopped and tensed, his hand resting on the doorknob.

"Marie has been in New Orleans her entire life and, has even been sleeping with one of the Devereux brothers for nearly a year, yet she had no idea they were hunters. They have apparently done a flawless job of becoming an integral part of the community while concealing their identities. It's a curious thing that you would know about them, and she would not, don't you think?"

"I suppose it is."

"You know if there is something you want to get off your chest, I am an excellent listener. I also have no issue killing someone who may have slighted you in any way. In fact, the thought sounds rather appealing, especially given the mood I am currently in."

Sawyer lowered his head, relaxed his shoulders, and smiled. "I know! Thanks, boss!"

As soon as she was alone, Harlow got up and locked the door. Being two steps behind this witch, or anyone for that matter, was not going to cut it. It was time to turn the tables on this little game.

Strolling over to the bar along the wall, she opened the utensil drawer and rambled through it until she located a sharp knife. Closing her hand around the blade, she pulled it until it drew blood, before reciting a few ancient words.

A gust of wind blew open the balcony doors, announcing his arrival. Nearly seven feet tall, he was dressed in a snugly tailored leather tunic, black pants, and boots, accented by silver metal cuffs adorning his arms. "You summoned me?"

Harlow turned. "Yes, Zane. I need some information from a recently deceased vampire by the name of Matthew Broussard."

"What do you need to know?"

"Where his girlfriend is hiding out for starters—well, former girlfriend, specifically, the one who murdered him along with anything else that might potentially be helpful."

"Do you want me to obtain this by any means necessary?"

"Of course! Use your own discretion, but given how things ended, you may find he is more than a little willing to cooperate!"

"Is there anything else I can do for you?"

Harlow thought for a moment, glancing towards the door Sawyer had just departed through. "Yes, as a matter of fact, there is, but this will prove to be a little more difficult, if you feel you are up for the job."

She went on to explain what she needed as he listened carefully.

"As you wish!" Zane bowed his head. "As always, I am here to serve in whatever capacity you need."

With that, he was gone.

He returned shortly before dawn, standing before her with his hands folded in front of him giving her the answers she requested.

"Would you like me to smite the witch for you?"

"No! This is personal, and to be quite honest, I am rather curious to see how it all plays out. What about the other matter?"

Zane lowered his gaze. "It seems that particular request will have to be escalated to someone higher in the hierarchy than myself."

Harlow groaned and rolled her eyes. "That's what I was afraid of."

"Is there anything else I can assist you with?"

"That will be all. Thank you, Zane."

A short time later, Carter knocked on her door and hand-delivered an invitation that had mysteriously appeared on his desk. It was addressed to Harlow and requested her presence as the special guest at an exclusive Mardi Gras Masquerade Ball.

She quickly typed out a text message, grabbed her coat, and headed out the door. It was early and the streets were still empty, but there was one place she knew would be open.

"Well, welcome back," Jacquelin said when she saw Harlow taking a seat at one of the empty tables with her back to the door. "I guess you didn't get a chance to finish that business with Matthew Broussard after all."

"No, I didn't, but that's alright, I have other business that needs tending while I am in town."

"What can I get you?"

Harlow rested her forearms on the table. "I can't seem to get your café au lait and those freshly-] made beignets off my mind."

"Coming right up!"

"Join me?" she offered when Jacquelin returned with her order.

Wiping her hands on her apron, she looked around to see they weren't that busy yet. "I suppose I can for a bit."

"I wanted to thank you again for your help the other day," Harlow said sincerely. "I appreciate your concern for my welfare."

"As much as I hate to speak ill of the dead, I think our fair city is a little bit safer without Matthew Broussard in it." "I daresay you are correct." Harlow bit into one of the pastries and moaned. Brushing the powdered sugar off her hands, she asked, "Did you grow up here?"

"I have lived here all my life. I can't imagine calling anywhere else home."

"I had the pleasure of spending the night with your son, Chase."

"I'm sorry, you what?"

"We somehow managed to find ourselves in the middle of nowhere at the same time when the storm blew up and were forced to take refuge in an abandoned home."

"Oh, I see!"

"Don't worry, he was a perfect gentleman," she clarified.

A slow smile spread across Jacquelin's face. "I would not expect anything less of him. He has always been a good boy."

"I actually met two of your sons yesterday. Allow me to say you did a remarkable job raising them on your own."

Jacquelin looked back at her inquisitively.

"Chase mentioned your husband passed many years ago," she explained.

"I am surprised to hear that. He doesn't speak of his father very often."

"Really? We had time to kill, and he spoke of him at great lengths. It was obvious he looked up to the man and loved him very much." Harlow watched for the older woman's reaction and then continued. "He did mention he was with him when he died, but he didn't say exactly what happened. I didn't have the heart to ask."

The older woman visibly tensed. "It was a tragic accident. My husband was alone in the kitchen after the boys went to bed. He slipped on something and hit his head. I found Chase with him when I returned home from work. He had been there for at least an hour. That poor boy never got over it." "Alone? That's odd. I thought Chase said he heard another voice coming from downstairs that night."

Jacquelin shook her head. "No, you must be mistaken. There was no one else in the house that night." It was clear she was lying.

"I am sure you're right—I must have misunderstood. Did you at least have family here to help you with the children?"

"My parents were both alive when the boys were younger, but they have since passed on. Ryland, my husband, had several aunts and uncles who pitched in and helped me a great deal, as well as the community in general. I don't know what I would have done without them."

"Your husband was an only child?"

"No, he had several brothers, but they had all moved away over the years and we had lost touch."

"That's a shame."

"Some things, and people, are best left forgotten." Jacquelin stood up. "Can I get you anything else?"

"Another order of what I am having for my friend who just came in."

Jacquelin's eyes went over Harlow's shoulder to the door, which had not made a sound when it opened. A fleeting expression of bewilderment crossed her face before she broke into a smile.

"Marie! Good morning!"

"Good morning, cher!" Marie kissed her on the cheek. "I see you have met my friend, Harlow."

"Well, not officially."

"You are correct. Please, forgive my appalling lack of manners!" Harlow blotted her lips with a napkin. "Harlow Thornhart, and it has been a pleasure to make your acquaintance."

Jacquelin nodded. "Let me go get you something to eat, Marie."

Taking off her own coat, Marie pulled out a chair. "Making nice with your new boyfriend's mother," she snickered.

"No, I was making nice with YOUR boyfriend's mother who is going to be thrilled to find out her son is dating a two-hundred-year-old witch. I am assuming you will not be giving her grandchildren." Harlow wrinkled her nose. "It took you long enough to get here."

"I had to slip out," she said, shifting in her seat. "Randy is a light sleeper," she whispered, after making sure Jacquelin wasn't nearby. "I take it from your message there is new information?"

Harlow produced the formal invitation.

Marie unfolded the envelope and read it over. "Why would she invite you to a party?"

"According to my sources, she intends to kill me in front of an audience and take my place as 'The Purveyor'."

"Wait!" Marie held up her hand. "She doesn't have the kind of power you do. What makes that bitch think she is qualified for such a thing?"

"She's not, but what she does have are nine or ten pints of vampire blood, and for someone who has had access to my client list, it would be enough to get her started in the trade. Besides, she also happens to now hold a sword that can kill anyone who disagrees with her. It's not the worst business plan I have ever heard of."

"You know what I don't understand?"

"Why you've gone and fallen for a human? I don't understand that, either!"

Marie rolled her eyes, ignoring the snarky comment. "Why does she have it in for you specifically?"

"I haven't been able to figure that out, either. However, I am sure she intends to tell me before she runs me through with the sword. Isn't there some sort of unspoken rule about having to lay all your cards on the table and explain your reasons before killing your sworn enemy?"

"In the movies, but this isn't one of those. How do you plan on stopping her?"

"Who says I will?" Harlow replied quietly before taking a long sip from her cup, savoring the flavor. "Damn, that's good!"

"Harlow, what are you saying?"

Resting the cup back in the saucer, Harlow sighed. "I have been making deals longer than most civilizations have endured. I have raised them into existence and razed them back down again, and for what? Just to watch the same shit show on repeat because everything in this world is entirely too predictable. I can honestly say, this is the one thing I never saw coming. I am also more than a little curious to see how it will all play out."

"So, what's the plan?"

"There isn't one. We are winging it, but I suppose we do need to go shopping!" Harlow tapped the invitation with her fingernail. "After all, Cinderella, we have a ball to attend tomorrow night."

Chase was awakened by the beams of bright morning sun hitting him in the face. He rarely slept past dawn, but it had been a long night.

Immediately sensing he wasn't alone, he sat up on the edge of the bed and pulled on his sweats.

"When did you slink in?" he asked Logan as he walked to the kitchen, relieved his little brother was indeed safe.

"A couple of hours ago." Logan was stretched out on the sofa with a beer bottle in his hand.

"Is my couch more comfortable than your bed?" Chase opened the refrigerator and took out a carton of orange juice.

"Nah, but I was all out of beer," he held up the bottle, "and you weren't. Besides," Logan shifted, "I need you to take a look at this."

Setting his juice aside, Chase's face filled with concern when he saw the ripped shirt and dried blood on his upper arm. "What happened?"

"I just grazed it on a tree limb. I figured you had something around here to clean it up with."

Reaching up and taking out a first aid kit from the cabinet, Chase took it over and sat down on the coffee table in front of Logan. Using a pair of scissors, he cut open the fabric and peeled it away. The wound wasn't that deep and appeared to already be healing. "I think you will live," he remarked, cleaning it out with some peroxide. "Where have you been the past couple of days?"

"I stayed at the fish camp and just as I was getting ready to leave, this wicked storm blew up out of nowhere, so I had to stay a little while longer."

"Randy and I got caught out in it, too, but we were out at the old Broussard place."

"What were you doing all the way out there?"

"Coming to look for you after Randy checked on a case. I was starting to get really worried." He began to bandage the wound. "I'm just glad you are alright."

"Bro, I have never felt better! I am also starving. Loan me a clean shirt so we can go downstairs and grab some breakfast."

"Aw man, I love Mardi Gras," Logan whispered when they rounded the corner. "It brings all the freaky women out. Check that one out over there with Marie."

"Careful little brother!" Chase warned when he saw he was referring to Harlow. "You have no idea what you are getting into with that one."

"Think I have a chance?"

"Not a chance in Hell! That one doesn't fuck humans."

"Humans?" Logan turned to face him curiously. "What is that supposed to mean?"

"I am fairly sure she eats men for breakfast—literally. Come on. I'll introduce you."

"Morning ladies!"

"Morning Chase," said Marie, "and good morning to you, Logan. Glad to see you are alright."

"Why wouldn't I be?" Harlow regarded him curiously. "Why not indeed?"

Chase cleared his throat. "Logan, this is Harlow Thornhart. Harlow, this is my brother, Logan."

"It is a pleasure to meet you," Logan purred.

Harlow simply stared back at him, two fingers resting on her cheek studying him.

"Join us?" Marie offered.

"As much as I would love to," Logan glanced at his watch, "I have to be at work in a few minutes." He waved to his mom and indicated he needed food to go. "But I guess I can sit until then." Logan took the seat closest to Harlow.

"Where's Randy?"

"He was sleeping in," Marie replied. "I am sure he will find his way down here soon enough. I swear your mama keeps this place open just to feed you boys."

As if on cue, Randy came through the door.

"Where the hell have you been?" he asked Logan as he pulled up a chair next to Marie and kissed her. "Morning, baby!"

"Got caught at the cabin in the storm. Um—" he waggled his finger back and forth between the couple, "did I miss something?"

"We all did," Chase answered. "What's that?" he asked Harlow when he saw the invitation.

"This was delivered to my room this morning." Handing it over for him to read, she explained, "It seems I am to be a special guest."

"You did say she would find you," he passed it to Randy. "What's her endgame?"

"She wants Harlow's job," Marie replied.

"What do you do?" Logan asked all smiles.

"I will explain later," Chase said in a muffled voice, tugging on his shirt as their mother approached.

"This is a pleasant surprise!" She handed Logan a bag and a cup. "I hardly ever see you boys all together at one table anymore."

"Sorry, but I have got to run. Thanks, Mama!" Logan stood and kissed her cheek. "It was nice to meet you, Harlow. I hope I will see you again soon."

"I am sure you will and Logan," he waited as she sipped from her cup, "take care of that wound. Sometimes when you pick up nasty little things in the swamp, they tend to grow and fester into bigger problems than you realize before you even know what has happened."

"What's she talking about?" asked Jacquelin. "I just got a little scratch from a tree branch. It's no big deal. Chase has already looked at it." He turned and addressed Harlow. "Can I ask how you knew?"

"There's blood on your hands," she pointed to a tiny spot on the side of his little finger.

"Oh, would you look at that! I must have banged it." Licking it off, he continued on his way.

Harlow and Marie exchanged looks of concern.

"Shouldn't you boys be getting to work, too?" asked Jacquelin.

Randy shook his head. "I decided to take the rest of the week off. I have accrued too much vacation time, and I am going to start losing it, so I figured why not? Thought I might go fishing or something."

"Good for you! You work too hard as it is! What about you, Chase?"

"I am not due back in for a couple of days, but I do need to run by the hospital and take care of some paperwork."

"Let me grab you some coffee." As Jacquelin went to the counter, Chase leaned in close. "We need to meet somewhere else. Our mom worries enough as it is." "I have an idea." Marie smiled. "How about dinner at my place tonight? We can put our heads together, make a plan, and then blow off some steam. My place is in a perfect spot on the parade route." "Sounds good to me," Randy slipped his hand over on her thigh.

"Fine!" Harlow agreed. "I will call the hotel, fill Sawyer and Mitchell in, and then Marie and I need to do a little shopping." Eyeing Chase up and down, she asked, "What size are you?"

"What size what?" he asked warily.

"Never mind!" Harlow patted his cheek. "I'm pretty sure I've got your number."

"On that note, I am going to head out." Chase stood, wary eyes on Harlow.

Randy sighed. "Speaking of paperwork, I need to clean up a few things too. Why don't I walk out with you? I will see you lovely ladies later."

"We need to get going, as well." Harlow stood and reached for her coat. "Come on, Marie, there's lots to do!"

"It's last minute, but we can probably rent tuxes for the guys at Donivan's, the men's shop," Marie said as they started up the street. "You and I will have to grab something off the rack this late though."

"Bite your tongue!" Harlow scolded. "I have already sent for everything we need, and it will arrive in the morning from Vegas. You are going to love what I picked out for you, by the way!"

"Then what the hell are we doing?"

"A little this, a little that, maybe I will even manage to add a little sparkle to your day."

"Oh, my Lord!" Marie stopped and folded her arms when she looked up and realized where they were. "What are you up to, Harlow?"

"I am slightly curious about the woman."

Harlow had learned from a search she had Mitchell conduct, that Amber Sparks ran a little boutique in the French Quarter. The big glittery sign read, '*ADD A LITTLE SPARKLE*'.

"Don't tell me you aren't the least bit curious."

"No, I'm not, mostly because I already know the story and the bitch behind it."

"Well, why didn't you say something?" Harlow scolded, waving her to a nearby bench on the street. "Do tell, and don't leave out any of the sordid details!"

"Why do you care so much?" Marie asked amused. "Is Chase starting to look interesting to you?

"Pish-posh!" Harlow grumbled. "I'm just bored and want to see what kind of trouble I can stir up. Besides, Chase wouldn't tell me what happened, so I thought I would come straight to the source."

"I'm going to tell you something, but it stays between us. There is a reason he didn't want to talk about their breakup. The handful of people who knew the truth kept it quiet so Jacquelin wouldn't find out, but Randy told me."

"Alright!" The excitement was written all over her face. "I give you my word it will be our little secret."

Marie sat down and sighed. "The guy Amber was screwing was Logan."

"His brother?" Harlow gasped. "Really?"

Marie nodded towards the shop. "That chick in there is a spiteful bitch. She grew up a wealthy socialite, her father a plastic surgeon and her mother a pediatrician. Her sole purpose in life was to land a handsome young husband who was on his way to being someone important. Chase fit the bill perfectly. He was the youngest head of the ER the hospital had ever had, and the administration was grooming him to run the whole place. Amber was giddy at the prospect. They had been seriously dating for two years and had already been talking about getting married. This was all she had ever wanted, but when the board offered him the job, he turned it down. He wanted to stay right where he was and continue to look after his patients."

"That was very noble of him," Harlow acknowledged as she took the seat next to her.

"Chase IS one of the good guys."

"So, how did she end up with Logan?" Harlow glanced towards the window, her contempt towards the woman she hadn't yet met growing as a strange sensation of protectiveness for Chase overcame her.

"Her daddy had a friend on the board who told him Chase was being offered the job that day. Amber rushed over to Chase's apartment, cooked a romantic dinner, dressed in something sexy, and popped the cork on a bottle of champagne. Chase called to let her know he had been offered the job but had turned it down. Amber was furious and was still there when Logan stopped by after work that day to have a beer with Chase. She invited him in, plied him with whiskey, and took advantage of the situation. Poor Chase walked in on them in the middle of the act."

"That's quite the betrayal coming from someone you are so close to."

"Not that it is an excuse for his behavior, but Logan can barely manage more than a six-pack, and, after a few shots of the hard stuff, I expect Amber's fake boobs would have been hard for even Gandhi himself to resist. After sobering up and realizing what he had done, Logan felt horrible and begged Chase to forgive him—promised to do whatever it took to make things right. Amber, on the other hand, laughed in his face and told him his brother was ten times the man in bed he was, and that she could never love a man with no ambition. According to Randy, Chase was crushed. Not only had he lost the woman he loved, but his brother played a big part in it."

"He and Logan seem alright now."

"They are, but it took a long time for them to get to this point."

Harlow sat quietly for a moment before announcing, "I don't like this bitch, not one bit. Let's go have some fun!"

"What do you have in mind?"

A set of chimes on the door rang as Harlow and Marie stepped inside the boutique. *ADD A LITTLE SPARKLE* was one of those specialty fashion shops where there was only one of everything and it was all grossly overpriced. Having come from money, there was no doubt this was used as a tax write-off for Amber's family and a place for her to spend her days doing something she called 'work'. More likely than not, there was a luxurious layout in the back where she sat drinking and gossiping with her friends, while the other businesses on the street struggled to stay afloat, barely paying their bills. Harlow spied Amber when she popped out of the back, cocktail in hand.

The woman was just like a thousand others she had seen in Vegas—long, bleached blond hair, breasts two sizes larger than normal, on an unusually thin frame, and little to no ass to go with it. Her makeup was flawless, except for her fake eyelashes that were a bit too large for her face. The tightly fitted flowery dress with excessive cleavage she wore over her newly freshened spray-on tan, along with the nude-colored four-inch heels, accented her long legs, but also gave the impression of being doll-like in a way. "Let me know if you need anything," she had said before vanishing again.

"What do you think?" asked Marie, holding up a gaudy, gold, backless halter top against her chest, basically consisting of a triangle-cut piece of fabric and two strings.

"I think it would be perfect for the new 'Barbie Whore Collection' never to be in production," she replied with disgust.

Marie burst into laughter and placed it back on the rack.

Harlow wandered over to the shoe section, picking up a purple flat with a large daisy on the toe and dusted in glitter. "What the fuck?" she muttered as she dropped it to the floor and brushed off her hands.

"Is this better?" Marie tried on a pair of oversized rhinestone sunglasses, looking into the mirror, wincing when she got a look at the price tag. "Damn! I know I overcharge the tourists, but this is highway robbery at best. Pointing to the jewelry counter, "See anything you want to buy?" she goaded.

"Yes, the entire store so I can burn it, and all of its contents, to the ground. It would be a service to this fine city."

"Did you find anything you like?" Amber called unenthusiastically as she returned to the front, her drink now topped off.

"You have a most unusual and eclectic array of items here," Harlow said, choosing her words carefully.

"Thank you!" Amber straightened up, exuding a sense of pride, "Each item is one I handpicked personally to match my own sense of style."

Harlow and Marie exchanged horrified looks.

"I was just admiring the lovely Mardi Gras masks hanging on the wall there behind the counter," Harlow turned her attention to them.

"Oh, you have an excellent eye. Those are handmade by a local artist, all one-of-a-kind and true miniature masterpieces."

"Might I see the blue one there?"

"Of course." Amber rolled over a ladder and climbed to the top rung in her heels and tight skirt to retrieve it, having some difficulty moving around, so she had to twist and shift to make it work. "Don't I know you?" she said to Marie over her shoulder.

"I own a shop here in town as well—*THE ENCHANTED CHALICE.*"

"Oh, yes, that little tacky tourist trap. I am amazed it has been around so long." Marie flexed her hands by her side, preparing to turn Amber into something a little more befitting her personality, like a cockroach, but

Harlow intervened. With her back to the shopkeeper, she rested her hand on her friend's arm and winked with a wicked grin on her lips. "Patience," she whispered.

Amber climbed back down and brought it over.

"It's lovely!" Harlow exclaimed as she carefully picked it up, looking it over. "What do you think of this one for Chase?" She asked Marie, discretely pointing out the 'made in China' tag on the back Amber had forgotten to remove.

Marie lowered her head to conceal the smirk on her face, now understanding the cat wanted to have a little fun with her prey before moving in for the kill. Clearing her throat, she lifted her chin and stepped closer. "I don't think it's him."

"You're right! You can put this one back, but may I see the white one—please?"

"Sure thing!" She walked back over to the ladder. Hiking her skirt this time, she went up, replaced the blue one, and reached across for the white one, having to bend at the waist because one was far from the other. Returning, she placed it in front of her."

"This one?"

"Nah!" Marie shook her head. "It's not him."

"It's a good thing you are here to help me! I just thought with him being a doctor and all, the color would be a good fit." Harlow perused the others. "Let's try the red one next."

Amber huffed, now out of patience and breath, snatching the white and crossing the room to the ladder once more. This time, when she went up, her shoe hung, and she slipped, having to grip the rails awkwardly to keep from falling, leaving her teetering precariously. Harlow wagged her finger, and the heel snapped, falling to the floor. Cursing under her breath, the owner finally made a grab for the red one and paused. "Any others you think you might be interested in while I'm up here?"

Harlow shook her head innocently. "No, I don't believe so."

Once she got down, Amber exhaled sharply, straightened her skirt, and traipsed back, clapping unevenly with the missing heel before dramatically slamming it down. She blew a long strand of hair out of her face. "Well?"

"Perfect!" Harlow smiled and picked it up. "Yes, I believe this is the one."

"Will that be cash or charge?"

Harlow's smile faded upon closer inspection. "Oh dear, there seems to be a speck of something here. This simply won't do!"

Amber leaned over. "I don't see anything!" "Right there," Harlow pointed, "surely you see it?"

"That's a piece of dust!" Amber brushed it away with her finger. "See, it's fine."

"Well, I can't give him a gift that is all dusty. That would be rude, and he has allergies! I can't have him sneezing while I am sucking his dick tonight. It would be a real mood killer. Take it back!"

Amber seethed. She tossed the mask aside and rested her palms on the counter. "Will there be anything else before I throw your asses out of my shop?" she snapped.

"No, thank you!" Harlow turned.

"Actually," Marie rested her arm on the counter and drummed her fingers, "I think the blue might look good on his brother, Randy, you know, being he is a police detective and all."

"You're absolutely right!" Harlow agreed. "Why don't you shimmy on up there and retrieve it?"

Amber cocked her head to one side, blinking hard. "Are we talking about the Deveraux brothers?"

Harlow nodded. "You know them?"

Amber swallowed hard and smoothed her hair back. "Chase and I used to see each other," she announced spitefully. "We even talked seriously about getting married."

"What in the world happened?" Harlow pretended to be extremely interested.

Amber eyed Harlow haughtily. "He was happy being a lowly general physician barely scraping by, but I could NEVER love someone satisfied with making such a paltry amount of money and with no ambition to climb the corporate ladder."

"Really? That's funny because he never speaks of you. I guess you weren't all that memorable," Harlow's gaze drifted around, "and he certainly never mentioned the overpriced shithole you have here. Given the severe snake infestation, I can understand why!"

"Snakes? What the hell are you talking about? I don't have snakes!"

"Oh, I believe you do, after all, birds of a feather always stick together!" Harlow lowered her sunglasses, glaring icily back at her, and growled.

Seeing the red in her eyes, Amber was startled and stumbled, falling backward, landing hard on one side. "Get out! GET OUT!" she screamed like a toddler having a meltdown.

"As you wish!"

"Snakes?" Marie questioned as they started for the door.

Harlow put her arm around her old friend and smiled. "Oh yes, snakes!"

Once they were outside, they returned to the bench to watch the show. Harlow flicked her hand to open the front door as the hissing, slithering creatures began to emerge from the most unusual of places, including up from the concrete sidewalk and down from the rooflines, almost like the children coming to the pied piper. It seemed they all had a single destination in mind.

"Those relatives of yours?" asked Marie, amused by the entertainment.

"Maybe a cousin or two," she countered.

Amber clambered to her feet, using the counter to pull up on. Picking up the phone to call the police on the two women who just left, she froze when she saw the sales floor start to move. Limping over for a closer look, she screamed when she saw the sheer number of snakes flooding into her shop through the opened door. Slowly retreating, her hand landed on one when she tried to steady herself on the counter. Screaming, she ran for the back room when they started to seep from the walls and cascade from the ceiling.

"Now this is the best shopping trip I have been on in years!" Marie laughed as they walked past a man sitting on a stoop strumming a tune, his guitar case top propped open for tips.

Harlow stopped, a devilish thought occurring to her.

"What are you up to now?" asked Marie when her friend folded her arms and regarded the musician.

"I am just recalling Amber's words. What did she say? Something about never being able to love a man with no money or ambition?"

"Something like that! Why?"

"Never is a long time, and karma is a bitch!" Starting that way determinedly, Harlow called out to the man, "What's your name?"

"Archie!" he responded, concentrating on his chords.

Archie looked to be about forty. Slight of build, he was pale, thin, in desperate need of a shave, and reeked of body odor.

"What's your story?"

"Why do you care, lady?"

Harlow reached in her bag and pulled out a hundred-dollar bill, holding it over his case as an incentive. "Call me a curious creature."

Stopping and resting his arm on the top of the acoustic, he sighed. "What do you want to know?"

"You live around here?"

"I don't have a regular place if that's what you're asking. I move around a lot."

"What about a regular job?"

"Nope, just me and my guitar. I haven't worked for someone else since I was a teenager. Why work for the man when I can live off the land? Capitalism kills the spirit, right along with the planet. I do what I have to do to get by—no more, no less—and I leave as little a carbon footprint as I can."

"So, it is safe to assume you do not aspire to get any further in life than where you are now?"

"You are quick on the draw, lady!" Archie went back to playing as Harlow dropped the bill into his case.

"What do you have in mind?" Marie asked.

"Have I ever mentioned what a whiz I am at conjuring love spells, especially when one of the parties is less than enthusiastic about the other?"

"You are going to make him fall in love with her?"

"Oh no, even better! I am going to make HER fall in love with HIM!" With a wave of her hand, the spell was cast. "Now all she has to do is see him and the magic begins."

Reaching into her bag, she produced two more bills. "Archie, these are yours if you will take your little show up the street to that fancy boutique." She pointed him in the right direction.

He accepted the donation and stuffed it inside his sock. "Whatever you say."

"You know what, you might want to wait a couple of days," she added. "I have a feeling the shop may be closed for a bit."

After their shopping adventure, the ladies returned to the restaurant for an afternoon pick-me-up. As they enjoyed their coffee, Harlow watched a couple in the corner back booth with fascination. The man, who appeared to be in his mid-thirties, wore a burgundy frock coat, trimmed in black lace, atop his black breeches and shiny, tall boots. Additionally, he was wearing a pair of red-tinted John Lennon-style glasses. A formal walking cane, topped with a silver handle, the kind not used for support, only presentation, rested against the table. The pale, thin young woman accompanying him, who couldn't have been more than eighteen, was dressed in a long-sleeve black flowy dress and platform heels. She sat on the inside, leaning her head against the wall, her eyes only half-open. It was clear she was high on something. The walking stick slipped, and when he reached for it, Harlow noticed an odd silver device, with a sharp-pointed tip, slipped on the end of his left middle finger, and the metallic smell of blood clinging to it.

"You need to eat," he said, pulling the plate over in front of her. "You're no good to me if you are starving to death."

"I'm not hungry."

"But I am!"

Taking her hand, he looked around before using the contraption to discretely prick her wrist. Lifting her arm to his lips, he suckled the blood.

"What the actual fuck is going on over there?"

Marie glanced over her shoulder. "Hump! You know how Vegas has their freaks? New Orleans has their own. Ever since that lady wrote that book series about vampires being in the French Quarter, these people have been running around here, drinking each other's blood and acting out their wildest fantasies like lunatics."

"Oh, I liked those books!"

"So did I, but now there's a whole group of these people who choose to live like this, believe it or not."

"Wait! They are humans pretending to be vampires?"

"Do you know New Orleans is the number one vacation spot for real vampires?" Marie waved her hand in the couple's direction. "Why do you think they come here? They have all the willing victims they can handle, running around in the middle of the night, playing dress-up in the cemeteries just begging for someone to bite their necks. It's New Orleans's version of the unlimited Vegas buffet, only it's for vamps."

"Why?"

Shrugging, Marie looked back at the couple. "It's a high for them. Think about it, if you were human and living in your mama's basement, wouldn't you want to escape into another world?"

"Not this one," she muttered. "But they are not vampires. They get absolutely nothing out of drinking blood."

"HE looks pretty happy."

"She sure as hell doesn't. That poor girl is as high as a kite."

"To each their own." Marie shrugged. "I'm not complaining. For every couple sucking down each other's blood like that, I sell one of those cheap vampire hunting kits to another pretending to be a hunter. Do you know how much I made off their kind last year? It tossed me into a higher tax bracket."

"Stop, Dylan!" they heard the young woman say. Her hand was on his chest, and she was attempting to push him away. "You're taking too much."

He gripped her wrist tighter and aggressively jerked her close. "Baby, if you want me to keep feeding your habit, you're going to have to keep feeding mine." She stopped struggling and turned her head towards the wall with tears in her eyes, letting him have his way.

"That's all fine, well, and good, as long as they are both consenting adults," Harlow said before finishing off her cup and standing, "but, she's neither. I think it's time this guy got a little dose of his own medicine."

Marie pressed some cash into the passing waitress's hand for the bill, before shifting to the now unoccupied chair. She wasn't missing this show for the world.

Harlow walked over to the booth and slid in opposite the couple.

"What the hell are you doing, lady?" Dylan snapped, annoyed by the interruption.

"Making you an offer you can't refuse."

Addressing the girl, she asked, "What's your name?"

Hesitating, she looked to the man as if asking for his permission.

"It's alright," Harlow cut him a nasty look. "I won't let him hurt you for talking to me."

The girl looked down. "Nicole."

"How old are you, Nicole?" "Lady, that is none of your fucking business!"

Harlow's hand shot out and grabbed him by the arm, twisting it into a painful, awkward position. "I am making it my business!"

His face contorted, the pain unbearable, yet he refused to cry out for fear of bringing attention to the table.

"How old are you, Nicole?" she repeated.

"Seventeen," she whispered, tucking her hair behind one ear bashfully.

"What does he have you hooked on?" "Tell me what you want, lady!" Dylan demanded angrily.

Harlow tightened her hold. "I want you to shut the fuck up. You can do it willingly by closing your mouth and letting me have a conversation with this girl, or I can rip off your dick and shove it down your throat to quieten you down. Personally, I prefer option number two, but the choice is yours!"

Her eyes went back to the girl. "What's your poison?"

Nicole curled into herself and tugged her sleeves down.

"Heroin?"

She nodded.

"Are you from New Orleans?"

"No, Jackson."

"How did you end up with this prize?"

Nicole eyed him with reservation.

"Don't tell her anything!" he muttered through gritted teeth. "Just remember, you will have to deal with me later."

"No, she won't! I am going to make sure of it."

Nicole swallowed hard. "I met him online. He told me he was a vampire, that he loved me, and we were meant to be together forever. Things weren't good at home, and he came all the way to Jackson to get me out of there. After he's drained enough of my blood to purify me, he is going to give me his to drink so I can live forever, too."

"And the heroin?"

"It supposed to help with the pain of transforming."

"Is that what he told you?" Harlow growled and squeezed until blood appeared on his arm. "Have you had sex with him?"

"I am warning you, Nicole, shut the fuck up!"

Harlow applied pressure until she heard the snap of the bone. He cried out and everyone turned in their direction.

"He stubbed his toe on the bottom of the table," Harlow announced to the room. "He's fine, he just has a low threshold for pain!"

Nicole lowered her head shamefully, her eyes shifting back and forth. "I needed to prove to him I was pure before he would turn me."

Harlow kept her right hand on Dylan, holding out her left across the table, offering it to Nicole. "He lied to you. This piece of shit is not a vampire, only a disgusting human playing dress-up and using it as a means to prey on young women like you. Let me guess—he told you your parents didn't understand you the way he did, and that no one could love you the way he could. He said the heroin was for your own good because it would help you feel better and forget all about what life was like before he came along. He made you think giving him your virginity would keep your souls connected forever."

Nicole wiped her nose with the back of her hand and nodded.

Harlow narrowed her eyes at him and relinquished her hold. "LEAVE!" she commanded.

Dylan didn't have to be told twice. Not bothering to give Nicole a second look, he fell to the floor as he scrambled away, holding his arm close to his body.

"Where's he going?" Nicole asked anxiously.

"Are you just going to let him get away with this?" Marie questioned as she came over to join them.

"Hardly!" Turning her attention to Nicole, "I have a friend who is a doctor. I want him to have a look at you. Dylan took far too much blood, and I am afraid he may have done more damage than that."

Nicole wrapped her arms around herself and shook her head back and forth vigorously. "No, Dylan wouldn't do that. I need to go find him." She started to get up, but Harlow rested her hand on her arm.

"If you go back to him, you will be dead by the end of the week. Your health is not good, and he doesn't care. As soon as you aren't serving him in some way, he will leave you for dead and move on to another underage victim. Let me help you so that doesn't happen."

"She's right, cher," Marie agreed. "We have way too many of his kind around here and it never ends well for the girl."

Tears flooded the girl's face. Harlow helped her up and the three women walked to Marie's car.

"I don't like this place," Harlow muttered under her breath, wrinkling her nose, after sitting Nicole down in a chair in the ER waiting room. "It smells of disease, shit, and piss," she said for only Marie to hear.

"Well, it is where the sick people are," she replied dryly.

"Stay with her. I will be right back." Going up to the desk, she went over to the first nurse she saw typing into the computer. "I need to see Dr. Devereaux."

Not bothering to look up from the screen as she furiously typed, the nurse stated matter-of-factly, "If you aren't currently at death's door, you need to sign in and wait your turn. As far as Dr. Devereaux," she cast a brief glance sideways at the white board on the nearby wall, "he is not officially on duty."

"I don't care! Get him!"

The nurse huffed. "I don't know who you think you are—" she finally looked up to find Harlow glaring back at her and instantly froze mid-sentence. Filled with an overwhelming sense of fear, she took two slow steps back, crossed herself, and shouted at the top of her lungs, "I—um—CHASE! CHASE! SOMEONE GET CHASE! NOW!"

Carly, the other nurse on duty, turned around from doing her paperwork when she heard the commotion. Upon seeing Harlow, her eyes widened, her hand flew to her chest, and she flung herself against the wall behind her. "Oh, sweet Jesus in Heaven!"

"I didn't ask for HIM and there is no need to bring HIM into this conversation!" Harlow spat.

Chase suddenly came around the corner. "What's going on out here?" When he saw Harlow, he immediately understood. "It's alright, Carly," he said with a chuckle, "she's a friend."

Carly lifted her finger in the air to say something, thought better of it, and walked away mumbling under her breath. "Nope! Not getting involved! This sister is minding her own damn business for once in her life!"

"Harlow, what are you doing here?"

"I have a young lady I would like you to take a look at," she explained as they walked. "Some little fucker pretending to be a vampire got her hooked on heroin before taking too much blood from her and, given the scents I detected, he has given her hepatitis and gonorrhea just for kicks."

"Shit! Unfortunately, I see way too much of this. Runaway?" he asked as they stopped in the hall, his eyes going to the trembling young woman Marie was talking to.

"Yes. She is only seventeen. Her family is in Jackson."

"They have probably been looking for her. I will get Randy to track them down. Where did YOU find her?"

"In your mother's restaurant?"

He appeared confused.

She tapped her ear. "My sense of smell and ability to see in the dark aren't my only talents."

"Ah! I'm assuming the guy has already made a run for it?"

"He has, but don't worry about that. I will make sure he never does this to anyone ever again."

"What are you going to do?"

"The human police force's job for a change. Consider it a little repayment for all the ones you have done for The Diverse."

"You know what?" Chase held up his hands. "The less I know, the better." Waving Marie over, "I will take care of the girl, and I will see you later tonight." "Don't spare any expense on the girl. Get her whatever she needs, no matter the cost, and have the bill sent to Black Thorn Enterprises—and Chase—thank you!"

"Chase!" a sobbing and disheveled Amber called from across the waiting room as soon as he returned from getting Nicole settled into a bed.

"Shit!" he muttered under his breath.

Holding her arm close to her body, his ex-girlfriend hobbled over on one shoe, making a loud clanking noise with the four-inch heel. Usually so finicky about her appearance, he had never seen her in such a state before. Her lipstick was smeared, mascara blackened the area beneath her eyes and one of her false eyelashes was hanging on by a thread.

"What on Earth happened to you?"

"I fell," she cried, wiping her nose with the back of her hand and sniffling. "I think I may have broken something in my arm, and my ankle is hurting really badly."

Chase waved for a wheelchair. "I will get Dr. Stevens to take a look at you."

"I want you," she said imploringly, grabbing onto his hand. "You are the best doctor here."

"I think it's best if you see someone else."

"No! Look, I'm sorry! I know we didn't end on the best of terms, and it was all my fault, but please don't take it out on me now when I need you the most. You have taken an oath, after all."

Sniffing the air around her, he asked, "Have you been drinking?"

"NO!" "Amber, I smell it on your breath."

"Okay, so I had a couple of mimosas, but that's all, I swear. Chase, I really need you!"

He blew out a hard breath as Carly approached with the wheelchair, dropping her head and pressing her lips together in a tight line when she saw Amber. "Take her to exam room four and order x-rays. I will be down to check on her in a few."

"Dr. Rainer is free," she stated with emphasis through gritted teeth. "Don't you want me to get her to look at this *particular* patient?"

"Please, Chase? I really want you!" Amber begged.

"Alright," he shook his head, "I will do it myself, but first I need to take care of that other patient. Get Amber started, will you?"

"You sure are a popular man with the ladies on your day off," Carly mumbled.

"I guess it's just my lucky day!" he commented and started down the hall.

"Get your skinny ass in this chair!" Carly ordered to Amber, pointing to the seat once Chase was out of earshot.

"How's the girl?" Carly asked when he returned to the desk an hour later.

"She'll live but might wish she hadn't by the time it's all said and done. We need to find her a bed in a top-notch rehab place that can handle providing additional medical treatment."

"All the low-income ones have a waiting list and only a few of those will take juveniles."

"Lucky for us, for once, money is no object. Find the best private facility closest to Jackson and make the arrangements."

"I will take care of it! Why don't you get out of here? It IS your day off."

"I have one last thing to do. Are the x-rays back?"

"Yeah, and nothing is broken. Give the bitch an aspirin and send her sorry ass down the road."

Chase cut his eyes over at her.

"Oh, I'm sorry, did I say that out loud. My bad!" Carly rolled her eyes.

Chase snatched up the report from radiology and sighed. "Let's get this over with."

Amber carefully reapplied the makeup from her compact and took a brush from her bag to tidy her hair. That woman from the shop had royally pissed her off and she couldn't think of a better way to get back at her than by using Chase. Practicing her pouty face in the small mirror, she quickly snapped it close and put it away when she heard him approaching.

Chase took a deep breath before pulling the curtain back. Amber must have gotten a good look at herself because she had cleaned away the mascara and righted her wayward eyelash. She was curled on one side when he came into the room.

"Good news!"

Amber lifted her head off the pillow and sat up.

"The x-rays are all clear. Nothing is broken, so you probably just have some sprains. All you need to do is go home, ice the sore spots, take some ibuprofen, and get some rest." Chase started making some notes on the chart. "What happened anyway?"

"I slipped off the ladder," she lied, intentionally making her voice sound weak. "Chase," she clasped her hands together attempting to appear penitent, resting them on her knees, "I have been wanting to talk to you for a long time, but I haven't been able to work up the nerve. I never apologized for what happened between us, and the horrible things I said, but I should have. It was entirely my fault, and it was wrong of me to become so upset with you for doing what you thought was best. I hope someday you can forgive me." "I forgave you a long time ago," he replied, not bothering to look up.

"You did?"

"Yes, I did, but I didn't do it for you. I did it for me. Carrying around that kind of anger and bitterness will eat you alive inside," he snapped the file closed, "and honestly, you weren't worth it."

"I wasn't worth it?" His words stunned her. Somehow, in the back of her mind, she had convinced herself he would always carry a torch for her, believing her to be the one that got away. "We were together for three years!"

"Three wasted years," he clarified, "because if you had any feelings for me whatsoever, you would have never slept with my brother."

Amber's face clouded. "Well, look who grew a pair, or maybe that new girlfriend of yours loaned you hers," she spat vehemently. "We will see how high and mighty she is when I have her arrested."

"What the hell are you talking about?"

"I wasn't going to say anything, but she's the real reason I'm here!" Amber's true temperament spilled forth like a raging river. "She and that friend of hers came into my shop, pulled me from the ladder, and then shoved me to the floor before releasing hundreds of snakes in my store. I am filing charges against her and then I am going to sue her for all she's worth."

He turned and leaned against the counter. "Then I will be forced to testify that you showed up here drunk, claiming to be injured with no visible signs of injury, and rattling on like a mentally unstable person about hundreds of snakes being in your store, put there no less, by another woman. It all sounds a little—well, insane. I think, from a medical standpoint, it is best if I go ahead and recommend a psych evaluation. I'm sure after I consult with Dr. Stevens and Dr. Rainer, we will all agree it is in your best interest. By law, we can hold you here for seventy-two hours for monitoring. So, the decision is yours—let it go or stay here for a while. Which would you prefer?"

Amber screeched. Throwing the covers back, she leaped from the bed and started reaching for her clothes. "Fuck you, Chase! Fuck you and that new girlfriend of yours! Oh, and by the way," she started to pull her dress over her head, struggling when it got stuck, "I am NOT sorry I slept with your brother. I am only sorry I didn't do it sooner."

"Goodbye, Amber," he said and started towards the door. "I hope you get all you deserve in life."

Chase slapped the file down onto the nurse's desk. "Carly, will you put that in the computer. I am going home."

She cautiously flipped it open, and a slow grin formed as she read it. "You recommended her for a psych eval?"

"I did and get the two on-shift doctors to sign it, as well, for good measure. After all, you saw how erratic her behavior was."

"I sure did. I think I might just need to add a note, too!" Carly breathed a sigh of relief. "You had me worried there for a minute with that one." Her eyebrows raised, "Now, would you care to fill me in on the big scary woman? I have a whole lot of questions about that one."

"Maybe later."

"Aw, come on, Chase, I'm married with three kids. I live a boring life. Toss a girl a bone!"

"I'll think about it," he reached over and rubbed the side of her arm, "but, right now, I have somewhere to be. Call me if you need me, just don't need me."

"Enjoy your few days off!"

"Let's just hope I can!"

Marie decided to stay with Nicole and wait for Randy.

Harlow, on the other hand, was on a mission. Getting the address of where they had been staying from the girl, she borrowed Marie's Jeep and drove to it. Dylan had rented an apartment in a shithole of a building. This place made a Vegas flophouse look like the Ritz Carlton.

Standing in front of the marker that read '1B', she could hear him inside, tossing things around. A slight push of the door with her strength and it fell forward from the hinges. Striding across it, the metal tips of her heels echoed eerily throughout the barren room.

Dylan looked up from the suitcase he was haphazardly packing one-handedly.

"We were just playing a little game. If the police ask, I'm going to swear that bitch came with me willingly and begged me to fuck her. As far as I knew, she was eighteen and just wanted to come to New Orleans to party for Mardi Gras.”

“And the heroin?”

“All her idea. I personally never touch the stuff. That’s my story and I’m sticking to it.”

“Why the blood? What kind of perverse pleasure do you take from it?”

“Do you know how powerful it makes you feel to drink someone’s blood?” He stared at the floor. “And to do it when you are fucking makes you feel like a god because you know there is not one part of that person you don’t have control over. It’s exhilarating!”

His arrogance incensed her beyond reason.

“I have known a few gods in the bedroom, and blood was never a part of it. Games are meant to be fun, played by consenting adults who know what they are getting into. No one is supposed to get hurt.” The image of Cherise’s friends came to mind and her anger erupted once more. She didn’t have Broussard to take her revenge on, but this human was another story. “You lied, pretended to be something you weren’t,” she dragged her fingers across a dusty table, slowly stalking towards him, “drugged that girl, stole her innocence, and left her to deal with the aftermath. Ironically, you are the second piece of shit I have seen do this in the past week. I didn’t get to express my disapproval to him, but it seems fate has given me a worthy substitute.”

“Look, I don’t want any trouble! Send the little bitch back to her parents,” he slammed his suitcase shut, “I am leaving New Orleans, and I am never coming back.”

“You’re right on both counts.”

Harlow grabbed him by the scruff of his shirt and flung him across the floor. He landed on a cheap coffee table, and it collapsed beneath his weight. Groaning, he rolled to his side and tried to get up. Seeing the cane across the bed, she picked it up and jammed the silver ferrule into his groin, drawing blood when she pierced his scrotum.

He howled.

Crouching down, she cocked her head to one side. "How powerful and exhilarated do you feel now?"

"Please lady!" he cried. "I don't know you! Just leave me alone."

"How many?"

"How many what?"

"How many innocent girls have you done this to?"

"She was the first."

Harlow used the handle of the cane to crack him across the bridge of his nose. The bones shattered and blood ran down the side of his face as he screamed. "You're lying. Try again!"

"You want to know the truth?" he sobbed. "I will tell you the truth. The truth is...," he broke into a bout of manic laughter, "I have done it so many times, I have lost count." "That's what I thought!" With one back-handed slap, he fell unconscious.

It was nearing dusk when he came around. His blurry sight started to focus. He could see Harlow leaning against what appeared to be a tombstone. Realizing he was in a cemetery, he rolled to one side and onto his knees.

"Good! You should be awake for this!" She sauntered over to him. "I was just going to kill you, but somehow, it didn't seem like enough. I decided it would be more fitting to first introduce you to a few of the souls you like to impersonate."

"What the fuck are you talking about?"

As the words left his lips, he noticed several shadows moving from behind the stones. "What is this place?"

"This is where my friends like to hang out at night. It's so rare for them to have a full gourmet meal to share these days, so I thought I would treat them." The creatures slowly moved into sight, closing in on him like a pack of wolves surrounding a lonely, helpless lamb. "Did you know, most vamps have a strict moral code they abide by? They don't kill their victims, they never take more than what they need, and children are strictly off-limits. When I told them what you had been up to, they weren't very impressed by you. In fact, they are all in agreement that they should take their time and do everything to you that you did to those girls. Dylan, I have to break it to you, but I don't think it's going to be a pleasant evening." Addressing the locals, "He is all yours. Just be sure to clean up after yourselves when you're done."

Eleven vampires closed in on him as Harlow walked away. A slow smile spread across his face when she heard him scream.

Chapter Thirteen

"Thanks for letting me borrow that," Harlow said as she tossed the keys to Marie, who stood at the kitchen sink with her back to the door. Wiping her hands on a towel, she turned and deftly caught them mid-air.

"What did you do with him?"

Harlow smirked. "Let's just say he is attending an exclusive dinner where he is the guest of honor—and the main course." Helping herself to a bottle on the table, she poured herself a glass and sat down.

"Couldn't happen to a better person!"

They tabled the conversation when Chase and Randy came from the living room into the kitchen looking for a couple of beers in the fridge.

"How's the girl?" Harlow asked.

"Better than she was before you brought her in," Chase replied, leaning against the door frame. "You were dead on with your diagnosis, by the way. I got her started on some meds and Carly is finding her a bed at a treatment facility for the heroin addiction. It's not going to be easy by any stretch of the imagination, but thanks to you, she's on the right road."

"I was able to track down her family." Randy handed a beer to his brother and popped the top on his. "They have been worried to death and looking for her for weeks. With Nicole's help, we were able to identify him. It seems he's wanted for a long list of charges in six states, all related to drugs and underage girls. We've got an APB out across the city for him."

"You might not want to waste too much time on that," Harlow remarked as she lifted her glass to her lips. "Let's just say he won't be adding to those charges."

Randy frowned, scratching his forehead. "You know what?" He took a swig from the bottle. "I don't need to know the details. It would just mean more paperwork for me anyway." Changing the subject, he slipped his hand on the small of Marie's back, "You need any help, baby?"

Marie smiled and kissed him. "I got it, babe. You and Chase go relax and watch the game. I'll let you know when it's ready."

"I do have one little question," Chase lifted his hand in the air. "Did you two lovely ladies by chance pay a visit to my ex's boutique today?"

Harlow and Marie looked to each other and both half-shrugged, attempting to appear innocent.

"We did a little shopping," Marie admitted.

Harlow smirked. "I did a little matchmaking."

"Hmmm!" Chase nodded. "Did that matchmaking involve snakes by any chance?"

"Snakes?" Randy exclaimed, puzzled.

"Why do you ask?" Harlow questioned.

"Amber came to the ER today, saying two women attacked her, pulled her from a ladder, and shoved her to the ground before unleashing hundreds of snakes in her shop."

"That lying bitch! No one laid a finger on her!" Marie grumbled.

"I DID unleash the snakes," Harlow confessed. "I thought she might like being around her own kind for a change."

"So, it WAS the two of you!"

"Yes!" Marie scoffed. "So, what if it was? She deserved it after she called my shop a 'tacky little tourist trap'!"

"No, she didn't!" Randy instantly became defensive. "Babe! That lady has got some fucking nerve."

"I know, right?"

"She is threatening to call the police and sue you for all you're worth." Chase continued.

"She can try," Harlow remarked dryly, "but I'm worth a lot of money and that bitch isn't going to see one dime of it. I will TURN her into one of those snakes before that happens. Besides, I have a feeling she's going to find a new purpose in life in the coming days."

"What is that supposed to mean?"

"Why do you ask? Do you still have feelings for that trashy whore?"

"No! Not at all!" Chase inhaled deeply and scratched his forehead. "You know what? I think Randy has the right idea. The less I know, the better!"

"Damn straight!" Randy grabbed Chase by the shoulder. "Come on, we're missing the game."

Harlow refilled her glass as Marie fluttered around the kitchen. "You really do get off on this 'Susie homemaker' bullshit, don't you? Where is that witchy woman with the snake around her neck I know and love? I remember when men used to cross the sidewalk and turn away because they were afraid of pissing off the all-powerful Madame Laveau."

Harlow recalled with fondness the first time she met the 'Queen of Voodoo'. Marie Laveau was born the granddaughter of a priestess from Sainte-Domingue, and already a powerful sorceress in her own right. Not only did she excel at conjuring, casting spells, and the mixing of herbal potions, but she possessed the deadly combination of having both beauty and brains. When she wasn't conducting rituals, she had to earn a living and did so by becoming a hairdresser to the wealthiest of the townspeople. She supplemented that income by learning their dirty little secrets from their servants and playing upon their fears. Often, she would make midnight visits under the cover of darkness to deliver her famous gris-gris amulet bags or a specially made potion for some ailment, or husband's mistress, the buyer didn't want to be mentioned in front of polite company.

Harlow found herself in New Orleans in 1850. Marie had performed a ceremony requesting spiritual assistance with a rival by the name of Rosalie who was trying to steal her title. Having heard so much about the woman, Harlow had come to town to witness the Voodoo queen for herself and happened to intercept the call. Watching one of the midnight services from the shadows, she had been impressed by Marie's enormous amount of influence over the people. The priestess was indeed a sight to behold, dressed in her long white robes, with a large serpent draped around her neck, working herself into a frenzy to the beat of a rhythmic drum. Offering up her services that same night, the two had struck a bargain, where Marie would become Harlow's supplier for magical potions in exchange for ridding her of her nemesis. It was also the beginning of a great long-standing friendship. Harlow returned to New Orleans several years later when she received word Marie's natural life was coming to an end. Moments from drawing her last breath, Harlow had helped her to drink from a glass containing vampire's blood—and watched as she transformed back into the woman she had been in her prime, with one slight difference—she was now a member of The Diverse.

"Who has time for that now?" Marie turned, stirring brownie batter in a mixing bowl. "I'm too busy running a business, volunteering, and keeping up with this old place. You know how it is!"

"Unfortunately, I do. If I am being completely honest, I don't hate the fact Broussard lured me down here. It has been a nice little change of pace."

"Change is good. Trying new things keeps us young, makes us feel alive," she inclined her head towards the living room where Randy and Chase were drinking their beers and watching a basketball game. "Some days I am as giddy as a schoolgirl!"

"Leave the details of your kinky roll playing sex games out of this. I don't need that image in my head," Harlow derided. "Why do you want me to hook up with him so badly anyway? Do you want to double-date? Or maybe you had an orgy in mind?"

"I am not sharing MY man!" Marie lifted her spoon from the batter bowl, pointing it at Harlow. "And maybe, just maybe I would like to see my old friend cut loose and have a little fun."

"Who says I don't have fun?"

"You did! You just admitted that chasing after a vampire who royally pissed you off was a 'nice change of pace'. Face it, cher, you need to get out more. Besides, I saw how you looked at Chase when you first met him. You were attracted to that human." Opening her mouth, Harlow started to reply, rethought her remark, and pretended to gag instead. Her eyes, however, drifted to Chase—and lingered.

Chase felt the weight of her stare and looked up. He smiled as he lifted his beer bottle to his lips.

"That looks like more trouble that you can handle," Randy whispered when he noticed the two watching each other so intently.

"It sure does," Chase muttered with a tinge of excitement in his tone.

"You are not really considering this are you? She is the type we usually hunt down and kill."

"I hate to break it to you," Chase leaned over, "but I am pretty sure your girlfriend is, too." "Yeah, I know, but as long as she isn't hurting anyone, she is off-limits. That's the rule, right? I guess I'm just going to have to keep her out of trouble."

Chase leaned back in the chair. "You're serious about her, aren't you?"

"Marie is definitely something special and, if I am being completely honest, I can't imagine my life without her."

"Are you sure she hasn't cast some sort of love spell on you?"

Randy grinned. "If she has, don't take it off, okay?"

"I will make a deal with you. I won't give you a hard time about Marie if you don't give me one over her friend in there."

Sawyer and Mitchell were the last to arrive.

"I'm sorry we're late," Mitchell apologized. "Traffic was a mess."

"It's actually my fault," Sawyer handed a bakery box to Marie. "I didn't want to come empty-handed. It's not really Mardi Gras without this."

"King cake from Lavigne's Bakery." Marie beamed when she saw the label and opened the box. "They are the best in town. Thank you, Sawyer, that was very thoughtful."

"I haven't found a better bakery in the world than Lavigne's."

"How do you know about them?" asked Chase as he and Randy came into the kitchen. "I thought they were the local's best-kept secret."

"It's not my first Mardi Gras, though it has been a few years since I was here last," he replied. "I was surprised to see they were still around after all this time."

"In that case," Randy handed him a beer, "welcome back!"

Sawyer half smiled and accepted the bottle gratefully.

"Your timing is perfect!" Marie waved her hand towel towards the dining room table. "Supper is ready."

"What is all this?" Harlow questioned as they sat down at the table for dinner, Chase just to her right.

"This is shrimp gumbo, that is crawfish etouffee, and in the big pot is smothered nutria."

"Nutria? You mean those river rats?"

"They're not rats exactly, but they are good eating," argued Marie.

"They are fucking rodents!" Harlow scoffed. "What's the matter? You couldn't find any rattlesnakes to throw in your pot?"

Marie grinned. "I could have, but I would have hated to have accidentally served up one of your relatives to you! Besides, I think they are all visiting Amber right about now."

Harlow hissed good-naturedly in response.

"Everything looks great, baby!" Randy assured, patting her on the behind as he pulled out her seat.

Sawyer inhaled and smiled. "This all smells so wonderful! I haven't had food like this in years."

"How long has it been since you were here last?" asked Chase, passing a dish to him.

"Decades. I have been all over the world and have yet to find anywhere with better food."

"If you don't mind, I will have a double helping of that nutria." Mitchell held up his plate. "God knows I have eaten worse in the military."

"What branch?" asked Randy.

"I was a Navy Seal before I came to work personal security for Ms. Thornhart." Marie handed him back a full helping. "Thank you, ma'am!"

"You're welcome. Enjoy!"

"How long have you worked for her company, Sawyer?"

He slowly chewed his mouthful of food before answering. "Twenty-nine years."

"Sawyer is the best assistant I have ever had. I only wish I had found him sooner."

Chase opened his mouth to ask Sawyer another question. Harlow could sense the attention was making her assistant uncomfortable, so she decided to intervene. Feeling a little mischievous, she crossed her legs, slipped her foot out of her shoe, and let her toes roam until they found Chase's inner thigh. He jumped, startled, his focus on Sawyer sufficiently diverted as he let one hand slide to his lap, preventing her from further advancement.

Marie noticed the exchange and discreetly winked at Harlow.

The conversation finally turned to the matter at hand and the group discussed the upcoming ball over their meal. Putting their heads together, they kicked around ideas for getting Cherise to safety and taking down Daphne. Everyone had their own suggestions that they took turns expressing as they went around the table. After the last person spoke, they all turned to Harlow who had remained uncharacteristically silent.

"Well?" asked Marie.

Harlow exhaled sharply. "I appreciate the consideration you have given to this, and I am beyond grateful for what you are willing to do, but this is my fight, and I intend to do it alone. For the ones in this room, Cherise is the only mission. Nothing else matters! Once she is safe, I want you all OUT! If the creatures at that venue figure out you are the only humans there, after a few drinks, they very well may rip you to shreds. The Diverse are passive enough when they are alone, but in large groups, they can easily be riled up and become downright dangerous. Let me make one other thing perfectly clear—I want no interference whatsoever when it comes to the battle between me and Daphne. If my time has come to leave this world, don't try to stop it, just let it happen.

"That really isn't a plan," Chase rebutted. "It sounds like more of a suicide mission."

"Haven't you heard? 'The best-laid plans of mice and men often go awry'," she quoted, resting her hand gently on his leg.

"I don't like it either," added Sawyer.

"I think we are all in agreement!" Marie was visibly upset. "Harlow, please tell me you aren't giving up so easily."

"I have not given up on anything," she fired back, "but I will not see any of you hurt or killed trying to protect me. I would lay down my own life for each person at this table," she cut her eyes to Chase and Randy hoping to lighten the moment, "well, except for these two. I haven't known them long enough and they ARE humans."

Mitchell cleared his throat to remind her once more.

"Oh, can't we just turn you into something else?" she addressed her bodyguard jokingly. "What would you like to be? Werewolf? Vampire? Warlock? How about a troll or a fairy? Take your pick. I can make anything happen, and you will never have to remind me you are human again."

"I think I will pass," he responded with a cough, quickly turning into a bout of laughter.

"Harlow, we need to talk about this," Chase said in a serious tone, turning the conversation back to the situation at hand.

"We are done talking. This subject matter is closed for the night." She patted his leg. "The only thing we need to discuss is dessert. I seem to recall something about cake."

After clearing the dishes from the table, Marie warmed up the king cake, sliced it, and served it.

"Ooey-gooey goodness! Now, this is something I can get on board with," Harlow said as she took a bite.

"You do seem to have a bit of a sweet tooth," Chase muttered.

"And?" she snarled.

Chase raised his hands defensively. "Just making a mental note."

Harlow glared at him, before stabbing the cake with her fork, meeting some resistance. Looking down, she noticed something sticking out of her piece. Using the tines, she picked at it.

"Sawyer! You should get your money back. There is a hunk of plastic in my slice." "It's supposed to be there. You got the baby, boss!" he said with a huge grin.

"Baby? What baby?"

"The baby Jesus!" Sawyer reached across, pulled it from the cake, and held it up. "See!"

A repulsive look crossed her face as she pushed the plate away, "Why in the world would I want THAT?" Picking up her napkin, she started vigorously wiping her tongue. "Bleh!"

Everyone at the table laughed.

"It's tradition, cher," Marie explained. "Whoever gets the baby has to host next year's party."

"Well, it's a ridiculous tradition. Who in the world thought it was a good idea to ruin a perfectly good piece of cake with something like that?"

"A Catholic baker," Marie muttered under her breath.

"Figures!" Harlow scoffed. "They ruin all the fun things!"

"Well, Harlow, next year I guess you're it. I can't wait to see what YOU cook up!" Sawyer teased.

"I wouldn't hold my breath if I were you!"

As they cleaned up, they could hear the sounds of revelry coming from outside. Marie's house was on the main parade route and had the perfect view from the second floor.

"Sounds like the party is getting started." Marie motioned towards the staircase. "Shall we?"

"Have you ever seen one of the processions?" Chase asked as they walked up the stairs to the second-floor gallery.

"No, I have not. The last time I was in New Orleans this time of year was before they had such a thing."

"When was that?"

Harlow paused to think. "As I recall, the year was 1788. I came to town and stayed for some length of time. I attended a few high society balls, made some deals, and collected some outstanding debts. Overall, it was a lucrative business trip. I liked the city a great deal and decided to hang around for a little while longer. Good Friday that year seemed a suitable time to depart, especially after I paid a visit to Vicente Jose Nunez, the Spanish army paymaster, regarding a personal matter. For some reason, he felt the need to embark in a great deal of prayer and light fifty candles after I left. I suppose he should have blown them out before going to dinner."

"Wait! That was because of you?" Marie rested one hand on her hip and pointed at her. "You were the reason for the Great Fire of 1788?"

"No, not exactly! After all, I didn't tell the fool to light all those candles and leave them unattended. They have warnings about how dangerous that is now, you know? It's right on the label."

Marie shook her head before flinging open the doors to the balcony overlooking the street. The laughter and howls from the crowd below flooded in, ushering in the festive mood.

Randy slipped his arm around Marie and escorted her over to the elegant wrought iron lining the landing. Offering his hand gallantly to Harlow, Chase dipped his head and said, "Please, allow me."

Harlow good-naturedly scowled at him before accepting his invitation and stepping out onto the landing.

New Orleans may have been quiet in the mornings, but this was its time to shine. The blend of colorful floats, neon lights, and fast-paced jazz music was a joy to behold even for the hardest of hearts. Harlow laughed despite herself. Who couldn't love a city full of sinners doing what they do best? Even Sawyer, who claimed to loath this place, had a huge grin on his face along with a wistful light in his eyes as he took it all in. Mitchell had managed to catch the attention of several women on the street below who were waving and shouting to him. His eyes widened when, in unison, they all lifted their shirts, exposing their bare breasts.

"Give those ladies their due," Marie ordered, nodding to a large basket of beads at his feet as she lit a couple of lanterns hanging from above. Grabbing a handful, he hollered back and tossed a pile to the group, who scrambled to catch them.

Harlow shot him a stern look to which he cleared his throat and replied contritely, "Sorry, boss!"

The ladies below began to chant, demanding the presence of his company, to which he looked longingly.

"Oh, go and have some fun! Tomorrow will be a long day. Just make sure you are sober and ready to work."

"I will be ready!" He grabbed a handful of beads and hurried towards the door. "Thanks, boss!"

"Wait!" Sawyer called out. "I had better come with you. This city will chew you up and spit you out if someone isn't watching your back."

"Have fun, Sawyer," Harlow winked.

"I think I just might."

With that, the two couples were all who remained.

"This is the first time I have ever taken any time off during Mardi Gras and, given what might be coming tomorrow, I think we could all do with a few drinks," Randy announced. "Laissez les bons temps rouler!"

Marie took his face in her hands, planting a huge sloppy kiss on his lips. "Oui, cher! Let's go bring up the bar."

Taking him by the hand, she led him through the door, casting a mischievous glance over her shoulder at Harlow.

"I guess this doesn't hold a candle to the shows in Vegas."

Harlow removed a cigarette from its case and tapped it against the side. "No, it doesn't," she lit it and inhaled, "I think this might be better. The appeal of Vegas is that nothing stays the same. People, money, attractions, even memories come and go all the time. It's fleeting and that's why folks who are looking for a good time flock there. New Orleans is different—an old city with timelessness to it. Everything that happens here is based on its history and familial roots. It's appealing to everyone for individual reasons."

"Does that include you?"

"Yes, even me." Harlow blew out a ring of smoke. "I had forgotten what a great city this is. One of the many disadvantages to running a corporation is that you're virtually chained to your desk. You know that old saying about all work and no play."

"I know the feeling, only my tether is to the ER. I daresay your job pays better."

Harlow pointed to his scuffed boots. "Judging by those, I would have to wholeheartedly agree."

"Well, my Jimmy Choo heels tend to slide on the hospital floors," he joked.

Harlow laughed. "You're not so bad, you know—for a human."

"And you're not so bad for—well, whatever you are."

A slow, sultry melody drifted outside, coming from an old record player inside the house. Combined with the soft glow emitting from the outdoor lamps, it created a romantic ambiance as the sounds of the rowdy crowd seemed to fade away.

Chase held out his hand. "May I have this dance?"

Harlow stubbed out her cigarette and slipped her hand in his. "Careful Dr. Devereaux, if you keep this up someone might mistake you for a gentleman."

"Banish the thought!"

Gently pulling her closer to him, she rested her hand on his shoulder, and he placed his chastely on her hip.

"I'm impressed," she complimented when she noticed his form.

"My mom and dad used to dance in the living room all the time. I paid attention. I think it's one of the things my mom misses most about him being gone."

"The last time I danced like this was with Sinatra," she reminisced as they started to sway.

"You knew Sinatra?" "Sinatra, Sammy Davis Jr., Joey Bishop, even Elvis—I knew them all once upon a time. You see, one can't reach legendary status on talent alone, no matter how lucky you are. Some of them may have had a helping hand along the way."

"That was you?"

Harlow's eyes lit up. "Back then, Vegas was a vastly different place, and it needed a little something extra to help make it truly special. That's where I came in. Too bad it didn't stay that way. I own a nightclub there now, and I keep it exactly like it was when Vegas was golden."

"I would like to see it sometime."

"Maybe I will give you a private tour one of these days."

Resting her cheek against his, she savored the moment, not recalling a time when she felt more content. When the song ended, she gently pulled back.

Chase searched her eyes before moving his lips closer to hers.

She did not attempt to stop him.

The two shared a slow, tender kiss—abruptly pulled apart by the sound of the door opening, Marie and Randy returning with a tray of bottles and glasses. Harlow turned away, towards the street, and closed her eyes. Chase covered his mouth with his palm.

"Here, let me help you with that," he offered, taking it from Marie's hands.

Marie noticed the tension and smirked. "We aren't interrupting anything, are we?"

"Yes, you are interrupting my drinking because my hand doesn't have a glass in it. What kind of hostess are you?"

"Well, let's fix that!"

The four partied until the wee hours of the morning before agreeing they should all get some rest.

The group returned to Marie's house the following evening to get ready for the Masquerade Ball. Harlow had suits and masks sent in for the gentlemen. Sawyer dressed early so he could help the others and was waiting in one of the spare bedrooms when they arrived.

"I am pretty sure this tux cost more than I made last month," Chase remarked as he admired himself in the mirror.

"Probably more than you made last year," Sawyer corrected, smoothing out the back along the shoulders. "Harlow had it flown in from Vegas this afternoon." Standing back, Sawyer folded his arms and took a good hard look. "That woman is never wrong."

"What do you mean?"

"Harlow said you would look best in a Brioni, and she hit the nail on the head. James Bond is going to have to move over because he doesn't hold a candle to Chase Devereaux in one of these. Even her measurements were dead on."

"I don't think I have worn one of these since prom, and my rented one was certainly not as nice as this one," Chase said as he held up the bowtie by the end. "I don't really remember how this part works."

"I've got your back," Sawyer took it from his hand and spun him around. "Don't you ever attend any formal hospital events?"

"No, I leave the schmoozing to Administration. I didn't spend all that time in medical school to attend fancy parties and entertain wealthy donors. Give me a good boil to lance instead any day."

"You certainly sound like you enjoy your work," Sawyer said as he knotted the satin fabric.

"I really do. I feel like I make a difference here."

"I'm sure you have made your parents proud." Sawyer turned him back toward the mirror and reached around him to make the final adjustments on the tie. "Perfect! It's a shame you don't dress like this more often. Maybe now you will start." Chase stared at the reflection, not at himself, but at Sawyer. "Are you sure we haven't met? I swear you look so familiar." Sawyer shook his head and stepped away. "I must have one of those faces."

Randy came through the door, unbuttoning his shirt. "Marie told me to get my ass in here and let y'all dress me," outstretching his arms, "so here I am! Pretty me up, boys!" Seeing Chase, he grinned. "Hey, look at you in the monkey suit! If you dressed like that more often, you might actually get laid."

"No danger of that—I can't afford it."

"Fortunately for you, Harlow only buys the best." Sawyer handed Randy a zippered bag. "At least you will have one extremely nice one to wear."

"What do you mean by that?" Chase questioned.

"It belongs to you now."

"I can't keep this!"

"Yes, you can. Harlow wouldn't dream of taking it back, especially after she sees you in it."

"I wouldn't advise arguing with the boss," Mitchell added as he came over to the mirror. "That never ends well. She always gets what she wants."

"Has she bought you any of these?" asked Randy.

"More than I can count—or even wear in one lifetime. Ms. Thornhart is extremely generous."

"You're her bodyguard. How do you feel about all this tonight?" Chase's tone had turned somber.

"Personally, I am not thrilled about it." Mitchell inhaled sharply. "I have seen the boss do things that will blow your mind, but I have never once heard her mention anything about dying. I am not going to lie, this has set my teeth on edge."

Addressing Sawyer, Chase asked, "And what about you?"

Her assistant slowly sat down on the bed. "I trust Harlow and the rest of you should, too."

"Has she ever told you what she is? I mean, is she capable of taking on this witch and winning?"

"I don't know what she is—I've never asked, and I don't need to know. What I do know is that she is the strongest creature I have ever met," Sawyer looked down and nervously picked at a handkerchief in his hand, "but if this Sword of Lucifer can kill anything..." he trailed off and turned away.

"You were right!" Poured into a royal blue, fitted evening gown, low cut and trimmed in silver sequins, Marie adjusted her cleavage. "I ADORE this gown! No one can ever accuse Harlow Thornhart of not having good taste. Are you almost dressed?"

"Almost!" Harlow answered from behind the screen.

"Harlow, I am worried about you! I am afraid your head is not in the game. Any other time, I wouldn't give it a second thought, but with this mysterious sword in play, I'm starting to wonder if we should go. It feels like we are walking straight into a trap."

"Because that's exactly what we are doing, which is why I want all of you out of harm's way. I won't have your deaths on my conscience."

"You won't have a conscience if you're dead!"

"That's true, but then again, I'm not certain I have one now."

"You have more of a heart than you are willing to admit."

"I do NOT!"

"Whatever you say!" Marie sat down in a nearby chair. "Well, come on! Don't keep me in suspense. Let's see how it turned out!"

Stepping from behind the divider, Harlow held out her hands. "What do you think?"

Marie smiled, "I think Chase is going to get another boner as soon as he sees you, and probably keep it all night. You really should offer that man some relief as a kindness, the same way you would offer a stray dog a drink of water!"

Harlow had had a little something special thrown together for the occasion. She wore a black Venetian ballgown, sleeveless and fitted on the top, with a full ruffled skirt, complete with a bustle in the back, appearing as if she had stepped straight off the streets of Victorian London. Her hair was up but curled with ringlets hanging down. Her gown, however, concealed a little secret. The skirt was attached with snaps and could easily be ripped off for unfettered movement.

"You look stunning, cher!" Marie clapped her hands lightly.

"As do you, my friend!"

"Are you sure about this?" Marie asked as she poured two small glasses of sherry.

"I am! This must happen, and what will be will be. Promise me you will look out for yourself."

Marie handed her a glass and held hers up in a toast, "Only if you agree to do the same."

Harlow tapped the rim to hers. "Cheers!"

The men were waiting in the foyer when the ladies came downstairs.

"BABE!" Randy howled when Marie appeared. Stepping to meet her, he took her hand and placed a kiss on her palm. "How did I get such a gorgeous thing to give me a second look?"

"It was your lucky day!" she said with a chuckle and kissed him.

Running his hand over her backside, he leaned forward and whispered. "I can't wait to get you out of this." "Let's survive the night first." Turning, she called up the stairs, "Harlow, you coming?"

"Yes, I just had to grab my phone."

Slowly descending, a collective gasp filled the room when she came into sight.

"Harlow!" Sawyer's hands covered his face. "Look at you! I wish Mason was here to see this. Wait!" he patted his coat, "Let me get a picture. He is not going to believe it unless he sees it."

"Who's Mason?" Randy whispered to Marie.

"Sawyer's husband."

"He's gay?"

"Duh!"

"You look great, boss!" Mitchell said as he went towards the front door. "The limo is here for the five of you and I will follow in the Suburban for later."

"Thank you, Mitchell!"

"What do you think?" Marie nudged Chase, who was speechless, his eyes fixated on Harlow who had stopped on the landing.

"Well?" Harlow's eyes drifted to the protrusion in his trousers. "I take it you approve?"

Chase moved across the floor and stepped up to meet her, completely beguiled. "You are the most beautiful creature I have ever laid eyes on."

Chapter Fourteen

Daphne Savant sat at the vanity, fluffing the feathers on her red lace mask in the mirror. Her perfectly coiffured hair covered partially in black netting was reminiscent of the style glamorous movie stars wore back in the forties. It seemed appropriate given the spectacular way she planned to introduce herself to the world of The Diverse that evening. For far too long, she had hidden in the shadows, waiting until the time was right to take down the one and only Harlow Thornhart. Tonight, that bitch would pay for what she took from her all those years ago.

"Why are you doing this?" demanded the human in the cage behind her.

"Power, money, glory," she smoothed back an errant strand of hair, "you know, the usual. But mostly," addressing her through the reflection, "I just want to see Harlow Thornhart dead."

"Then why am I here?"

Sighing, it occurred to her she should have probably cleaned her up for the occasion, especially given she was still wearing the same, now filthy, dress they had taken her in. Oh well, by the end of the night, it wouldn't matter anyway, so why waste the hot water and clean clothing? Daphne's eyes drifted to the syringes next to her makeup. "You have an especially important job to perform. With your blood, this world will begin anew—and believe me when I say, it's about damn time."

The two golems she had brought to life from clay came into the room. They weren't very smart, but they did obey orders without question.

"She's here," the larger one said. "The magical rocks are glowing."

Using a strand of Harlow's hair she had been hanging on to, Daphne had cast a spell, using them as a supernatural motion detector fashioned strictly for her honored guest.

"Excellent!" Daphne took one final look in the mirror, stood, and handed the syringes to the other golem. "Inject our friend Cherise here and wait for my signal to bring her out. It's time to get this party started."

Harlow and Chase stood along the back wall, masked and close, as if they were a couple absorbed in each other to conceal their presence.

The location of the masquerade was on the edge of town in an old, abandoned movie theater. The inside, however, had been transformed into a dark, seductive den of iniquity. At some point, the seats had all been removed and replaced with a black hardwood floor. Red curtains framed what was once the stage and the old-fashioned candelabra lighting had been intentionally set low. A bar lined one side and a food buffet the other. A Hollywood designer could not have done a better job. Upbeat, party-going music played in the background. The room was filled with nearly two hundred party goers, and they were enjoying the freedom of hiding behind a costume-themed event.

Marie and Randy mimicked them from the other side of the room, while Mitchell and Sawyer searched for Cherise.

"Are these all Diverse?" he asked.

"They are." Harlow exhaled sharply and dragged the back of her hand along his cheek as if they were lovers. "Control your breathing and keep your heartbeat steady or they will know you are not one of them." Closing his eyes, he took in a deep breath and let it out slowly.

"You cleaned up extremely well, Dr. Devereaux," she whispered into his ear as she tightened his bow tie, "for a human."

"I would say the same about you," he rested his hand on her hip to keep up the facade, "but I have a feeling you always look this beautiful." Wearing a simple, wrap-around lace mask with the Victorian theme, she looked like someone who could have stepped straight out of his wildest dreams.

A bump from a reveler from behind sent him deeper into her arms. Steadying him, their eyes met. Whether it was the adrenaline from the excitement of the moment or the buildup of the sexual tension over the past few days, something akin to a spark ignited. Whatever had been brewing between the pair over the past few days unexpectedly rose to the top. The two were just about to kiss when the music was dialed down, and a woman dressed in a red gown appeared on the stage with a microphone.

"Welcome friends! I want to thank you for coming. Tonight, you are here to raise your glass to our new beginning!" she announced. "For far too long, our kind have been forced to hide in the shadows, afraid to be who we truly are for fear of how we would be judged by humankind. Humans have overtaken this world. We have adapted to their society and their rules because we were told it was better that way. Well, I am here to tell you it is not. We are by far, the superior species, and it is time they come to know who we are. We will no longer fear them. Instead, we will have them bow down and cower at our feet."

The crowd erupted into a cheer. Chase looked at Harlow nervously as she and Marie locked eyes across the room.

"We all know who Harlow Thornhart is. She has made a fortune, taking our gifts as payments for what should rightfully be ours to take. I say, why should we pay to be who we truly are? Just so humankind won't know we exist. Maybe it's time to let them know we are here, and I mean to do it in a big way. After tonight, they will know who, and what, walks the Earth in the dark. I am Daphne Savant, and I will be your leader in this new world." Grasping a rope behind her, she yanked down a cover, revealing a large screen television.

"Is she out of her mind?" Chase questioned.

"Yes! But in addition to that, the sword is corrupting her. It is giving her false confidence in a plan that is doomed to fail." "Is it doomed?" Chase noted the room full of creatures who seemed excited by the prospect.

"Creation will not allow it to happen," she explained. "Most things are left to chance in this world, but creatures ruling humankind was one of the things expressly forbidden when the world was made, a pact formed by the powers that be, agreed to by both sides. These fools don't realize if they attempt to eliminate humans, they will only succeed in destroying themselves. What I do with Black Thorn Enterprises manages to keep the two worlds apart, and has since the beginning, in turn preventing its self-destruction. I will be damned if I let this bitch ruin it now."

"We come together this night to declare our independence!" Daphne continued, walking back and forth across the stage like an overly confident motivational speaker, "Our revolution begins with two acts of defiance. The first," she pointed to the screen, "will be the destruction of the old world that maintains the barrier and the second," she waved out two of The Diverse pushing a cage, "will be a group toast where we feat on human blood."

"Damn it!" Harlow muttered when she saw a dazed Cherise slumped back in the enclosure.

"One person for all these people?" Chase looked at Harlow. "What's wrong with this picture?"

"It's not the human, it's what's inside of her. I can smell it from here. She has been pumped full of LSD."

"Let me guess," Chase eyed the room, "given the metabolism and high sensitivity of The Diverse, one little taste of blood will send them into a psychedelic frenzy?"

"And when unleashed in New Orleans during Mardi Gras," Harlow confirmed his assumption, "the casualties will be astronomical. This will be the beginning of a war no one will be able to stop, not even me. This world will be destroyed in the process within a matter of months."

"Let's get started, shall we?" Daphne turned to the screen and pressed the button on a remote. A live video feed of Blackthorn Enterprises appeared.

Harlow's head snapped up. "What the fuck is this bitch up to? Why is my company being shown?"

Lifting another controller into the air, Daphne tossed her head back and laughed. "Join me as we say goodbye to the machine that keeps us divided." Clicking the button, the room watched in disbelief as the live feed showed Black Thorn Enterprises exploding and erupting into flames.

"You fucking bitch!" Harlow snarled, enraged. Swallowing hard, she composed herself before starting towards the stage, ripping the skirt part of the ballgown off and tossing it aside, revealing the black leather pant suit she wore underneath.

"Well, well, what do we have here?" she asked, freeing her hair and shaking it loose.

The Diverse collectively gasped and parted as Harlow sashayed towards the stage, clearing the way. "A thieving assistant with plans of grandeur trying to make the world her own."

"I thought seeing your beloved company turn to ash would force you out in the open. You see, you have been sitting on that throne of yours for far too long," Daphne fired back, "being judge, jury, and executioner, and it's time for a change of management. You don't do anything for anyone unless there is something in it for you, and you just sit there, letting people die because they are simply too poor to afford your help. None of our kind should have to suffer because of you."

"Is that the best you've got?" Harlow stopped and crossed her arms. "Surely, there is a ridiculously boring story driving you, in there somewhere, you are just dying to reveal. Isn't that the way this works? Why don't you tell me what I did to set you on the path of vengeance? My time is precious, and I have better things to do than worry about the ant crawling on my shoe."

The crowd began to murmur among themselves, unsure of what might happen next.

Marie and Randy worked their way over to Chase as Sawyer and Mitchell slipped into the back of the room, waiting for an opportunity to get Cherise out.

"Patricia Englewood was my mother!" she announced vehemently. "Who the fuck is Patricia Englewood? Is that someone I am supposed to have heard of?"

Daphne's nostrils flared angrily. "You don't even remember her name? Allow me to refresh your memory. The year was 1792. My mother and her coven lived near the coast of South Carolina. They moved there from Massachusetts to escape persecution for their beliefs, but one of the locals started making trouble for them, blaming members of their group for her own misdeeds. My mother was arrested for a crime she didn't commit and accused of witchcraft. I was beside myself and used what little magic I had learned to send out a call for help, only to have you appear."

Harlow regarded her intently as she began to recall the event herself, having never given it a second thought.

Daphne, on the other hand, had been chewing on it for centuries, now becoming emotional.

"I begged for anyone who was listening, but you were the only one to appear, and when you did, you refused to lift a finger. Instead, you just stood there in the crowd, watching her burn without batting an eyelash. I distinctly remember that stupid smirk on your face as she screamed in agony. I was six and I have never forgotten that smug expression."

Harlow tapped her fingers on her cheek. "Now that you mention it, I do seem to recall something about that day. The problem was that your mother didn't have anything she was willing to trade. The first rule of barter is that you must have something that someone else wants. And let me guess the rest. The coven took you in, taught you all their ways and you vowed revenge against the horrible creature who stole your mother from you at such a tender age, so here we are."

"Fortunately for me, the coven raised me, and one of the members recalled hearing vague rumors of a weapon that could kill anything. From the moment I heard mention of it, I made it my life's mission to find it and make you pay. I discovered how to keep myself alive using vampire blood. I traveled the world learning everything I could from the best of the worst perfecting my craft to a level unlike any other. It was then I heard you had set up shop in Las Vegas, wheeling and dealing, making a fortune off those with nothing else to lose. I made certain when I interviewed for the job you had no idea who I truly was or what I was really after.

"I cannot tell you how much it turned my stomach every day to pretend I liked working for the bitch who let my mother die. But it was worth it. By watching you, I learned your ways and when you finally trusted me with the keys to the vault, I spent every free moment searching. That's where I found the diary of Gordon Mandeville where, in two sentences, he mentioned moving here with the precious religious item his family protected. That led me to Matthew Broussard.

"I easily seduced him and convinced him to help me take you down. The poor fool had no idea the kind of power that was just sitting in his own home. It had taken me over two hundred years, but I finally found it."

Daphne pulled the sword from a holster concealed in the back of her gown and hoisted it into the air. "Behold, The Sword of Lucifer, the one thing that can kill anything that walks the Earth, even you, and with it, I will destroy you and take my place as the leader of The Diverse. Know this! The monster standing before you is one of your own making, simply because you let her die."

"Oh, I didn't LET her die. That was her own choice." Harlow took a step closer. "You see, I made her an offer directly the morning she was to burn, after all, it was her life, not yours. Even I, in good conscience, cannot strike a bargain with a child. Where's the fun in that? Your mother simply refused."

"You're lying!"

"I am many things, but a liar is not one of them."

"What kind of offer?" Daphne was clearly taken aback, caught off guard by her words.

Harlow leaned in and whispered in her ear. "I told her I would save her in exchange for her six-year-old daughter, who I would take in and train to serve me, to be my assistant in the years to come. You see, I saw something in you, even back then and I knew, taking you in at such an early age with your mother's blessing, would have instilled a sense of loyalty which you obviously lost as an adult. I offered to take care of you, keep you alive and by my side for centuries, but she adamantly refused, not wanting such an existence for her only child. Patricia preferred that you live and die as a normal human, getting married, having a family, and scrounging in the dirt to survive. She thought she was saving you from a life of darkness with me by choosing to burn at the stake. Isn't it ironic that she DIED to prevent what you became anyway? Even I couldn't have planned it better."

"You're making this up, just trying to save your own skin!" "You know damn well I NEVER lie. It's bad for business."

Daphne screamed and shoved her away. "I will kill you for what you have done!"

"If you must," Harlow goaded, holding out her arms in a dramatic fashion. Daphne awkwardly lunged towards her with the blade raised, her anger making her clumsy.

Harlow deftly side-stepped the move.

Turning, Daphne came at her again, stumbling.

Harlow took the opportunity to shove her forward, sending her to the floor. Crossing the stage, she used the heel of her stiletto to stomp on her calf, causing the witch to howl in agony. Grasping the back of her hair, Harlow slammed her forehead into the floor, just enough to stun her before dragging her to her feet. Slapping the sword away, she forced her to stand and heaved her forward. Daphne landed hard but rolled on her side in the direction of the blade. Harlow scoffed and looked to the crowd. "This is your leader? She's a piss poor example if I ever saw one."

With her back turned, Daphne scrambled forward and laid hands on the weapon.

"Harlow! Look out!" Chase yelled.

Her head snapped up. When she turned in his direction, she could see Marie and Randy were holding him back. She found the worry in his eyes and the distress in his voice touching. She smiled, a warmth filling her from within.

Distracted for mere seconds, it was just enough time for Daphne to swing the sword. Feeling the sharp tip grazing her upper thigh, her anger and full focus returned to the fight at hand.

"You are going to pay for that!" Harlow snarled.

"No, you are!" Daphne had taken advantage of the momentary lapse to plant herself in a stable stance on one knee. As Harlow came at her, she plunged the sword upward into her midsection, folding her over.

"NO!" Chase shouted and tried to rush forward. Marie and Randy tightened their grip, Marie whispering something in his ear as she looked to the crowd nervously.

Harlow dropped to her knees, gasping for air, her trembling hands hovering on either side of the blade as blood dripped to the floor.

"I win! Die you fucking bitch!" Daphne whispered in her ear. Clamoring to her feet, she held up her hands, presenting the blood as a trophy, and announced to the room, "Harlow Thornhart and Black Thorn Enterprises are no more. It is time to take this world for ourselves."

Harlow roared, writhing in pain. Howling, she rested back on her haunches, the sword having gone all the way through and out of her back, the tip resting on the floor, holding her in place. She cursed before her head rolled to the side, having seemingly gone still.

Daphne laughed and danced around on the stage as the crowd began to cheer. But she stopped when she heard something that terrified her, sending chills down her spine—the sound of a chuckle. Turning, she saw that Harlow's body had begun to shake and the laughter was coming from her.

The dumbfounded crowd went silent, the only sound to be heard was that of Harlow erupting into a full-on belly laugh. Wrapping her fingers around the handle, she pulled it from her middle and whipped it in the air, before dramatically swinging it around and allowing the blade to come to rest along Daphne's throat.

"What made you think this would be powerful enough to kill me. There is only one thing that can destroy me, and this ain't it!" Whispering for only the witch to hear, "My father would NEVER allow harm to come to me from his own weapon." Pulling back the fabric, she revealed the wound in her abdomen was already healing itself.

"Your father?" Daphne repeated, her eyes wide with disbelief, stunned. "That's what you are? You are the daughter of—?"

"Now you see where I get my devilishly good sense of humor." Shifting the blade into her left hand with a fiendish smile on her face. "And I don't need a weapon to deal with the likes of you."

Harlow's right hand shot out, her fingers encircling Daphne's throat. "Some things are more satisfying being done the old-fashioned way." Tightening her grip, she lifted the witch from the floor, leaving her feet to dangle as she thrashed about. Daphne struggled, grasping for anything to fight back against her sworn enemy, to no avail. Her opponent was simply more powerful than she could have ever imagined. The nefarious sneer on Harlow's face only increased with each gasp of air. Before Harlow allowed the woman to expire, she decided to intensify the suffering, just for the hell of it. Leaning forward, she uttered a few words. Daphne's skin turned bright red, and bubbles began to form. Burning from the inside out, the flames shot out from her chest, her agonizing screams piercing the air.

Harlow held firm, refusing to relinquish her grip until all that remained in her hand was a blackened skull. Turning, she pitched it into the crowd.

The Diverse parted like the Red Sea as it bounced twice and came to rest on the floor.

"I am Harlow Thornhart, the one, and only Purveyor, and you would all do well to remember that. This world does not change as long as I am in it to maintain order. There will be no uprising, no killing of humans, and in turn, no killing of The Diverse. You all have good lives now. You should give some thought to what you are willing to give up. Now, get the fuck out of here before I smite you all for the hell of it."

The crowd immediately began to move towards the back doors, the pace picking up, soon turning frantic. The building cleared within moments, leaving Harlow, Marie, Randy, Sawyer, and Chase alone.

"See to Cherise," she said to Sawyer and Mitchell.

"Yes, boss!"

Chase rushed to her side, taking her by the arm and urging her to sit on the steps, appalled by the amount of blood on her clothes and the surrounding floor.

"Hey, we could use some help over here with this lock!" Mitchell shouted.

Randy hurried over to help. "I will come with you," Marie added. Touching Harlow on the arm, she asked, "Are you alright?"

"Never better!"

"That had better be the truth!" Marie warned.

"Let me take a look at that," Chase said with some urgency in his tone once they were alone.

Not bothering to see for herself, she waved him off. "That's not necessary. I am perfectly fine!"

"Humor the doctor in me?" he pleaded. "Please? I was fairly sure we lost you, and still not sure how we didn't."

That's when she noticed how badly his hands were shaking. The normally level-headed doctor was in a cold sweat and his heart was racing.

Harlow gently touched his face before she leaned back, allowing him to see for himself.

"What the hell?" he muttered, stunned when he saw the wound had essentially mended itself.

"I am a fast healer."

"How is this possible?" He shifted to face her. "I thought that sword could kill anything that walked the Earth."

"Apparently, I am the exception."

"Did you know it wouldn't hurt you?"

"I never said it didn't hurt," she pursed her lips, "in all honesty, it stings quite a bit, but to answer your question, I may or may not have had a slight inkling it wouldn't kill me."

"Want to elaborate?"

"I think it is best I don't! I am not sure you are ready to hear that answer."

Chase helped her to her feet. Removing his coat, he draped it around her shoulders gallantly. Nodding to the blade, he asked nervously, "Do you want me to take that?"

"I think I will hang onto it." Holding it out and twirling it back and forth, she smirked. "I have heard stories about this thing all my life. Somehow, I expected it to be bigger—and engulfed in flames. Not as impressive as I thought, but I think it will look nice hanging over the fireplace."

"You really are one of a kind, aren't you, Harlow Thornhart?"

"In more ways than one."

"Are you sure you are alright?" His apprehension was palpable. Harlow reached over and cupped his cheek. "I am fine, but I am truly touched by your concern."

"I am sorry about your building."

Glancing over her shoulder to the screen, she growled. "It's alright. I had been considering making a few changes anyway. Now is as good a time as any."

"Harlow?" Cherise laughed as Mitchell helped her out of the cage, still dazed and confused about where she was and what was happening. "Why are you wearing a pink tutu and riding a unicorn?"

Harlow pressed her lips together in a line, suppressing a smile.

Chase went over and checked her pulse, dodging to one side as she reached out and grasped for something nonexistent behind his ear. "She's stable but she needs to get to the hospital."

Mitchell removed a blanket from her prison, wrapped it around Cherise, and picked her up, carrying her towards the door. "On it!"

"Keep me informed," Harlow called out, "and after she has been cleared, I want both of you on a plane back to Vegas. Don't let her out of your sight until we can make arrangements for a shaman to wipe her memories of the past week completely clean. I can't undo what has been done, but there is no need for her to have to re-live it."

"I suppose I should call and have the jet readied so we can be getting back home, as well," Sawyer remarked, scowling at the live feed. "We are going to have to deal with that and it's not going to be pretty."

Staring at the burning rubble, Harlow waved it off. "There's nothing to be done while it's on fire. It is the middle of the night, so we know no one was inside. We can deal with it after it has been put out. Call Mason and let him know you are safe and, while you are at it, check in with Samuel at the club to make sure he is alright. Right now, I think I need a drink."

"I know I could definitely go for one," Marie added. "There is a great little bar up the road not far from here."

"Yeah, alcohol seems like a good idea," Randy agreed.

"That's the best plan I have heard all day!" Harlow theatrically waved the sword in the air, and it disappeared.

"Where did it go?" Chase asked looking around.

"It is somewhere safe and out of the hands of anyone who could cause trouble with it." She reached over and yanked his bowtie free. "Come on, I'm buying."

They spent the next three hours drinking and celebrating their victory.

Chapter Fifteen

Harlow sensed him as soon as she returned to the room in the early morning hours. Crossing the way, to the cart of alcohol, she poured herself a glass and regarded him. He sat with his hands resting on his crossed legs, gazing into the fireplace, a smug expression on his face. His wings were put away for the occasion. He was even dressed like any other ordinary human, wearing a pair of black trousers and a blue button-down shirt.

"Imagine my surprise getting an invitation from Harlow Thornhart of all people. I don't remember the last time you requested my presence."

"That's because I have NEVER requested your presence, Michael, and I didn't send YOU an invitation this time either," she fired back. "I cast a spell to summon Azrael."

"You are one of the few people whose requests must be vetted—rules and such. In order to speak to her, you must convince me first." He finally turned to acknowledge her. "What can I do for you?"

Harlow cocked her head to one side, already feeling the beginning of a knot forming in her neck. "I need to speak with Ryland Deveraux."

"Now, why would you need to speak with someone who hunts your kind?"

"You know very well I am the only one of my kind. If you are referring to The Diverse, you also know I walk a fine line."

"I stand corrected," he offered a penitent slant of the head, "my apologies. Allow me to rephrase the question. Why do you wish to speak with Ryland Devereaux?"

Harlow bit down on the inside of her cheek. She loathed having to ask any of them for a favor, but this one especially chapped her ass—and he knew it. And with his appearance, she knew the price just went up.

"I need to know some details about his final moments—for his family's sake."

Michael seemed truly intrigued. "Why would Harlow Thornhart care about such a thing?"

"My cares are none of your concern." She downed her drink. "What's it going to cost me?"

"It always comes down to business with you, doesn't it? Whatever happened to doing things for the sake of family?"

Harlow refilled her glass and moved to stand next to the fire. "I am not the one who came here with a price in mind. Stop wasting my time and tell me what you want in exchange."

"Very well," Michael stood. "It will cost you the Sword of Lucifer."

"No!"

"That's the price if you wish to speak with Deveraux. Come now, Harlow, you know as well as I do that thing cannot be allowed to fall into the wrong hands. It must be secured."

"It is secure—with me. No one is more qualified to protect my father's sword than I am. YOUR people are the ones who entrusted it to a bunch of humans leaving it vulnerable to begin with."

"It was safe for centuries."

"Until one of your good seeds went bad. It was sheer luck it was not found sooner. You should be thanking me for removing it from that witch's hands. It will go into my personal collection."

"That is unacceptable! You would be able to take over the world with the power of that weapon." "Why in God's name would I want to? A world full of humans? Please! Hell would be more pleasant to rule."

"Yet here you are asking to visit with one you claim to bring some peace to his family. The question is 'why'?" He stepped closer to her. "Have you come to care for a human, dear niece?"

"NO!" she lied.

"I have named the price. The choice is yours, but know this, that sword will not be allowed to remain in your possession. We will get it one way or the other." He started towards the door.

Harlow swished around the liquid in her glass. "If I give it to you, what will you do with it? Surely not make the mistake of putting it back into human hands."

Michael stopped and smiled, his back still to her. He had her right where he wanted her. "No. It will go directly to Raguel. As you know, it is his job to keep angels and demons in check. It will serve him well and when it is not in use, he will store it away safely."

"And where will he do that? You and I both know it cannot enter Heaven, and it will never be allowed in Hell. That leaves the middle ground, which puts us right back to the humans."

"Over the centuries, Raguel has procured several places where he keeps his weapons, guarded against angel and demon alike. What happened this time will not happen again, I give you my word," he exhaled sharply, "and even if it does, as you well know, you are safe from its effects. We both know you only have one weakness, and if what you have told me is the truth, you have nothing to fear."

Harlow closed her eyes, choking down the vomit rising in the back of her throat. "Very well! The sword for a conversation with Ryland Devereaux," she paused, "PLUS three personal favors from you, yet to be determined."

"You must be joking!" he scoffed.

"The sword is worth far more than a conversation with a dead human. I am the Purveyor, and I never lose on a deal. I guess the real question you need to ask yourself is—what is it worth to you? After all," she took a long, slow sip from her glass and looked him directly in the eye, "what's a few favors for the sake of family?"

Knowing he was in no position to disagree, Michael's nose angrily flared. What he thought would be an easy mission had just become a great deal more complicated. "One!"

"Three, or the sword stays with me. I don't need to speak to the human that badly."

"What kind of favors?" he growled.

"I haven't decided yet," she said cheerfully. His presence and his response told her he had been told to do whatever it took to get the sword, and that his orders had come directly from the top. "I won't tie you to a bed and cover you with prostitutes for my own amusement while holding a video camera if that's what you are worried about. But understand this, when I call for a favor, I expect that call to be answered and in a timely manner."

"Very well!" he said through gritted teeth.

Harlow smashed her glass against the table, shattering it into shards. Taking the biggest piece, she slit open her palm and held it out. "Forgive me, I am a little gun shy when it comes to my own family. I will need a blood pact."

With a repugnant expression on his face, he stuck out his hand and let her slice it open. Grasping their hands tightly together, the bargain was struck. With the wave of her hand, the sword appeared, and Harlow reluctantly handed it over. "Take good care of this, or I may just be inclined to take it back."

Michael accepted the blade. With the snap of his fingers, a doorway of blue flames appeared. "Azrael is waiting for you." The two parted with no further words.

Harlow cautiously stepped across the threshold and into a bright white light. Shielding her eyes, she followed the rock pathway that was illuminated, as well. Finally, she came upon a tall golden fence, the only foreseeable entrance through a wrought iron garden gate being guarded by two stone-faced warriors on either side. As she approached, the warriors, dressed in all white, moved into a fighting stance, crossing the ends of their spears at her throat.

"Stand down!" Harlow ordered as she shoved them away. "I have special permission from Michael to visit with Azrael. She is expecting me."

The pair moved back into their original positions and made no move to stop her as she lifted the latch and went inside. Following the pathway through the forest of live oaks and across the bridge where the babbling brook flowed beneath, she smiled when the majestic gardens came into sight. This was the space between, where souls journeyed, waiting to make the transition, giving them time to acclimate to their fate before climbing the stairs to the pearly gates.

Azrael took a great deal of pride in maintaining them, wanting those who were about to enter Heaven to be comforted with the joy of their beauty, not fearful of what was to come next. Taking the path to the left to a different section, Harlow recalled fond memories of playing there as a child when her father had business with Azrael regarding a soul that was on the fence. Stopping to admire a bright purple rose, she took it in hand and smiled when the bloom seemed to become more vibrant from her touch.

"It never gets old," she heard someone whisper just over her right shoulder. She turned only to be handed a stunning black rose. "I grow these in your honor and keep them close to my heart because they remind me so much of you. Hello, Harlow."

Her smile widened as she accepted it. "Hello, Azrael. Are we completely alone?"

"Yes! This is my personal space and no one else is allowed in without my knowledge or permission."

The two embraced tightly, Harlow holding onto her for a little bit longer than usual. "It's good to see you, old friend."

Azrael took her by the hand and led her to a nearby bench, her long white gown a stark contrast to Harlow's black ensemble. "And you, as well! It has been far too long!" Gesturing for her to sit, she said, "I hope you know I had nothing to do with Michael showing up when you summoned me. I would never have done that to you of all people. Things have been a little strange around here lately."

"How did that happen?" Harlow questioned. "I thought our communication methods were secure."

"So did I, but the message you sent me was somehow intercepted. I still haven't figured it out, but as soon as your father's sword surfaced, a tension formed in the air, and even minor matters are now being questioned. I have never seen things here in such a state before."

"Well, Michael has the sword now, so everyone can go back to having their usual, boring sticks stuck up their asses as opposed to adding that additional one."

Azrael chuckled. "Oh, how I have missed you! We really need to plan a night to sneak out like in the old days. When was the last time we were together anyway?"

Harlow thought for a moment. "I believe it was when we slipped into that party King Henry the VIII was having."

"That's right! As I recall, you remained behind while I came back home to work. Didn't he get the son he so desperately wanted shortly after that night?"

"When have you ever known me to pass up an opportunity to make a deal?"

"Never!" The two women leaned into each other and laughed.

"Tell me, Harlow, what brings you here?"

Sighing, she explained, "I need to speak to Ryland Devereaux regarding his death. There seem to be some inconsistencies in the story, and I just want to hear it straight from the source. I also may need an additional favor after he and I talk."

"Of course! If it is within my power, it is yours. You know that! Out of curiosity, may I ask why?"

"I think the family is in need of some closure and if I am able to bring them a small measure of peace, I would very much like to."

"I suppose wonders never cease! I do believe Harlow Thornhart may be coming fond of humans."

"Banish the thought!" she scoffed. "I have my own selfish reasons for doing this!"

"Whatever you say!" A sly smirk crossed Azrael's face as she stood. "Wait here while I go get him."

A short time later, Harlow emerged from the garden with the black rose in hand and strolled back through the door into her room. The portal disappeared behind her. Taking out her phone, she called Marie and made some arrangements.

Chapter Sixteen

"I need some caffeine," Harlow announced late that evening. "Sawyer, I found this delightful little place up the street. Marie and the Devereaux brothers are meeting us there for a late dinner."

"Of course! I will get my coat. Shall I call an Uber?"

"No, let's walk instead. It's close by and it's a lovely night."

"I will never understand how you walk in those things," Sawyer said as they strolled up the street.

Harlow took him by the arm, holding on to him as they maneuvered around the people in their path. "You know I am a glutton for punishment!"

"I know you are a glutton for the whips and chains in the bedroom, but six-inch heels are an entirely different type of torment and there is no pleasure to follow it."

"I beg to differ. I feel a great deal of orgasmic delight when I take them off at night," she joked. Becoming serious, she shifted the conversation. "Sawyer, I want you to know how much you, and our friendship, mean to me. I know I don't always show it, and I can be a bit of a hard ass to work for, but you are a treasure to me. Please remember that, even though it may not seem like it at the time, I always have your best interests at heart."

"Oh my God, am I dying?" he asked dramatically.

"No, you aren't dying."

"Are you dying?"

"NO! Why would you think that?"

"Well, those are the only reasons I can think of for a declaration like that from you," he teased. "What's going on? Don't tell me you are going soft on me!"

"No, I'm not. The only reason I told you those things is because I am about to inflict a little tough love on you, and I prefer if you didn't hate me for it." Harlow steered him across the street into the restaurant. When he saw the name across the window, he stopped and turned to leave. Harlow grasped him firmly by the arm, holding him in place. "Where do you think you are going?"

"Harlow, I have to go," he whispered, "I just remembered there is some work I need to do."

"Nonsense! As your boss, I am giving you the night off." Dragging him inside, she waved to Marie and the brothers as she helped him to the table and forced him into a chair.

Chase stood and pulled out a seat for Harlow.

"Oh, thank you, Chase."

"I hope y'all are hungry," Jacquelin said as she came out of the back. The older woman stopped short when she caught sight of Sawyer. Grabbing onto the nearby counter, she staggered, and her face drained of all color. Chase and Randy were immediately on their feet, rushing to her side.

"Mama, what's wrong?" Chase demanded, helping her into a chair and dropping to one knee at her feet.

"YOU!" her eyes were fixated on Sawyer. "How dare you come in here after all this time and after what you did? You have no right to be here!"

"Jacqueline—I—" a miserable Sawyer stammered. "I am—so sorry!"

"Sorry for what? What's going on?" Randy asked, looking back and forth between the two. "Mama, do you know Sawyer?"

"Of course, I know him," she spat. "That man is your uncle, and he is the one who killed your father!"

Marie looked around the room, thankful she had been able to convince Jacquelin to close the place before their arrival.

"Killed Daddy?" Randy shook his head. "I don't understand!"

"That's where I recognized you from when we first met," muttered a stunned Chase as he slowly stood and turned towards Sawyer, "It's because it was you that night. You were the one who came out of the kitchen and ran off into the woods. You showed up at the park that day. I saw you talking to Daddy while I was sitting at the picnic table eating my hot dog."

Sawyer nodded, unable to form words.

Chase started towards him, ready for a fight.

Harlow stepped between them and rested her hand on his chest, stopping him cold.

"Sawyer is under my protection, and I will never allow you or anyone else to harm him."

"You will protect the person who murdered my father?" he demanded angrily.

"No, I won't," she replied calmly, "because he didn't murder your father."

"What? How would you know? I was there when it happened. You weren't!"

"He's right," Sawyer confessed, his voice starting to crack. "We were arguing. I came to the house that night to tell him I was leaving New Orleans. I grew up in a family of hunters who saw our kind as an abomination. I loved your father more than anything, and I didn't want to bring trouble to the family because of what I truly was. Back then, I couldn't get it completely under control and I knew it was a matter of time before I made a huge mess of things. I didn't want to bring that kind of shame to him. He and Jacquelin were the only ones who knew, and when I told him I planned to leave, he begged me not to go."

"You were born into it—a true rougarou," Harlow stated sympathetically.

Sawyer wiped a few tears from his cheek. "Most born into it learn to control it right away because it is a natural part of who they are. For some reason, no matter how hard I tried, I could not."

"That is true at the beginning for the strongest of your kind, and what you and the ones like you don't understand, is that it is emotion-based. The deeper the feelings, the harder it is to maintain your composure," she clarified. "You didn't have anyone to help you figure things out. If you had been around others of your kind, it would have made all the difference in the world."

"He accepted you for what you were and loved you anyway because he knew it wasn't your fault," Jacquelin cried, "and you killed him for it."

"I didn't mean to. When we started to argue, I transformed. He grabbed me by the arm, and I just meant to break free, but I pushed back too hard, and he fell, hitting his head on the table. I didn't know what to do. I tried to calm down enough to call for help, but it wasn't working." He addressed Chase. "I heard you come down the stairs and I tried to communicate with you, but it only came out as a growl. I knew if I ran away, you would immediately go check on your father and it was his best chance. I spent the night in the woods and after I returned to my human form the next day, I learned he was dead. I left that same day. I caught a flight to Europe and wandered aimlessly, even trying to put an end to myself for the sake of others, but each time I did, the wolf would emerge and stop me. I had given up all hope until I heard rumors of a place in Tibet, a monastery that specialized in teaching The Diverse how to transition into human life by helping them master their nature. I spent years there, but finally, I got it under control. They never taught me how to forgive myself though, and I was too much of a coward to come back to my family in New Orleans. I am so sorry for what I did."

"You did not kill me, baby brother," a voice boomed from nowhere.

The group nervously looked around until slowly, a shape took form next to Jacquelin.

"Ryland?" she gasped.

"Hello, sweetheart." The specter tried to take her hand but was unable to. Turning to Harlow, he asked, "Would you be so kind?"

"It would be my pleasure." Harlow waved her hand back and forth and she recited a few words given to her by Azrael until Ryland became corporeal once more.

"Oh, my Lord! How is this possible?" Jacquelin crossed herself and stood, moving into his arms where they embraced each other tightly.

"You can thank Ms. Thornhart for pulling a few strings, and at great personal expense, from what I understand." He offered a nod of gratitude. "I can only remain in this form for a very short time, but you need to know what really happened that night."

"You did this?" Chase whispered to Harlow who had moved to stand next to him.

"It's time the truth was told. You all have been carrying around an enormous amount of baggage for no reason whatsoever. It must be that flawed human part in all of you. It's time to put an end to this once and for all."

Ryland moved to stand in front of Sawyer and rested his hands on his shoulders. "Brother, you did not kill me that night. I did hit my head when I fell, but that was not the cause of my death."

"I don't understand."

"I guess you could say poor timing did me in. You see, before you came to the house that night, I was nursing a terrible headache—the worst one I have ever had in my entire life. What I didn't know at the time was that I had developed a slow brain bleed."

"You had a stroke! We left the park early that day because you weren't feeling well." It hit Chase like a ton of bricks. "That's why you couldn't communicate with me when I found you. You were paralyzed."

"Maybe the fall set it off," Sawyer reasoned.

"It doesn't work that way," Chase countered. "It would have just been a matter of time—more like a ticking time bomb."

Ryland grasped his brother's face with his hands. "You were not responsible for my death, and I want you to stop blaming yourself for it. I am proud of all you have done and what you have become. I only wish you had been here for Jacquelin and the boys as they grew up, but I understand why you had to leave. You had your own path to walk. They do let us take a peek down here once in a while and, for the record, I really like Mason. I think he is good for you." Sawyer leaned against his brother's chest and broke into a sob, releasing years of guilt in a torrent of tears. "I have missed you so much! I love you, brother!"

Ryland kissed the top of his head and pulled him to him. "I love you, too!"

Turning to Chase, Randy, and Logan, he waved them over and took them into a giant group hug. "I am so proud of my boys. You have chosen to do more with your lives than I could have ever imagined or hoped for my own. Not only do you serve other people in your professional lives, but you protect the innocent in your off time, and you do it with a conscience, a thing many hunters often forget they have. The fact that it came naturally and didn't need to be taught speaks volumes as to your character. I love you all and I cannot wait to see what you do next. Please tell your other brother I am sorry I missed him, but that I do keep an eye on him, as well. Now, if you will excuse me, I think I would like to have one last dance with my wife in the few moments I have left."

The brothers quickly moved a table out of the way.

"Any musical requests?" Harlow asked.

"*What a Wonderful World* by Louis Armstrong," Sawyer whispered in her ear when he saw the couple already lost in each other's eyes. "It was their song."

"Excellent choice!" she snapped her fingers and the old jukebox in the corner that hadn't worked for years dropped a 45 and lowered the needle.

Marie inconspicuously rubbed the back of her neck, using it as cover to use a little of her own magic to dim the lights. They all stood back and watched as the couple shared one special last dance together. When the song ended, Ryland took his time kissing his wife tenderly. "I love you, sweetheart, and I will be waiting for our next dance when you meet me in Heaven." Jacquelin held onto his hand as he began to fade out of sight. In the final seconds, he addressed Harlow.

"Please look out for my family and, thank you, for all you have done!"

"Go in peace," she quietly replied with a nod. The lights flickered and he was gone.

The room remained silent for what seemed like an eternity.

Clapping her hands together to break the tension, Harlow announced, "Well, this has been an enlightening evening. Who wants a drink?"

One by one, each hand in the room rose.

Harlow cranked up the jukebox as the brothers quickly rounded up all the alcohol in the place. Sawyer and Jacquelin talked as they worked together to lay out a spread of food. The family spent the rest of the night mending fences and closing up old wounds.

"That was a really great thing you did," Chase said as he sat down next to Harlow, "you know, given the fact we are lowly humans and all."

"I couldn't have my assistant too down in the dumps to work," she countered, "after all, I do have a pile of rubble waiting at home in Vegas to clean up. The paperwork alone is going to be hell."

"So, I suppose there is no rush to get back," he pointed out, cautiously letting his hand drift over on hers.

She looked down at it, rather surprised by his forwardness. "What do you think you are doing?"

Stroking her fingers lightly, he replied, "I was hoping we might, I don't know, spend some time together, alone, in a place where we won't be interrupted like we always are."

"And where might that be?"

"My apartment is upstairs." "You live above your mother's restaurant? Does she not have a basement with its own couch and fridge for you to not pay rent in?"

"I don't know. Maybe one of these days, something might change, and I will start looking for another place," he took a swig from his beer, "if I have the right incentive, that is."

Harlow turned her head and smirked. "I told you I don't sleep with humans."

"Who said anything about sleeping?" Leaning closer, he whispered, "Come on, why don't you take a chance and let me be your first—human, that is? Who knows, you might be surprised?"

"If I am being completely honest," she sighed, "I have to admit, my curiosity is more than a little piqued." Harlow regarded him for a bit, struggling with herself. "Oh, what the hell?" Offering her hand, she conceded, "Take me to your shitty little apartment."

Randy leaned over and rested his chin on Marie's shoulder. "So, how old are you really?" Marie lifted a beer bottle to her lips and took a sip. "Twenty-nine."

"No, I mean really?"

Rolling her eyes, "Alright, I just turned thirty."

"No!" he gently turned her face to his, "I mean—REALLY!"

"Thirty plus a couple of hundred, give or take," she mumbled.

He paused and smirked. "I guess that makes you a cougar."

"How do you feel about that?"

He gently pressed his lips to hers. "Well, they do say older women make good lovers. I suppose I am a lucky man, but at some point, we are going to have to have a serious conversation, after all, I want to know everything about the woman I love."

A slow smile spread across her face before her eyes drifted to Harlow and Chase who were now sitting incredibly close together. Randy followed her gaze. "How old do you think she is?"

"Let's just say if a woman's age is any indication of how good she is in bed, Chase very well may end up in a coma, provided he survives the night, that is."

"Well, this really is horrendous," Harlow remarked dryly as she looked around.

"It serves its purpose," Chase replied as he poured two glasses of wine.

"Doesn't it bother you that you can see the front door from every room?"

"Not really."

"Well, it should!" Harlow snatched the glass from his hand, downed it and tossed it aside. As she turned to him, the look of disgust on her face turned into something more carnal.

Grabbing him by the waistband of his jeans, she urgently pulled his body to hers and kissed him. Chase dropped his glass and took her face in his hands, stopping to grin as he returned the favor. A primal intensity took over as the two began tearing at each other's clothes, her strength far outweighing his. Harlow slammed Chase roughly against the wall, knocking several pictures down, shattering the frames. Smirking, she yanked his tattered shirt over his head and tossed it aside, before slowly dragging her sharpened nails across his chest, taking a moment to appreciate the view. Sucking in breath, the tantalizing action simply urged him on. Turning the tables, he enveloped her in his arms, flipped her around, and pressed her towards his bed.

"Straight to the bedroom?" she teased. "What kind of girl do you think I am?"

"I don't you are a 'girl' at all," he hissed, his eyes locked on hers, his hands gliding over her the curve of her thighs. "I think you are the most beautiful creature I have ever laid eyes on."

"Right on both counts!" she smarted before thrusting her tongue down his throat.

He fumbled around until he found the zipper on her dress. Down it went, pooling at her feet, revealing the perfect outline of a goddess standing in stiletto heels. He forced her backwards on the bed. Harlow relaxed on her elbows as she watched him remove her heels, tossing them over his shoulder one by one. He paused to take one ankle in his hand, encircling it with his tongue, upwards, his gaze locked on hers.

Secretly delighted by the gesture, her head rolled to one side, and, for a brief second, her eyes drifted to the curtains. "What the fuck?" she cringed and mumbled with disgust. Squinting for a better look, she added, "You need a new decorator! Your current one sucks ass!" Her thought, however, was quickly dismissed when his attention turned to a much more important matter, a little higher up.

He looked up dreamily. "There's something else my decorator would like to suck on at the moment, if you don't mind terribly!"

Taking his meaning, Harlow forgot about the curtains as her hand went to the back of his head. "Please, be my guest!"

Her back arched and she exhaled as several sensual waves overtook her. Her hands slid downward towards his ass, and, with little effort, she tore his jeans clean in half.

"Damn!" he exclaimed when he realized what happened. "That was my favorite pair!" he teased, shoving them aside, glad to be rid of the constraint between them.

"I will buy you some new clothes tomorrow, if you are a good boy! And Gucci..." she wrinkled her nose as the denim next to them, "none of whatever 'this' is."

"I guess I will have to earn my prize," he replied, laughing.

"Yes, I think you will," she exclaimed and rolled him over onto his back.

Harlow shifted and landed atop him, splaying her fingers across his chest, chewing on her bottom lips as she contemplated her next move. She had never seen this much of a human this close, and she didn't hate it. Chase waited with bated breath for what was to come.

Harlow took her time, licking and teasing his member, using her sharpened nails to graze his shaft, just to add to the intensity. She had been with creatures of all kinds, even a Fae god, yet nothing intrigued and excited her the way Chase did.

"Mmmm!" she mumbled after licking a drop from his tip. "Takes like mortal."

"What was that?" Chase's eyes closed and his head lobbed to one side. He appeared caught in a dream he couldn't explain and would never be able to escape—not that he would ever want to. Something about that vulnerability made her desire him even more.

Harlow replied by taking him all the way in her mouth, holding him in place, and suckling him until he could no longer form words. When she felt him nearing the edge, she replaced her lips with what he really wanted, taking him all the way inside in one, demanding move. Her hips swayed, shifting up and down with a strength and intensity no human had ever experienced before. He was the first and likely the last. Finding their rhythm and moving as one, they came simultaneously with a shudder strong enough to buckle the pine floors.

They continued on, slowly making love, taking the time to thoroughly please each other—many times and on multiple levels.

Three hours later, Chase rolled off the bed and went into the kitchen.

Feeling more sated than she ever had, Harlow couldn't help but smile as she watched him go. She could get used to this. Pulling the sheet to the side, her hand happened to brush along her leg. Drawing her hand back, she was stunned to see a red spot on the covers. Lifting it for a closer inspection, she frowned when she saw the place where Daphne had cut her with the blade. It had not healed completely and was oozing a bit. Blotting it with her finger, she held it up for a closer inspection. "Well, that's a problem."

"What's a problem?" Chase asked as he came back into the room carrying two full glasses of wine.

"It's a problem that you are using your tongue for all talk and no action," she replied, discreetly covering her leg with the sheet. Settling against the headboard, she accepted the glass and took a sip.

"Well, let's see what we can do about that!" He sat the glass aside and crawled onto the foot of the bed. Harlow reclined and closed her eyes as she waited for him to satisfy her again.

Logan woke with a start, in the middle of the night, his heart pounding and with an unbelievable thirst that needed quenching. He had been having a horrible nightmare and when he awakened, part of him still believed it was real. Pulling his knees to his chest, he raked his hair back and took several deep breaths as reality started to fill back in. His dream had started well enough, happy even, as he sat around the dinner table with his whole family, including his father and uncle. They joked, laughed, and told old stories about what he and his brothers did as children, his father gripping Chase's shoulder tightly and thanking him for looking after the family while he was gone. They all stopped and applauded when his mother appeared, smiling and carrying a cake with writing on it, welcoming Sawyer back to the family. The light in the room started to dim and they all stopped to look at the single light bulb above the table that was now flickering. "I will get that!" his mother announced. Before she could move, Logan found himself filled with a gnawing, insatiable hunger. Leaping across the table, he shoved the cake aside and went for his mother's throat, tearing it open. The others sat still and watched, emotionless, as the blood began to pool on the floor. He, on the other hand, jumped down on all fours and began to lap it up from where it ponded. Looking up, he could see Sawyer peering over the edge, smiling as he said, "Welcome to the family!"

Desperately trying to shake it off, he shoved the covers aside and went into the kitchen for a beer. He jumped, startled when the light came on unexpectedly and he saw Harlow leaning against the wall with her arms crossed watching him intently.

"Jesus! You scared me! What are you doing in my apartment? How did you get in here anyway?" "There isn't anywhere I can't get into. You and I need to have a chat while no one else is around."

"About what?" He took a bottle from the refrigerator and popped the top. "If you are sleeping with my brother, stay far away from me. I don't want there to be any question about my loyalty to him."

"You were bitten," she stated.

"I was scratched," he corrected.

"You can tell yourself that all day long, but I sensed and smelled it the first time we met. You are turning whether you want to admit it or not. Your hair is growing at a rapid rate, as are your fingernails, and you are emitting a strong musky odor. Soon, your appetite will grow, as will your senses and your ability to tolerate things like pain and alcohol. The transition is not going to be easy. In fact, it will be hell. You will need help."

"No way! I don't want my family to know!" he snapped.

"Then, for once, we agree. I also believe it is best if they don't."

Logan regarded her peculiarly.

"They should not be forced to live with your curse," she explained. "Chase already feels an absurd amount of responsibility to look after all of you, given he was forced to become the man of the house at far too early an age. Your brother will blame himself for leaving you up at that camp alone and, given his outlandish notions of maintaining a certain moral code, the guilt most certainly will eat him alive. I think you have caused him more than enough grief for one lifetime, and I simply will not allow you to do more of it."

"I will deal with this alone."

"And how are you going to do that? The same way Billy Harmon did?" Harlow walked over to the table. "What happens if you lose control and end up ripping your poor mother to shreds?"

Her words cut him to the bone, the dream still fresh on his mind.

"I will put an end to myself first," he said quietly.

"Yes, because suicide is always a good backup plan," she snarked. "Once again, Chase will take it the hardest. He has been through enough."

"Why are you so concerned about my brother's feelings all of a sudden?"

Ignoring his question, Harlow rested her hand on his shoulder. "You will allow Sawyer and Mason to teach you how to control yourself," Logan flinched as she leaned close to his ear and dug her fingernails into his skin, "or I will personally put you down like a rabid dog. Chase wouldn't be able to live with the survivor's remorse. I, on the other hand, have NO problem living with the death and destruction I leave in my wake. In truth, I relish it." Relinquishing her hold, she straightened up and smoothed out his shirt. "The thirst will not begin to overwhelm you until the next full moon. You begin your lessons tomorrow. I suggest you notify your job you are going to be needing some time off."

Harlow slipped back into bed.

Chase was fast asleep, but his arms came around and he planted a kiss on her shoulder as she settled in. Enveloped in the warmth of his arm, she found herself perfectly content laying there and listening to the beat of his heart.

"Good morning," he said when he felt her stir.

"Morning?" she raised, "Where did the time go?"

"You fell asleep." "I DID NOT!" she countered. "I don't sleep!"

"Every living thing has to sleep sometime."

"Not me!"

"Well, you did, and by the way, you snore!" Chase kissed the tip of her nose.

Harlow gasped, aghast. "Lies!"

"I don't, but for the record, it's not very loud and incredibly adorable." Tossing aside the covers, he got up and went into the bathroom. "I will be right back!"

"I never sleep, and I certainly don't snore!" Harlow grumbled as she slipped on one of his t-shirts from the back of a chair and went in search of her phone. After locating it, she curled up on the couch and began checking her messages.

Chase came out of the bedroom, leaned over the back of the sofa, and kissed her. "Everything alright?"

"Yes, fine. I am just making a few arrangements. I must get back to Vegas as soon as possible. The authorities need some answers and, honestly, I have a huge mess to clean up."

"Are you coming back to New Orleans?"

Harlow lowered her phone. "I suppose I will have to. My best assistant has decided to stay here for a while to get to know his family better and I am not sure how long I can do without him. Mason, his husband, has closed up their house and is already on his way." She took him by the hand and turned to face him. "Chase, about last night."

"Let me guess," he scratched his forehead awkwardly, "the human experience isn't for you."

"If I am being completely honest," lowering her head to conceal the grin on her face, "I didn't hate it, and I might just be convinced to give it another shot just to be sure."

"Oh!"

He leaned in for another kiss, but she stopped him by pressing her finger to his lips, "But it will have to wait. With Black Thorn Enterprises in shambles and my reputation in doubt, I need to let the world know I am still here and, more importantly, in control."

"When will you have to leave?" Coming around and sitting down, he slipped his arm around her.

Harlow rested her head on his shoulder and her hand on his chest. "Noon."

"That soon?" Chase was clearly disappointed.

"I'm sorry, but this is important." "I understand."

Harlow glanced out the window. "But I suppose it is still early, and we have a little time before breakfast," climbing over into his lap, "so, let's work up an appetite, shall we?"

Marie and Randy met them at the restaurant later that morning. Just as they arrived, so did a tour bus. The brothers jumped in to help their mother, who was shorthanded that shift.

"So, what now?" Marie asked, offering a little wave to Randy. "Are you going to rebuild Black Thorn Enterprises?"

"Eventually I suppose, although I may give some thought to a new location. Between the tacky tourists and our own home-grown freak shows, Vegas just hasn't been the same since formal evening attire went out of style. Maybe it is time for a change. Sawyer wants to spend more time here, getting to know his family, and I think it will be good for him. Mason has already located a place for them to stay and he is on his way." "Are we going to talk about the little fact that Logan is about to join The Diverse?" asked Marie, her eyebrows raised. "He is starting to smell like a wet dog after all."

"No! As far as the brothers are concerned, it is best if they believe you and I know nothing. Sawyer and Mason will sort him out."

"I am all for that, cher!" Marie stirred her coffee. "You know, Louisiana does offer some surprisingly good tax incentives if you are looking to relocate. And we have been known to do it up right come Mardi Gras. The locals aren't too bad, either."

"The humidity is awful for my hair," Harlow complained, her eyes cutting to Chase's rear as he leaned across the counter, "but the view with my café au lait and beignets here at Devereaux's restaurant is worth the trip alone. Perhaps I will give it some consideration, but first, there are some things I need to take care of back in Vegas."

"Like what?"

"For one, I need to retrieve my items from the underground vault. They are buried deep enough and protected with enough magic that the explosion will not have penetrated it, but I don't want to leave it unguarded for too long. I also need to check on my panther and, oh yes, figure out how to get the sword back."

"The sword? What happened to it?"

"It was the price I had to pay for the little family get-together last night, but don't worry, now that I know who possesses it, it is just a matter of time until I take it back."

"I have no doubt!" Marie sipped from her cup, paused, and blinked hard. "Did you say 'panther'?"

Harlow nodded. "Bathsheba—gifted to me by Queen Sheba herself."

"Wait, how old is that damn cat?"

"She's been around a while, but then again, so have you and me."

"What about Chase?"

Harlow's hand unconsciously drifted to her thigh where she found her wound still tender. "I am sure he will forget all about me as soon as I am in the air."

At that moment, he looked up and his eyes found hers. A slow, coy smile spread across his face—as did hers.

Marie looked back and forth between the couple, finding the star-crossed lover's gaze unbroken. "I wouldn't be so sure about that!" she remarked.

Excitement alight in her eyes, Marie leaned back and smiled. "So, I am dying to know—how did the great Harlow Thornhart find sex with a human?"

Her lips curled up. "Enlightening!"

Harlow said her 'goodbyes' to Marie and the Devereauxs at the restaurant before stopping by the hotel to get her things. Chase had been called into the hospital unexpectedly while they were having breakfast when a five-car pileup occurred, flooding the ER with patients. Sawyer chatted away in the back of the car about business as Harlow stared out the window, watching the streets of New Orleans fade into the distance, already missing it.

"Mitchell has all of the numbers here in New Orleans to reach me. Do not hesitate to call me, night or day, if you need anything," he rattled on as they walked towards the jet. "I have my laptop and can dial in from anywhere. I have also been in contact with the authorities, as well as the insurance company, getting the ball rolling on rebuilding. Mitchell will be waiting for you at the airport."

Harlow stopped and rested her hand on his shoulder. "Don't worry about me. I have everything under control. I need you to take care of Logan for the sake of the rest of your family." "Don't worry, boss. Mason and I will keep him close. I have already been in touch with the monastery I went to, and they are on standby if things get out of our control."

"Good!" Harlow took him into an embrace. "Take care of your family. I have grown rather fond of them—even if they are human."

"Thank you for all you did," he said as he squeezed her tight. "And for the record, I approve."

"Approve of what?"

Sawyer nodded just over her shoulder.

She turned to see Chase sitting on the steps of the jet. "I will keep an eye on him too," he whispered.

Harlow shook her head as Sawyer walked away.

Chase stood and met her halfway.

"What are you doing here?"

"I couldn't very well let you leave without saying 'goodbye'," he took her by the hands.

"What about the poor humans in the hospital who need your medical expertise?"

"They can wait for a little bit." "I suppose you are waiting for me to invite you to come along with me?"

"No, I'm not, though I must admit, I would have been extremely tempted if you had. I am not sure what, if anything, is happening between us, but I am willing to wait and see where it goes without pushing my luck."

"That's a very good answer."   Chase leaned in and the two shared a long, lingering kiss.

"Goodbye, Harlow."

"Goodbye, Chase."

They held hands for a long moment before reluctantly parting ways. Chase waved as she settled in at the window.

Fighting off a pang of emptiness as the plane took off, she decided to take her mind off him by doing some work. As she reached for her laptop, a jolt of pain shot through her thigh. Looking down, she was dumbfounded to see blood seeping through her clothes. Yanking up her skirt, the site where she was cut by the sword was now angry and inflamed.

"Damn! That really IS a big problem!"

Mitchell was waiting on the tarmac when she arrived.

"Welcome home, boss," he said as she emerged from the plane, engrossed in her phone screen.

"It's good to be home. Was the shaman able to get Cherise sorted out?"

"Yes, ma'am." Leading the way to the car, he went on ahead to open the door. "She has no recollection whatsoever of what happened. The shaman was even able to place a few false memories, so she now only recalls having a relaxing weekend in Lake Tahoe."

"Excellent! What about the other women?" Harlow slid into the back seat.

Mitchell closed the door and came around, taking his place behind the wheel.

"On their way to Reno for an impromptu girl's weekend, their car went off the road and burst into flames, burning their bodies beyond recognition. The IT department pieced together some old surveillance footage and planted it at a convenience store near Silver Springs, timestamping it twenty minutes before the accident."

"Tell Sawyer to find a way to take care of the families financially. I know it is little comfort, but it is also one less thing they will have to worry about."

Mitchell nodded and started the car.

"Damage assessment?"

"The entire building is gone."

"What?" Harlow looked up from her phone, her face full of disbelief. "The whole thing?"

"I am afraid so. I guess the witch picked up some extensive explosives knowledge somewhere along the way. She knew exactly where to put them to bring it down completely."

"What about the authorities?"

"It has been ruled accidental, caused by the rupture of the main gas line that ran through the building. Miraculously, given when it happened, there were no deaths."

"Not even one?" Looking out the window, she mentally assessed the timing. "What about the cleaning crews?"

"I checked. It seems they had several people out sick that week and had shifted their normal routine to the following night."

"That's rather odd, don't you think?"

"I prefer to think of it as 'luck'. It is Vegas, after all."

"I suppose."

"But the good news is, the fire doesn't appear to have gone any further. We won't know for sure until we get inside, but it seems the underground garage may have gone unscathed, and, of course, the vault should be fine as well. The Black Thorn and your home were left untouched. All your employees are currently working from home, and it is business as usual, minus the building of course. Do you want to go by the site now?"

"Maybe later. Right now, I just want to go home."

Harlow dismissed Mitchell for the rest of the day. Going inside, she was relieved to see Bathsheba stretched out on the sofa peacefully napping. Quietly slipping by as not to disturb her, she opened the door to the hall closet and waved her hand, revealing that it was a magically concealed entrance to her inner sanctum.

Inside, the walls and floors were made of slate rock, like a castle from days of old. Torches with flames that never extinguished hung in small cauldrons along the sides. An eternal blaze burned brightly in the large round sunken fireplace in the middle of the floor. It was surrounded by two circular black velvet sofas, one wide enough for sitting, the other large enough for other 'activities'.

The chamber to the left contained a full library with a wide array of her most beloved tomes, ranging from original Shakespearean works to the most wickedly powerful Books of Shadows. Another to the right was filled with her favorite medieval torture devices. Collecting them had become a hobby of hers.

Harlow walked past them, stopping to lightly touch the door of her very own 'red room'. The thought of getting Chase in there was one that pleased her greatly. Sighing longingly, she continued on her way, entering the final room at the end of the hall.

Opening the door, she smiled. This was where her true personal collection rested. Only the most powerful relics had the honor of residing here. Sorcerer's stones were displayed in partitioned cubbies while extraordinary volumes filled with powerful enchantments rested on their very own lecterns, opened to whatever page she had needed at the time. Shelves were lined with the rarest of potions and the scarcest ingredients to make them. A large cauldron, filled with a purple, incandescent substance, boiled and bubbled in the center of the room, ever ready for when it was needed. Harlow passed by it to go stand in front of a large gilded, floor-length mirror hanging on the opposite wall. Placing her hand on the glass, she spoke only one word.

"Larka!"

She stepped through when the familiar dark forest appeared.

The air was cool and damp here, a light mist still clinging to the vegetation, an indication it had just rained. Harlow walked along the barely discernible trail formed of decaying leaves, packed down so tightly, it kept anything else from growing beneath it. She didn't need it—she knew this place like the back of her hand.

Treetops had grown together, forming as one, blocking out the light from above, yet redwood ferns and other evergreens grew in vast abundance, though nothing bloomed. Her attention went to the whimsical cottage ahead of her, fashioned from the trunk of a tree that had been as wide as a three-story building. Smoke drifted from the chimney, warming Harlow's heart with fond memories from her childhood. She couldn't remember the last time she had visited and mentally vowed to not go for as long again.

Sensing a presence, she turned to see the hooded figure coming from the woods, carrying a basket loaded down with freshly harvested herbs and mushrooms. Closing her eyes, she inhaled, the scent of rosemary and mint wafting in the air. It reminded her of a simpler time when she didn't have a care in the world.

As the figure started Harlow's way, she pushed back the hood of her cloak and smiled. "My dear Harlow! It is good to see you!

"Hello, Larka, it has been far too long." The women warmly embraced.

Larka had essentially been Harlow's nanny growing up. Appearing to only be about thirty, the beautiful nymph was much older than Harlow but lived in one of the spaces between worlds, where time moved at a snail's pace. Long silver hair hung to her waist but was braided into a single plait, a streak of purple winding its way down the middle. Her enormous eyes burned violet, matching her lilac tinted lips and she wore a large chunk of amethyst around her neck. "I am sorry about your building," Larka said as they locked arms and started towards the door.

"How in the world did you know?"

"I get cable TV out here now."

"Really? I can't even get cell reception!"

"It's not easy, but it's not impossible. What can I say? I caved and worked a little magic. It was the only way I could watch that Game of Thrones show. I must admit, I am addicted to it." Harlow shook her head and laughed as they stepped inside.

Larka added a handful of herbs to a kettle of water and placed it on a grate in the enormous wood-burning fireplace, large enough to warmly illuminate the house.

The home was small but cozy. Just about everything inside was made from natural materials—wood, stone, grass, herbs, mud—whatever the Earth had to offer, except for a few, recently added modern conveniences, like the new sixty-inch tv hanging over the mantlepiece.

Harlow sat down on the sofa in front of it, clasping her hands together remembering the many countless nights she had fallen asleep after listening to a story, her tiny body snuggled beneath her caretaker's protective arm. That was back when sleep was a luxury she could afford.

"I had forgotten how much I missed this place," Harlow remarked with a warm smile, "and YOU!"

"You are always welcome here, you know that! Honestly, I would love to see more of you. I miss our time together."

"I know, I'm sorry. I have just been so busy lately. I haven't had time to do anything for myself. There is always so much to do and not enough hours in the day to do it."

"Which makes me even more curious!" Larka sat down on the hearth and poured two teacups, handing her one. "I haven't seen you in at least a century. Tell me, what brings you all the way out here now?"

Harlow hesitated. Setting the cup aside, she pulled back the fabric on her skirt to reveal the wound.

Moving closer for a better look, Larka's brow furrowed as she gently touched it. "Harlow, what in the world happened?"

"I was cut by my father's sword, and, for some reason, it won't heal. The strange thing is, I was run through with that very same blade," she leaned back and pulled up her top to reveal her perfectly healed skin, "and I can't for the life of me figure out why this little nick won't close up."

Larka got up and went to a nearby cabinet, perusing the shelves before making her selections and removing a few bottles of herbs. "What was happening when you were injured?"

"I was in the middle of a fight. Somehow, my opponent managed to momentarily catch me off guard."

"Give me the details." She returned with the herbs and a mortar and pestle, listening carefully as she ground them into a paste.

"She came at me, I side-stepped before grinding her into the floor with my heel, and when I looked away, she sucker-sliced me."

"What caused you to look away?"

Harlow thought back, trying to recall. Suddenly, she remembered. "Oh! It was Chase! He called out to warn me..." she trailed off. "I was distracted by his...."

"Who is this Chase?" Larka motioned for her to lie back across the couch.

"A human," she replied as she stretched out, "I met him in New Orleans when I was dealing with this witch. He was assisting me."

"So, he is a friend?"

Harlow opened her mouth to reply but snapped it closed.

"Ah! He is more than a friend." Larka started to slather on the mixture, her lips curled in amusement.

"I suppose?" Harlow nodded.

"Do you love him?"

"Love him? Why the hell would you ask me that?" Harlow became flustered. "Let's not get all crazy now! I have only known him a few days."

Larka set the paste aside. "Sweetheart, let's not play games, shall we? You forget who you are talking to. I may be retired, but I was your nanny, and I know you better than anyone, especially your own father. There isn't anything I don't know about you, including the one single event that will weaken you enough to allow you to be killed—falling in love with a human."

"Damn it!" Harlow mumbled. "I knew I shouldn't have slept with him."

"Did you sleep with him before this happened?"

"NO! It was after—but—FUCK!"

"I never thought I would see this day," Larka muttered, refocusing on Harlow's injury. Laying her hands over the wound, she said a few words, sending a ray of healing light into it. When she pulled away, the opening was closed, though a small, raised scar remained.

"What the fuck have I done?" Harlow sat back up and dropped her head into her hands.

"It's not what you have done, sweetheart," Larka moved next to her, rubbing her back comfortingly, "it's just what sometimes happens. We have no control over who we fall in love with."

"I shouldn't have allowed it to happen. I have avoided getting involved with humans like the plague because I knew falling in l—lo—well, you know—with one was the only thing in this world that could weaken me, make me vulnerable, and I let it happen anyway."

"I am afraid it happens to the best of us." "I can't even say the damn word, so it can't possibly be!" Harlow straightened up. "I just won't see him ever again. This—feeling—will fade, I will be indestructible once more, and I just won't get involved with another one ever again. Problem solved!"

"Sounds like a plan. There is only one flaw with it."

Harlow slowly turned her head to face Larka. "What's that?"

"Darling, the only love that can weaken you is 'true' love, and that is not always so easily dismissed."

"I can do it! I am certain of it! I am Harlow-fucking-Thornhart, after all!"

"Good luck with that!" Larka patted her leg and snickered. "You let me know how that works out for you. Since you are here, why don't you stay for supper?"

"Do you have any chocolate cake? No one makes them better than you."

Larka smiled. "For you, my sweet, I can whip up anything! And while you are here, I want you to tell me all about Vegas."

"Why?"

"I have been considering taking a vacation and I keep seeing all these commercials on cable. I think it would be a lot of fun!"

Hands on her hips, Harlow stalked around the charred remains of her building. Daphne had somehow managed to plant explosives in all the weakest points, and Black Thorn Enterprises had folded in on itself, leaving nothing to save. The little voice in the back of her head that originally whispered something was off was now shouting loud and clear from the rooftops—the witch had help from someone deep within her organization. This knowledge didn't come through a computer. As she pondered the thought, she noticed an old man dressed in shorts, wearing a gaudy Hawaiian shirt and sunhat surveying the damage as he approached.

"It seems you have quite a mess to clean up." Harlow's eyes widened when she recognized the voice. "Daddy?"

"Hello, sweetheart!" He held out his arms and she stepped into them, embracing him tightly.

"What the hell is all this? Why do you look like someone's deranged grandfather on holiday?"

"Isn't this what the tourists wear? I thought I would blend in better this way." "Well, I don't like it!" she snapped. "Not one bit! Change!"

"Can't you just be happy to see me?"

"Of course, I am! You know I miss you terribly, but this is a bit much to swallow, don't you think? I mean, we look nothing alike when you dress like this!"

Letting out an exasperated sigh, "Oh, very well!"

With the snap of a finger, he transformed into a handsome, dark-haired man dressed in a black Tom Ford suit, complete with diamond-studded cuff links and a matching pair of Bulgaria sunglasses. A slight tinge of silver streaked along the sides of his neatly combed back hair.

"That's better!" She smiled and hugged him again. "Though, what's with the gray?"

"Given I am Harlow Thornhart's father, I believe those gray hairs have been appropriately earned."

"What are you doing here, Daddy?"

"Can't a father just come to visit his daughter without a reason?"

"You haven't left Hell in two millennia?"

Slipping his arm around her, they started to walk towards her car. "Well, I did feel a substantial shift in the cosmos."

"Then you are aware your sword has surfaced."

"Yes, of course!" he replied with a sly smirk. "What else could it have possibly been?"

"Michael has it, but I did manage to negotiate three favors from him for it."

"Excellent! And what are we going to do about getting it back?" "Don't worry, I am already formulating a plan. I just need to deal with this mess first."

He stopped and looked around. "What's there left to deal with? It appears it's already been handled." "There is the matter of my vault beneath here that needs to be emptied and secured."

"It's warded and buried deep enough where no one can reach it. Have Zane and some of the other demons handle it. They have nothing better to do. That is why they are at your disposal, after all."

"I also need to find out who has betrayed me."

"Minor details!" Lucifer placed his hands on both of her shoulders. "You are looking tired, sweetheart. Are you not getting enough rest?"

"You know I never rest! I don't have time for such nonsense." "And that is the problem! Which is why I decided to pay an extended visit."

"You're staying?" Harlow was absolutely stunned. "What about Hell?"

"Hell is—well, hell! It's not going anywhere, and it can take care of itself for a while. Right now, I just want to spend some time reconnecting with my little girl."

"Really?"

"Really! I have missed you, darling!"

"If I am being completely honest, I have to admit," she eyed him warily, "I don't hate the idea. I have missed you, too, Daddy."

"Splendid! Then it's settled. What do you say we drive out to your place and find a room for me to stay in, and on the way, you can tell me all about what is new in your life?"

"Okay! I guess!"

A diabolical smile spread across his face as they climbed into the car.

He could hardly contain his excitement about the real reason for his visit.

Chapter Seventeen

The Vatican, Rome, Italy

Cardinal Victor Simone sat at his desk making notes in his journal. He stopped when a stack of papers on his desk shifted to one side. Laying his pen down, he gathered and stacked them, placing them neatly back in place. Going back to his writing, he frowned when they moved once more, this time falling to the floor. As he bent to retrieve them, he heard a faint rumble. Slowly straightening up, he noticed the cause. The top of his desk was trembling. Getting up and going over to the window, he looked out over the city to see nothing out of the ordinary. A sudden thought occurred to him.

Hurrying over to a bookcase in the far corner, he moved a statue of a cross aside to reveal a hidden pin pad. Punching in a code, a panel slid aside revealing a completely hidden room. Inside, covering an entire wall, was a map of the world with dozens of different colored lights to indicate where demons were most active in the world in real-time. Technology mixed with a little old-time religion had developed an advanced tracking system for The Diverse of the world. Based on the map and reports from the field, Victor would send out members of an elite team to handle the problem or quell the rowdiness, whatever the case may be.

Most of the colors were yellows, purples, and blues indicating minor activity, usually an area of multiple possessions, places where demons were making deals, or even The Diverse were wreaking a little havoc. However, one area was red and flashing. In all his years in this post, he had not once seen it red and never flashing, meaning something of great significance was happening at that moment. Taking out his glasses, he moved in for a closer look. The activity was occurring in New Orleans, Louisiana, of all places.

Lucky for him, he already had a man on the ground in that area. Going over to the nearby desk, he flipped through a Rolodex, punched in a few numbers, and waited for the call to go through. When he got his machine, he left a message and dialed the second number on file.

"Good morning! This is Nancy. Thank you for calling Saint Paul's Parish. How may I help you?"

"Yes, I need to speak to your parish priest. I have been unable to reach him."

"I'm so sorry, sir, but he has been up in Shreveport all week helping out a homeless shelter that just opened. He should be back tomorrow. May I take a message?"

"Yes! Please get in touch with Father Patrick Devereaux at once and tell him to call Cardinal Victor Simone. I need to speak with him on a matter of immense importance. It's urgent!"

Father Patrick Devereaux opened the door to his rectory, dropped his bag on the floor, and let out an exaggerated sigh of relief. It had been a long week, and it was good to be home. His work at the new homeless shelter had been rewarding enough, but the cot in the back room of the church he had been sleeping on left a great deal to be desired. Rubbing his sore neck muscle, he noticed a peculiar smell. Sniffing around for the source, he made a face when he realized it was coming from him.

"Whew! I think I need a shower."

Removing his collar and setting it on the table, he looked at the clock on the wall. It was 6:15 pm and he was starving for some of his mama's cooking. Hitting the 'play' button on his vintage answering machine, he listened to his messages as he unfastened his shirt. Pressing the button, he fast-forwarded through the usual list of church member prayer requests he was too tired to listen to at the moment but stopped when he heard Chase's voice.

"Hey bro, I think it safe to assume you left the charger to that ridiculously outdated flip phone of yours at home while you were away." Patrick winced when he saw it lying on the table by the door. It never occurred to him the reason it had not rung was because the battery was dead. *"Anyway, we need to talk. A lot of things happened while you were out of town and some of them are pretty mind-blowing. I assume you will be starving when you get in, so I will be at the restaurant around seven. See you then."*

Patrick shook his head and laughed. Chase always had an uncanny knack for knowing everything about his brothers and he wasn't sure that was a good thing.

"Oh, and by the way, I met someone. Anyway, we'll talk."

Patrick paused and stared at the machine in disbelief. "Did you just say you met someone? I can't wait to hear about this."

He hurried towards the bathroom, forgetting to hit the 'stop' button in his excitement. The messages played on while he showered.

"Patrick, it's Cardinal Victor Simone. I need you to get in contact with me as soon as you get in. It's extremely urgent. Some sort of event has occurred in your city that has set off our alarms here in Rome. In all my years in this job, I have never seen anything remotely close to this. We need to find out what is happening, and soon. You have my number. Call me!"

Patrick quickly dressed in his usual black pants and shirt, stopping only to run a comb through his hair. Retrieving his collar, he put it on using the mirror by the front door. That's when he heard a beep come from the machine. "I will check it later," he said to his grumbling stomach, before reaching for his keys and heading out.

Patrick arrived at the restaurant precisely at 7 pm. Chase was waiting, leaning against a chair he had pulled out with a grin on his face. The two brothers embraced.

"Welcome home, bro!"

"It's good to be home!"

They sat down.

"How did things go with the homeless shelter?"

"Fine! Fine! Everything there is wonderful. Forget all that. I want to hear about this woman you met!" Patrick reached over and tapped his brother on the chest. "Well, don't keep me in suspense. Tell me all about her."

Chase blew out a hard breath and scratched the back of his head. "I don't even know where to begin with that one."

"How about you start with a name!"

"Her name is Harlow Thornhart, and she is something special." Chase beamed.

Patrick leaned back in his chair and grinned. "She must be to put a smile on your face like that! How did you two meet?"

"That's a bit trickier to explain."

Their conversation was interrupted when Jacquelin saw Patrick and rushed over to greet him. Standing, the two hugged tightly. "Has your brother told you?"

"Told me what?"

"I haven't had a chance to yet, Mama."

Jacquelin grasped his hands tightly as tears came to her eyes. "We got to see your father in the flesh!"

"What?" Patrick was truly caught off guard. His face paled as he looked to Chase for an explanation. "What on Earth is she talking about?"

"You had better sit down. This is going to take a while."

Patrick listened with utter fascination as Chase told him about the visit from their father.

"Daddy was actually here?" he finally managed. "And not just his spirit? In actual corporeal form?"

"He was as real and as warm to the touch as the last time I saw him alive! Baby, it was wonderful! He cleared up all the misconceptions about his death and helped to bring our family back together. Which reminds me! We need to introduce you to your uncle, Sawyer. You were just a little thing the last time he saw you. He is going to be so happy to see you all grown up." Jacquelin patted his hand. "I'm sorry, I know you are probably starving. Let me get you boys some supper while you talk!"

Patrick turned to Chase who was sitting with his elbow on the table using his hand to prop up his chin. "Why do I have the feeling there is so much more to this story?"

"That's because there is!"

Chase told him about Matthew Broussard's death and the events leading up to the brothers getting trapped with Marie and Harlow at the Mandeville house."

"Marie Lavine and Randy are a thing? How did we miss that?"

"That's your takeaway from all I just told you?"

"Vampires, ghosts, and witches I'm used to, but Randy having a girlfriend is truly a wonder."

Chase shrugged. "Yeah, I was just as shocked as you are."

When he got around to the story of the Sword of Lucifer and the Masquerade Ball, Patrick found himself in uncharted territory and was greatly concerned.

"Wait! This woman, or whatever she is, survived all that and you're not the least bit concerned about what she might be?"

Chase sighed. "I admit, I had my misgivings in the beginning, but after spending some time with her and getting to know her, I don't anymore. Besides, we have all known Marie forever. If she vouches for her, that's good enough for me, and Randy feels the same way." "Did it ever occur to you she put a hex or a spell of some sort on you, or ALL of you? If she is as powerful as you say, it would be an easy thing to do."

"I don't believe she did," he replied quietly.

"But you don't know for certain."

"I don't think she is a bad person if that's what you are getting at."

"Chase, she makes deals with the creatures we hunt, and from what you have told me, it doesn't sound like she has much of a conscience."

"I never said that. In some ways, I have found her to have more honor than many of the people I have dealt with over the years."

"Chase, you are the most level-headed, clear-thinking person I know, and if you can't see…" he trailed off as a thought occurred to him. "Did you sleep with her?"

Chase's eyes lifted and he smiled as their mother approached with two plates of etouffee. "That smells great, Mama!"

"You boys eat up while it is hot!"

Patrick waited for Jacquelin to leave before sliding his plate to one side. "Answer me! Did you have sex with her?"

"Not that it matters, but, yes, I did."

"Chase! Of course, it matters! What were you thinking?" he chastised. "You slept with the enemy, and because of it, she has gotten in your head."

"She is not our enemy. In all honesty, without her, you and I would be in the middle of a war between humankind and The Diverse at this very moment. Instead, we are sitting here enjoying dinner together."

"This isn't right!" Chase rested his hands on the table, looked down, and sighed heavily. "I wasn't asking for your opinion, just hoping my brother might be happy for me. You know good and well, I haven't even been on one date since Amber and I split up, and this was a huge step for me. No one coerced me or forced me with a spell. I did it because it was what I wanted to do and for no other reason. I am sorry if you can't see that."

Patrick closed his eyes. Chase had been alone for a long time, and, under any other circumstances, he would have been thrilled, but right now, he was more worried than anything.

"I hope I am wrong." Offering an olive branch of sorts, he asked, "Do I get to meet her at least?" He pulled his dish back over in front of him.

"I don't know. She had to go back to Las Vegas to take care of some business. Look, this may not go any further than where it already has, but even if it doesn't, it was nice to feel something for someone else again."

Patrick nodded and decided to change the subject. "Randy and Marie, huh?"

"Yeah, and I can honestly say, Randy seems really happy with her. I wouldn't be the least bit surprised if you were conducting a wedding ceremony soon."

"It's that serious? How about that?" Patrick reached for his fork. "Tell me about this newfound uncle of ours."

"Sawyer is great, although, I have to warn you, he is married to a werewolf. His husband, Mason, is an art dealer."

Setting the fork back down, the priest folded his arms and rested them on the table. "A gay uncle who is married to a werewolf?"

"A gay uncle, who is also a Rougarou, married to a werewolf," Chase corrected. "Rougarou and werewolves, though similar, are two different creatures, something new I learned this week." He stuffed a forkful of shrimp into his mouth and chewed.

"Any other bombshells you need to drop on me before I eat my dinner?"

Chase thought for a moment and shook his head. "Not any major ones. I think you have had enough for one sitting."

"Good, because I don't think I can handle anymore right now."

As they enjoyed their meal, Nancy, the secretary at the church, came in with her husband.

"How was your trip, Father Deveraux?" she asked when she spotted him.

"Wonderful! The shelter is going to help a lot of people. I hope things were quiet while I was gone."

"They were, well, except for that one strange call earlier today. I left a note on your desk."

"Who was it?" Patrick picked up a napkin and wiped his mouth.

"What was his name?" Nancy tapped the side of her head. "Cardinal Simon—no Simone. Cardinal Victor Simone."

"What did he say?" Patrick was suddenly extremely interested in the answer.

"Just to call him and that it was urgent." "Thank you, Nancy. I hope you and your husband enjoy your dinner. I will see you tomorrow."

Patrick reached for his keys as they walked away. "I have to go," he whispered.

"What's going on?" Chase asked worriedly.

"I don't know, but if it's Victor, it's not good."

"Want me to come with you?"

"No! We will talk later!" Patrick stood, hesitating. "Chase, I don't want you to think I am not happy for you, because I am. I know what a number Amber did on you and to find someone who makes you smile like that is no small feat. I just don't want you to get mixed up with someone who is not good for you."

"I know!"

Patrick gripped his shoulder. "Leave your phone on. After I talk to Victor, I may need your help."

"Whatever you need, bro! I am always here for you."

Epilogue

"Lady, there isn't one single snake in that entire place," said the older gentleman with the words 'exterminator' and 'Paul' sewn across his chest as he came out of the store.

"I'm telling you, there were hundreds of them!" Amber argued. "They were everywhere!"

"Look, I don't know what you saw or what you think you saw, but I have been in this business a long time, and if there had been hundreds of snakes in there, there would be some signs of it—a shed skin, some scat, or at the very least, a distinct odor. You've got none of those things, not to mention the fact they wouldn't even be out on the street at this time of year. The only thing I found on the floor," he held open his hand, "was this."

Amber huffed and snatched her broken heel from his hand. "I SAW THEM! They slithered in right after that woman with the red eyes left!"

"First snakes, and now, a lady with red eyes." Paul forced a smile, nodding sympathetically as a slow awareness washed over him. "Do you see things like that often?" he asked cautiously. "I mean, it's okay if you do. I had an uncle who used to see things like that, but with the right medication, the doctors were able to get him sorted out." "I AM NOT CRAZY!" she snarled, stomping her foot.

"Of course, you're not," he said in a placating manner, using a tone he would have used to address a child. "I am sure the big, bad, red-eyed lady just wanted to buy some shoes from you."

"No, she didn't! She wanted to brag about fucking my ex!" "Now, there is no need for that kind of language, young lady," he lectured, picking up his bag. "No charge for the trip. I wouldn't feel right taking it—just make sure you get yourself some help."

"I AM NOT FUCKING CRAZY!" she screamed, pulling at her hair as he hurried away. "AHHHH!"

"Ok, there are no snakes," Amber assured herself, squaring her shoulders, "which means I should be able to walk right in there without any problem. None whatsoever!"

Hesitating, she looked up and down the street for encouragement, only to see a man with a guitar strapped across his back coming her way. She kept her eyes glued to him and was stunned when he stopped in front of her window. Taking a seat, he opened his case without saying a word, only offering a passing glance at her in the process.

"What are you looking at?" she snapped.

"Not a damn thing. I am just playing," he said as he unstrapped his guitar.

Stepping closer, she took a good look at him. Something strange and unfamiliar began to overcome her. Relaxing her shoulders and seductively licking her lips, in a more cordial manner, she asked, "What do you play?"

"A little bit of everything."

Twirling a long tendril of hair, "What's—um—your name?"

"Archie."

"Hi Archie," she smiled sweetly and offered her hand, "I'm Amber and it's nice to meet you. I have to say, I love musicians."

"Good to know," he muttered, ignoring her as he concentrated on plucking a few chords.

"You know, it's cold out here and, well, this is my store," she pointed over her shoulder with her thumb, "Why don't you come in and warm up? Let me make you a drink."

"No, thanks."

Placing her hands on her hips, she inhaled the fresh air and looked around. "You're absolutely right! It's a beautiful day. We should just stay out here and enjoy it."

Sitting down next to him, she inched over until she was practically sitting in his lap and casually laid her head over on his shoulder as she stroked his chest. He grimaced as he gently tried to push her away. "It's hard to play with someone so close."

"I have faith in your ability, my sweet love."

"My what? Okay then!" he exclaimed as he shoved her off and quickly stood up. "I think it is time to go somewhere else."

"That's an excellent idea!" Amber clapped her hands together eagerly. "We can have a picnic in the park where I can feed you grapes and you can serenade me for everyone to hear."

"Don't you need to open your store?" he asked hopefully.

waved it off. "It's just money and who needs that when you have love?"

"Love? What the hell?" he muttered.

"I have a bottle of champagne chilling inside that I have been saving for a special occasion. I think today is the perfect day to open it. I'll just go grab it!" "Yeah, why don't you do that?" he said, plastering on a fake smile.

"You wait right here, sweetness! Don't go running off!" she giggled, touching him on the nose. "I will be right back!"

As soon as she was out of sight, he grabbed his stuff and bolted down the street.

Returning with a bottle and two glasses in hand, she noticed he was gone. "Archie? Archie? Come out, come out, wherever you are!"

Frantically searching the area, she became upset when she couldn't locate him. Stomping her feet and letting out a high-pitched squeal, she broke the bottle against the sidewalk and vowed, "I will find you, Archie whoever-you-are, and I will show you just how much I love you, even if it is the last thing I ever do!"

www.ingramcontent.com/pod-product-compliance
Lightning Source LLC
Chambersburg PA
CBHW060358310726
48976CB00003B/872